THE
DARK
LADY

THE
DARK
LADY

Louis
Auchincloss

Houghton Mifflin Company
Boston 1977

Library of Congress Cataloging in Publication Data

Auchincloss, Louis.
   The dark lady.

   I. Title.
PZ3.A898Dar [PS3501.U25]   813'.5'4   77-3666
ISBN 0-395-25402-7

Printed in the United States of America
V 10 9 8 7 6 5 4 3 2 1

124498

FOR MY SISTER, PRISCILLA

Here is Belladonna, the Lady of the Rocks,
The lady of situations.

T. S. *Eliot*, THE WASTE LAND

CONTENTS

PART
ONE

IVY

❧ I ❧

Ivy Trask could never make up her mind which of the
Irving Steins' dwellings she preferred: the rather huddled
but comfortable Beaux-Arts town house on East 68th Street
or the great gray two-story Parisian *hôtel*, a rectangle enclos-
ing a glass-covered courtyard, which they had erected and
surrounded by flat, rich green lawns for their summers and
weekends in Rye. The delight of dinner parties in the city in
the Venetian dining room with its corner cupboards full of
Meissen and Spode and a fire in the grate on stormy winter
nights, the coziness about the round table that almost filled the
chamber and the pleasing relation of the iced champagne in
Ivy's cut crystal glass to the freezing temperature safely outside were all the least bit tainted by the knowledge that she
would have to return before midnight through snowy streets
to her lonely rooms at the Althorpe. In the country at Broadlawns, on the other hand, she could rest assured that when
Clara Stein should rise from the pheasant-tailed wicker chair
that she always occupied in the conservatory, Ivy would have
only to go to her bedroom, from the window of which she
would be able to gaze out, as long as she wished, over the
moonlit woods beyond the wide lawn and listen to the
soporific din of crickets. The two places, in any event, with
all their large assets and small liabilities, had comprised, before the advent of Elesina Dart, the major part of Ivy's emotional life.

She was, at fifty-five, and might be, with any luck, for
another fifteen years, the fashion editor of *Tone*, a monthly
magazine of limited but regular circulation in New York and
its suburbs. It had struggled to preserve the ideal of a
woman's role as a pioneer in art and elegance through the
worst of the Depression and now, in 1937, seemed moderately
sure of survival. Ivy epitomized in her own appearance the

incongruity between the ideal of her periodical and its average reader. She was short, even dumpy; her features were sharp, her lips thin, her abundant, red dyed hair difficult to wave. But her clothes, if subdued, were of high fashion and of deep colors, and her eyes were very fine, with large, pale green irises, capable, she liked to believe, of an arresting intensity. God had given her her eyes, as *Tone* had given her her clothes, and she had little better use for either than to bring them to the Steins.

Ivy had been an inner member of their circle, or salon, for a decade. Judge Stein, a lawyer and one-time surrogate, now an investment banker and collector of art, had married into the Clarkson family, one of the proudest of old Manhattan, but he had long since discovered, despite a fervent zeal for upper-class Gentiles sadly at odds with the grandeur of his imagination, and despite his eschewal of Jewish faith, that the doors of his wife's world were opened for him only grudgingly and on occasion. As he had with his marriage burned many of his own bridges, he had been constrained to put together a special society, but as an indefatigable and open-handed host, with beautiful things to show and great music to play, he had had no difficulty assembling about him a heterogeneous group of relatives — poor Clarksons and richer Steins — of people from his banking firm, of artists and musicians, some poor and hungry, some merely hungry, of decorators and art dealers, of old friends of Clara's who scorned the prejudices of their group and of others who through their own marriages or unacceptable conduct had run afoul of these prejudices themselves. Clara, pale, remote, serene, accepted each new recruit at her husband's suggestion; she viewed her fellow humans with an eye that seemed to relegate judgment to a higher sphere for which she was not responsible. Her husband, large and hearty, with a wide scholarly brow and thick gray wavy hair, responded to flattery with kindness and to beggary with generosity, so that their salon contained, in addition to some famous artists and composers, an occasional character who would have been chased from the door of a more conservative home.

Ivy had first come to the Steins professionally, when the Judge, who managed everything in his houses and who even chose his wife's dresses, had decided that his theory of how to present Clara would not survive her middle years. His idea had been to show her off as the centerpiece of his collection, the beautiful woman to whom the beautiful porcelains, the ivories and jades, the medieval tapestries and stained glass paid silent tribute, and to this end he had arrayed the noble, if rather ample, figure of his chestnut-haired wife in exotic robes, vaguely historical. It was Ivy's genius to see that Clara's importance to the collections that surrounded her could be enhanced by making her as different as possible from them. She had emphasized the priestess, the vestal virgin, and had put Clara in togas of gray or white or light blue, worn with large stones in old-fashioned settings. The result had pleased both Steins, and Ivy's position at Broadlawns had for a long while seemed secure.

On a Saturday night in the fall of 1937, as the Stein houseguests at Rye assembled in the courtyard where cocktails were served to await the arrival of those who came by automobile, Ivy was feeling less than her usual anticipatory pleasure. The evening did not promise to be one of the best. To begin with, the guests of honor, the young Albert Schurmans, were not true members of the Stein circle. They belonged to the interrelated world of rich German Jewish banking families who continued for business and family reasons to visit Irving, but who frowned upon his social ambitions. Albert Schurman was the son of an ambassador and the nephew of a senator; his wife gave herself airs. There was apt to be a row. But what made Ivy really uneasy was Elesina Dart. Elesina, her wonderful new young friend, was a stranger to Broadlawns and had only been asked at Ivy's suggestion.

"Do they always sit out here?" Elesina asked with a little shiver. "Don't they find it cold?"

"It isn't really. It's just that you think it must be. The plants wouldn't live if it were."

Elesina looked up doubtfully at the huge pale skylight and then at the beds of begonias and the pink marble benches. She beckoned abruptly to a waitress with a tray of cocktails.

"Oh, Elesina, do be careful."

"Ivy, you're absurd. Can't you see any difference between a girl who likes an occasional binge and a confirmed alcoholic?"

"Elesina, you promised me!"

"That I'd be careful. And I will. I'll limit myself to two." Elesina took a glass from the tray. "I can't be expected to face this crowd without a lift. Who are all these people, anyway? That old Shakespeare scholar who made a pass at me in the corridor upstairs, and the big, steamy lesbian poetess who ogled me all during lunch."

"They can't help being attracted to you, darling." Ivy took in with renewed admiration her young friend's dark beauty. Elesina was still too thin, even a bit haggard, despite Ivy's determined health program on her behalf, but her large agate eyes, full of a reserve that seemed half humorously, half irritably to expect the worst of a bullying world, her jet black bobbed hair with the long lock that kept falling across her ivory forehead and which she kept impatiently brushing back, her luminous skin and long loose limbs, her rather aggressive cross between carelessness and stubbornness seemed to suggest the nineteen twenties surviving into the thirties to say, "I told you so."

"Even our host has been paying me marked attention. You'd think I was in a *maison de passe*. What does Mrs. Stein feel about it? Isn't she jealous?"

Ivy looked across the little fountain pool to where Clara stood, in gray, fingering a long pearl strand. Nothing in their hostess' isolation seemed in the least either shy or inviting.

She might have been alone in her garden. Now her sons, Peter and Lionel, large, dark, hirsute, rather lumbering versions of their father, crossed the patio with their wives to greet her. The way Clara put her hand on the shoulder of each as he kissed her seemed designed to keep the bestial at bay.

"Nobody really knows if Clara is jealous," Ivy speculated. "But Irving's too clever to take her for granted. There's something sinister under Clara's passivity."

"You mean he's afraid of her?"

"I think we're all a bit afraid of her. Clara is capable of ruthlessness. You should see her put her husband in his place. Once, last winter, when he was boasting that he had declined a bid to join the Tuesday Evening Club because . they wouldn't play Wagner's music in the war, Clara remarked for all to hear: 'That's funny. I don't remember our being bid. I thought we were too Jewish for them.'"

"How she must hate him!"

"Oh, not at all. I think she loves him — as much as she loves anyone. She simply likes occasionally to set the record straight."

"Watch it. Here he comes."

Judge Stein was indeed on his way over to them, or at least to Elesina. He managed, with his shaggy gray hair and his prominent, faintly mocking gray eyes, his pince-nez with its dangling red ribbon and his portly, thrusting build, to suggest some great composer, some bust of a romantic, burly Beethoven in a winter park.

"I thought you might like to see my new Francesco Bibiena, Miss Dart. A baroque palace design. Really a gem. I've just hung it in the library. You will be the first to see it in Broadlawns."

Elesina went off on her host's arm, glancing back at her friend with the suggestion of a shrug. Ivy was amused. Watching them retreat across the patio, she proceeded mentally to mate them. That Irving in his still vigorous sixties should find a beautiful woman in her thirties desirable needed little aid to fantasy. But Elesina? Perhaps she was one of those women who were attracted to older men, men who represented things opposite to themselves, sterner things, paternal things. Might there not be a thrill to exposing herself as weak and vulnerable to something hard and crushing? Ivy knew that the Judge had a weakness for prurient academic paintings, quite inconsistent with his finer eye for Italian drawing. She remembered the little Gérôme in his library bathroom of the naked slave girl, her proud head averted in shame, exposed in a marketplace to a group of elderly Roman businessmen who were studying her contours with eyes which expressed a greater cupidity than lasciviousness. The girl could be Elesina. Why not?

"Ivy!"

She realized with a start that it must have been the second time that her name had been called.

"Yes, Clara?"

"You seem lost in thought. Come and sit with me. The Schurmans have just telephoned that they will be late."

Ivy went around the fountain pool to sit on the bench by Clara Stein's chair. Clara's plentiful chestnut hair rose from her head in a kind of fuzz that seemed inappropriate to the sedateness of her chalky oval face and blue gray eyes.

"Miss Dart is charming," Clara said, judicially.

"Oh, I'm so glad you find her so."

"Certainly the men do. Irving is quite infatuated. I hope she will not find us too dowdy."

"Clara! How could she?"

"Oh, very easily. To begin with, she is young. Her place is with the young. Of course, David is coming tonight, and the Schurmans, and that will help, but so far the weekend can hardly have been gay for her. Why did you bring her, Ivy?"

Ivy did not underestimate the criticism latent in her hostess' mild tone. "Why? Is that so surprising? That I should want to introduce her to the most brilliant salon in New York?"

Clara's eyes widened slightly as she weighed the extravagance of this avowal. "You're very fond of Miss Dart."

"Don't we care most about the people we can help?"

"And how do you help her by introducing her to Broadlawns?"

"Elesina has had great sadnesses. I'm trying to revive her appetite for life. For people."

Clara shook her head. "There you go, Ivy, with your eternal emphasis on people. Where do people get you to?"

Ivy began to feel aggrieved. "Of course, nothing seems much to one who has all that you have, Clara. You can be sufficient to yourself. But what have I got? People have been my life."

"People are a cul-de-sac. We all basically have to live in ourselves."

"I seem to remember a commandment about loving thy neighbor."

"It was the second. The first was to love thy God with all thy heart and soul and mind. It doesn't leave much over, does it?"

"We don't often hear you in so religious a vein, Clara."

"Well, I interpret God in my own peculiar way. But one thing he is surely not — he is surely not my fellow man."

"I don't see how you can love God and not his creatures. I have to love individuals. Like you. And Irving. And your dear boys."

"And Miss Dart?"

"Yes. And Elesina." Ivy's irritation dwindled before the continued rigidity of Clara's gaze. It was not like Clara to preserve this coolness so long. Usually she would break suddenly into a smile that would dismiss the topic as a shadow before the reality of the welcome, the weekend, the warm little world of the Steins. "What is it, Clara? What has come over you? Don't you like Elesina? Do you want me to take her home?"

"Of course not, dear." Clara leaned over to touch Ivy's hand with the tips of her fingers. "It's just that at times one happens to see things. Perhaps too clearly. There now. Let us forget it."

"Clara!" Ivy's world rocked. "You dislike me!"

"Don't be a goose, Ivy. Ah, at last. There are the Schurmans."

Clara rose and walked with her quick stride to where the guests of honor stood with her husband. There were little cries of greeting and exchanged snips of kisses. Albert Schurman, stout, grinning, balding, still a handsome young man though doomed to weight, looked about the patio with a gleam of mischief as though to set himself apart from Stein things. His wife, very blond and cold of countenance, seemed to be trying to make a formal greeting even more formal.

Ivy was interrupted in her gazing.

"I'm supposed to take an old bag called Ivy Trask in to dinner. Could you tell me which she is?"

"Oh, David, sweetie!" Ivy threw her arms around his neck.

David was the youngest and brightest of the three Stein sons. He was a bit on the short side, stocky and well built, and there was a fullness in the round nostrils of his small aquiline nose, a fleshiness in the red lips, a determination in the square chin that might one day make him too like his father. But at twenty-four David had still the aspect of a Romantic poet and some of the exuberant idealism that Ivy associated with her schoolgirl visions of Shelley. He had blond wavy hair and blue eyes, and when he grinned, he showed teeth so perfect they might have been capped.

"The old man's hopping mad," he told Ivy when they were seated in the dining room before the porcelain centerpiece of Arion charming the dolphins with his song from the fragment of a wrecked vessel. "You know the Houdon *Madame Vic-*

toire in the hall? Al Schurman put his derby hat on it for a joke. And Dad saw it!"

"Oh, David, no." There was no flaw in Irving's integrity as a collector.

"It's all right. Dad simply walked up, removed the hat and silently handed it back to him. But it makes a cool start for the evening." David's eyes were fixed on his father, who was talking to Elesina. As Ivy followed his glance, she saw the Judge's large hand descend upon her friend's. David smiled maliciously.

"Tell me about Miss Dart. It is Miss?"

"It's a professional name. Elesina is an actress. Actually, it's her born name. You must have heard of the Darts. They're old New York."

"You mean she's a lady, like Ma." David seemed to consider himself as his father's son, while Clara, however much adored, occupied her own cerulean sky. "Why do you make a point of it?"

"Because so few ladies can act. It goes against the central rule of their bringing-up — always to mute things, to tone them down."

"And Miss Dart doesn't?"

"If you'd seen her Hedda Gabler at the Columbus Circle Repertory, you wouldn't have to ask."

"Columbus Circle? Can't she do better than that?"

"Oh, I hope she will. Elesina has had her problems."

"Men?"

Ivy's glare was snubbing. "There always has to be that, doesn't there? Yes, I'm afraid she's been a bad picker. Bill Nolte was a total nonentity. And Ted Everett was putty in the hands of his old fascist father."

"Those were her husbands?"

"Both now shed. I trust there'll be no others for a while."

"Not while Ivy, the dragon, is on watch. Are there babies?"

"One little girl, who lives with Everett. He's poisoned the

child's mind against Elesina." Ivy put down her soup spoon to be able to turn to David for full emphasis. "My poor friend has nothing to show for either of her marriages."

"You mean no alimony?"

"Nothing!"

David chuckled. "Forgive me if I point out, Ivy dear, that in that case your protégée must have been on the wrong side in two divorces. And that in itself tells me something about the divine Elesina."

"You're a brute, like all your sex! No wonder Elesina is so bitter. Look, the table's changing. Talk to the lucky lady on your right."

Ivy, left in silence, compared the occupants of the great formal blue chamber with the handsomer, haughtier ladies and gentlemen who condescended to them from the walls, subjects of the art of Lawrence, Romney and West, in scarlet uniforms and billowing dresses, against Palladian backgrounds or hunt picnics or fashionable malls. But her pleasure in this, an old game, was spoiled by the recollection of her talk with Clara. It was curious how penetrating Clara's vision could be. A hundred women could come to her house and receive the tactile, breathy attentions of the Judge without causing the lift of one of her long penciled eyebrows, but she could flare at the least change of his tone of voice, even from the other end of the long table, when a special impression had been made. Oh, yes, Clara, for all her airs, for all her cultivation of Greek poetry and early American hymns, could be a woman and a cat! Ivy watched her critically as she chatted with Al Schurman. Did she and Irving still make love? Then she shifted her gaze to Elesina, and in doing so it crossed David's broad shoulders and half-averted profile. Now she mated David with Elesina. They were Paris and Helen on the ship, flying from Menelaus. Unashamedly on deck, oblivious of the sailors as they would have been of dogs, naked, they copulated, his hair long and blond, mixed with hers, long and black . . .

"Irving seems to admire Miss Dart," Fred Pemberton, the Shakespearean scholar, observed to Ivy with a throaty chuckle. "The lofty Clara may yet deign to pucker her noble brow . . ."

⇝ 2 ⇛

Elesina was seated on Irving Stein's left and Pat Schurman on his right, but as Elesina and her host occupied the two chairs at the end of the long table she was given the appearance of being guest of honor. The obvious interest of the table in this striking new member of their group, this repertory actress with an obscure reputation for disaster, was gratifying, but Elesina was still irked that dinner had interrupted her quest of a second cocktail. Why did one never get enough to drink in Jewish houses? She noted sourly that there was only a single wineglass at each place. And these people had millions! Suddenly she was restless, oddly elated by her own bad humor.

"It was so good of Ivy to bring you into our lives, Miss Dart." Irving Stein's full, warm handclasp enveloped the fingers of her right hand under the table. "We hope you will become a regular visitor to Broadlawns. I could tell by the way you studied my little Bibiena that you have the eye of a connoisseur. That is what we care about." The voice, soft and low, dropped to a rumbling whisper. "Tonight, however, is not typical. The Schurmans are family. Very fine people, of course, but with no eyes or ears for the things we love. Pat's idea of celestial bliss is to watch her boys play hockey."

"Judge, do you think I might have a glass of wine now?"

"Why certainly, my dear." Even in his surprise he failed to release her fingers. His free hand beckoned the butler. "Some wine for Miss Dart."

Elesina with a slight effort brought her right hand up to table level. Only then did he release his hold. "Oh, don't let go," she protested, smiling across him at the obliquely watching Pat. "I'm always proud to have my hand held, aren't you, Mrs. Schurman? Only I insist that everybody witness my honor!"

"Very amusing, I'm sure."

Elesina turned away abruptly from Pat Schurman's pert stare. Let the little minx have Stein's paw in *her* lap if she wanted! Did she think Elesina Dart cared? Mrs. Schurman, indeed! Did Mrs. Schurman know there had been a Dart at Valley Forge? And a Dart at the Treaty of Ghent? Wouldn't all the Steins and Schurmans in this pompous room have given all their purchased portraits for her own little Copley, now unfortunately sold, of Elisha Dart?

But Elesina could never long enjoy this kind of snobbish fantasy. She felt her spirits suddenly deflate. How petty it all was! What did these people care about the Darts? What was all her family's past but a few tattered albums of faded snapshots of ladies in big hats on broad verandahs, of bearded men at the wheels of unbelievable autos, a box of yellow newspaper clippings of weddings and funerals, a memory of memories, a story written on the opaque waters of the East River, gone with the dirty snows of yesteryear?

She had to beckon the astonished butler to refill her glass. Really, it was too much! And now she was aware of a louder voice, addressing her with heavily ironic politeness.

"Your little interchange with the Judge, Miss Dart, puts me in mind of that sonnet of the divine bard's where he contemplates his mistress' fingers on the keys, or jacks, of a spinet. It evokes this happy conceit which I presume, facetiously, to offer in my own behalf at our host's expense: 'Since saucy jacks so happy are in this, Give them thy fingers, me thy lips to kiss.' "

Fred Pemberton, on Pat Schurman's right, was leaning across her to gain Elesina's attention. His intrusive, watery eyes, his fixed little smile made her shiver in disgust. She decided to indulge the impulse to cut him down.

"But those dark lady sonnets were only a cover-up.

Wasn't it the 'lovely boy' whose lips he really wanted to kiss?" Elesina now glanced down the table to where David Stein was talking to Ivy. "The divine bard, as you call him, would have addressed himself to our host's son rather than to me."

Pemberton, to her surprise, cackled with pleasure. Apparently any attention pleased him. "Aren't you forgetting, Miss Dart, the evidence of the twentieth sonnet? Where our poet tells us that nature, in molding the body of the beloved youth, intended him originally for a girl, but then fell a doting and added 'one thing to my purpose nothing.'"

"You interpret that as a reference to the young man's sexual organ?" Elesina's question was designed to insure that Mrs. Schurman should understand the reference, which she clearly did, for her thin lips were now pursed into a ball of disgust. Irving Stein coughed loudly, uneasily. "I suppose it's clear enough. But the presence of such an organ might still have been 'nothing,' or no impediment, to the poet's particular taste. However, a truce to such speculations! I am not sure that Mrs. Schurman appreciates our scholarly freedom. Let me simply point out that this sonnet may have been intended to put the reader off the track. After all, sodomy was a serious crime in Elizabethan England. Even if it flourished at court, you could still be burned alive for it. A man in Shakespeare's unprotected social position did not lightly twit authority."

"But, my dear Miss Dart," Stein intervened, "you are a veritable mine of authority! I told you you'd be one of us!"

"Oh, I once played the dark lady in a comedy based on the sonnets." Elesina laughed deprecatingly. "I believe it had three performances. However, it gave me the chance to study the sonnet sequence and make my own guesses. Why not? It's a garden where nobody fears to tread."

"And I, of course, have been one of the nonangels in that enclosure," Pemberton told them. "I have even published a work on the subject entitled, perhaps optimistically, *The Riddle Solved*. It was my theory that Shakespeare's feeling for the youth was the most intense passion of his lifetime and the principal source of the high tragic mood that preceded the composition of *Hamlet* and *Othello*. Of course, it had a homosexual aspect, but not necessarily in any vulgar or physical sense. The young man was obviously of the highest birth — very possibly the Earl of Pembroke himself — and a corporeal liaison may not have been feasible."

"I suppose the Earl's family may have had something to say about *that*," the now utterly disgusted Pat Schurman put in sharply. "Shakespeare may be a god to you, Professor Pemberton, but to the Pembrokes he was probably a dirty old man."

"Hardly old, Ma'am."

"I confess I've had misgivings about the sonnets," Elesina interjected, to take the initiative from Pat. "To me there is something *malsain* about them. They are too crawling, too syrupy, too self-pitying."

Irving Stein seemed shocked at this. "But, Miss Dart, you are speaking of the greatest love poetry in the English language!"

"Oh, love, pooh, Judge. It's not love at all. It's a kind of crush. Or series of crushes, really. For if the sonnets cover a period of many years, as some scholars say, they must have been addressed to a series of young men. We all know that middle-aged pederasts keep changing the objects of their affection. After all, how long does a pretty boy stay pretty?"

Pemberton proved unexpectedly hospitable to this variation of his theory. "You have a point, Miss Dart! As a matter of fact, in *The Riddle Solved* I state that Shakespeare's great love could have been for two men, first Southampton and then Pembroke. But I fear we're going to shock Miss Cranberry." He lowered his voice as he glanced down the table at the poetess, a huge blond woman with straight hair pulled to a bun in back and a fleshy, pendulous, menacing face. "You know her theory, don't you? She claims there was no youth *or* dark lady. That the sonnets are a literary exercise, a novel in verse, a jeu d'esprit. But how can an old maid comprehend the eclecticism of the Elizabethan male?"

"We're talking about you, Miss Cranberry!" Elesina called boldly down the table. "Professor Pemberton doesn't believe that unmarried women can understand Shakespeare."

Miss Cranberry's heavy, square face turned, with slowly mounting hostility, to her critic. "As much as unmarried men, anyway," she retorted with a grunt.

"I understand that *you* are not married, Miss Dart," Pat Schurman observed suddenly. "But surely nobody could accuse you of naiveté where Shakespeare is concerned."

The acidity of the comment created a general atmosphere of embarrassment. "Oh, well, I'm an actress, and we don't count," Elesina responded with a shrug. "There was a time when we couldn't even be buried in hallowed ground. But the professor, Miss Cranberry, seems to imply that you turn Shakespeare into a sort of Kate Greenaway."

"Better than turning him into a sort of Oscar Wilde. I have often wondered if those critics who persist in finding evidence of inversion in the sonnets do not betray what I shall be polite enough to call their subconscious preferences."

"My friends, my friends!" interposed Clara Stein. "Please let us not be so heated. Erna, do talk to Mr. Simkins. He has told me how much he loves your poems. And David, you must help our end of the table to understand the sonnets." Clara, with a nod to her husband and a wink at David, signified that she wished the table divided into two sections to separate the combatants. It was an instance, Elesina supposed, of what Ivy had told her: that the detached mistress of the house always knew how to resume her rule.

"You must think we literary buffs have strange preoccupations." Elesina had turned now with affected humility to Pat Schurman. "The Judge tells me you're a great hockey fan."

"It doesn't mean that I can't read, Miss Dart."

"I never meant to imply it." Elesina glanced at her host, who, she was glad to note, had instantly resented Pat Schurman's insulting tone. "I'm sure you have just as interesting theories about Shakespeare as anyone here."

"I don't know if they're as interesting, but they're certainly a good deal cleaner. If that's a virtue, which I don't suppose you believe."

"Cleaner?"

"Yes, Miss Dart. I am frankly revolted at what I have heard at this table tonight!"

"Pat, my dear, you mustn't take that attitude," Judge Stein intervened earnestly. "It isn't as if there were young people present. I . . ."

"I'm sorry, Cousin Irving, but I cannot agree with you. I should not be honest if I did not tell you that I consider the moral tone of the conversation tonight very low indeed. And I deem it a fault on your part to permit and encourage it."

Irving Stein had turned quite red. "Am I to credit my senses?" he almost shouted, with a slight accentuation of Teutonic accent. "Surely you, a cousin by marriage, and a younger one at that, cannot be criticizing *my* moral tone?"

Patricia Schurman's self-possession was wonderful to behold. She had put down her fork and was facing her host with a small, steady, mocking smile. "I suggest you ask some of your other guests what they think of the dirty talk we've been exposed to tonight."

Her husband, at the other end of the table, was looking cruelly embarrassed, but it was still apparent that, if it had to be war, he was going to be on the side of his wife. In the silver-tinted air over the long table there hung a sense of the shivering jealousies between the two families. "Pat, will you drop it, please? What do we gain by bringing these things out?"

"I am only too happy to drop the whole distasteful subject," his wife retorted. "It was certainly not I who brought

it up. But in dropping it I wish to make it entirely clear that I
stand by everything I've said."

Something at this seemed to tear within the Judge. His
head sagged for a second, but when he raised it and faced his
opponent, his words came out in a rush that was something
between a bleat and a gasp. "It is an outrage for a woman in
your position to say such things! I will not permit it in my
house!"

"I'm perfectly willing to repeat it, Judge."

Stein rose from his chair, his face now scarlet. In a moment, with a rush of silk, Clara was at his side. "Come away,
dear," she said placatingly. "We can finish our dinner in the
library. No, David, you stay here. Please, everyone! Don't
get up. Go on with your dinner. Pretend that nothing has
happened. It is difficult, I know, but it's the only way to
handle these things. Sarah," she murmured as she passed
Peter's wife, "take over, dear."

There was a nervous bustle of conversation around the
table as the Steins left the dining room, her hands clasping his
arm. Everyone babbled the first thing that came to mind.
After dinner, when the ladies had retired to the drawing
room, Elesina went over to Ivy.

"Your friends are extraordinary. Do they put on this act
every weekend? It's like that party at the Macbeths'. Except
there it was the guests who had to leave."

Ivy sighed. "I seem to have brought the apple of discord to
the banquet of the gods. You're a very potent influence, my
dear."

Elesina smiled. Decidedly, the weekend was proving more
lively than she could have hoped.

৵ঙ 3 ৡ৵

Ivy always thought of herself as having had no individual
childhood, but as having been an amorphous part of the
jumbled noisy life of the Trasks in their ancestral shingle

mansion by the lake at Auburn, New York. For reasons that she never quite fathomed the Trasks, like a noble Italian family, seemed to cling to the same habitation, so that her memory of meals was of a long board at which several uncles and aunts, at least one grandparent and numberless cousins ate and chattered. Trasks would sometimes marry and leave the tribal roof, but they had a way of coming back, for long summers or Christmases, or even permanently, with the death or defection of spouses or with economic reverses. Some Trasks were poor and others well off, but all were indoctrinated with a sense of responsibility for fellow Trasks, or for persons who had married Trasks or whose mothers or grandmothers had been Trasks — Parkers, Sewards, Tremaines, Gardners, Sewells. The history of the family was a history of "upstate."

Yet as Ivy grew up she was soon made aware that, despite a good deal of evenly distributed affection, there were still social distinctions to be observed. Uncle Fred Porter, for example, was a "personage"; he had been lieutenant governor of the state, and even the little boys hushed up when he talked. Aunt Eleanor Sewell was "unfortunate," because her husband had been a gambler and because she drank. Julia Trask was "fast," so that no nice boy, at least no nice local boy, could be reasonably expected to marry her. Ted Tremaine was "smart," which meant that he would go far, and Blanche Trask was "too good for this world," which signified religious hysteria and an early demise. But what was Ivy? What was plain little Ivy, whose sharp green eyes took in so much more than was good for her? She seemed as much a part of the old house as the Duncan Phyfe dining room chairs and the languid ladies in the Morse portraits, as the horsehair sofa and the stillness of the dark dining room in midmorning, because she never went away, like the others, to other homes, or even for vacations. Ivy was an orphan, and she didn't have a cent.

It sometimes seemed to her that her parents had simply

been lost. She could not be sure whether she remembered her
mother or remembered only the photographs of that pretty,
pouting, perversely happy face. Her father, too, had been
beautiful, but he had been "weak," though whether this re-
ferred to his health or character Ivy had never been sure. He
had died of a brain fever when only twenty-five, and his
widow had followed him less than a year later. Ivy was told
that her mother's heart had given out, but in later years she
suspected that the words concealed a suicide. She was kindly
treated by everyone, but it was evident that her extra helping
of affection was inspired by the general sense of her aloneness.
What in the name of heaven were they going to do with
her?

Ivy conformed carefully to what she gleaned was expected
of her. She heard that she was bright, so she worked hard to
obtain good marks at school. She was told that she was
always a help in the house, so she made herself useful to Kate
the cook and Millie the chambermaid. She heard from beautiful Aunt Amy Porter that boys weren't everything in life, so
she accepted her plainness and obscurity and thought as little
as she could of parties and dances. She learned from
Grandma that unmarried women should be allowed careers,
so she asked to be sent to college and read every book in the
library from Cooper to Bryant. And she would indeed have
gone to New York City and to Barnard College had President
Theodore Roosevelt not named Uncle Fred Porter Secretary
of Commerce and had Aunt Amy not suggested that Ivy go
with them to Washington and be her social secretary. The
whole household at Auburn rang with the felicity of this
decision. The problem of Ivy was solved!

And so it was, for many years, even permanently, so far as
Auburn was concerned. Uncle Fred enjoyed his high office
for a decade, through the terms of Roosevelt and Taft, and
Ivy had a liberal education, not only in politics, but in the
social and cultural life of the capital. Such intellectuals as
Henry Adams, Senator Lodge and Lord Bryce, admirers of

Uncle Fred's *Constitutional History of the United States,* were frequent visitors. They rarely spoke directly to Ivy, but their words and manners were tucked away in her unwritten diary. Ivy had the combined reverence and cynicism of a London shopgirl watching royalty on parade. She saw that the great thinkers of the Theodosian court held themselves superior to the crude politicians, but she also noted that their pretensions were based, at least in part, on wealth and social position. The American Renaissance, it appeared, like the earlier Italian, had started at the top.

Ivy was smart enough to make herself indispensable to her aunt, who, like many of the Trask women, had little gift for organization. Aunt Amy was a gently indolent creature who nursed a rather faded blond beauty like a string of fine old pearls, but she was capable of noting even minor derelictions in subordinates. Ivy became adept at seating dinner parties, matching affinities without violating protocol, and her aid was soon sought by other Cabinet wives. "Get the little Trask to do it," the word went out. "See if Amy Porter can spare her for the afternoon." Sometimes, when Aunt Amy was ailing, Ivy acted as hostess for her uncle, and then she was always careful to conduct herself in such a way as to be appreciated without being overpraised. For she knew that her job would not survive the day when the first guest failed to miss Aunt Amy.

For a long time no man came into her life. Where would he have come from? Washington was not a town for romance; the men who came there were not only married but middle-aged, and many who dined at the Porters' were old. It never would have occurred to Aunt Amy or Uncle Fred to invite a "beau" for Ivy, and her looks were not the sort that made males leap boundary marks. Besides, she was shy with her contemporaries. She did not believe that she could attract them, and she could conceive of no greater humiliation than being detected in an attempt to do so. Yet on the whole she was not dissatisfied with her life. She considered that, judged

by her scanty equipment, she might be deemed to have done
well. Even a paid niece, she would tell herself with a private
smirk, was not too lowly to be occasionally smug.

Eventually a man, a sort of man, did come. Edouardo
Calabrese was a secretary in the Italian legation, a bachelor,
past fifty, of a well-to-do Florentine banking family whose
sisters had married into the nobility. Edouardo was charming; he had wide cultural interests, spoke perfect English and
knew America intimately. He even collected American art,
and his house in Georgetown had many samples of the work
of Hassam, Bellows and Eakins. He greatly admired Uncle
Fred's near classic book on the Constitution and was a constant guest at the Porters', one of the very few to whom Ivy
became more than the efficient, bustling little assistant to her
aunt. He would talk to her as if she were the equal of any
lady present.

"Tell me, Miss Trask," he asked her one night before dinner, "do you write down the things you observe? Do you
keep a journal?"

"No. Why?"

"Because I've been watching you. Those fine green eyes of
yours seem to take in everything and everybody. What a
record it would be, if you set it all down!"

"But then it would be somebody else's, wouldn't it? Now
it's mine. Because it's true. If I wrote it out it would become
a work of art — bad art, at that."

"Do you believe, then, that we can live just in ourselves?"

"Who else should I live in?"

"I see you're a realist, Miss Trask. And a very live one, too.
I sometimes feel that if I were to touch the tips of your
fingers, I should get an electric shock."

"*Merci du compliment!*"

"I mean it well." He held up a long thin hand to show her
his tapering fingers. "Don't you think this old Italian appen-
dage needs a stimulus?"

"Why do you call it old? Can it be older than you?"

"I wonder." He contemplated his hand whimsically now, as if it might suddenly disappear. "It goes way back. We are bourgeois, but we go back. Like the Medici."

Ivy laughed and touched her fingertips to his. "There! Did you feel the shock?"

"Oh, yes. I'm better already. I think we're going to be friends, Miss Trask."

Edouardo, it turned out, had a reputation most unusual for an Italian; he was not a ladies' man. The relationship that he and Ivy developed was accepted with a smile and a shrug by the Porters and their friends; nobody gossiped when he took Amy's old-maid niece to a concert or for a drive in Rock Creek Park. Ivy was too shrewd to be falsely modest. She divined at once that her value to Edouardo was more in what she was not than what she was, and she was perfectly willing to have it that way, to play Jane Eyre to his expurgated Rochester. She liked to sit by him in the old victoria that he rented for drives by the river or to walk with him by the cherry trees. His formal, balanced phrases, his velvet tones opened a new world for her. She noted now for the first time all the colors of spring and of sunset, and she learned the stories behind the lacquered diplomacy of the day. She even put together a picture of the Italy of his boyhood, replete to the ravens around the towers of the villa in Fiesole and the smell of incense in the damp darkness of the family chapel. Ivy hugged herself with delight at the realization that she was at last able to put her hard-won knowledge of human beings to good use. How many silly girls would have spoiled it all by trying to marry him!

One Sunday spring afternoon, as they walked by the bank of the river, in the full, damp, heart-moving air, Edouardo's discourse became more personal.

"It is not always easy to be Italian, you know. So much is expected of one. There are days when I curse our reputation for romance! My sisters are always ready to cut me to pieces when I so much as look at a lady who is not their candidate for Signora Calabrese."

"I guess it's lucky there's an ocean between them and me!"

"But you are sensible, my dear Ivy. I sometimes think you are the most sensible individual in all Washington. Or the only one. So many of your compatriots seem to view life through a kind of screen which converts individuals into types. Your old men become wise, your maidens innocent, your youths lusty, and . . ."

"And our Italians lovers!" Ivy interrupted with a sharp laugh to cover her tension. "Yes, my only asset as a child was seeing the world as it was. And my only education was learning not to tell people what I saw."

"But will you tell *me*, Ivy?"

"Yes!" she exclaimed with sudden decision, walking on quickly ahead so that she would not have to look at him. "I see that you are afraid that I may be a goose. That I may develop ideas about our friendship. That you may even find my uncle waiting on your doorstep with a shotgun in his hand! You needn't worry. *I'm* the one he'd shoot. But that's not the point, anyway: what he would think or what my aunt would think or what anybody would think. It only matters what *we* think. And here it is, Edouardo. I have no fantasies of becoming your wife. No fantasies about romance. I have no desires, no interests, in that field. All I care about is our friendship. It is important to me that it should continue. Unchanged." She stopped now and faced him, breathing hard. "And I feel I could murder any lumbering fool who interferes with it!"

Edouardo clasped her hand in both of his. "Dear Ivy," he murmured. "We will always be friends. I know that now."

Walking home, she trembled at the narrowness of her escape. It was as if she had been crossing a bare heath under the crack of thunder. Big ugly gods, like buddhas, glinted malevolently at her. They knew whom she loved! And was not love a thing to be revealed, to be leered at, to be opened up like a package on their dirty altar before prying eyes and held up, a bloody, aborted fetus to the humiliation of any man who had failed to respond to it, who had denied Venus? Oh, no, she would clutch the fetus to her breast, take it from the vile temple, bury it in the black, bare earth outside. And then she could defy the glinting idols, or at least fool them, dangerous game though it was, parading under their very eyes her heretic's game of unfleshly friendship, exulting in the whiteness, the spermlessness, the heady sanctity, the simple forbidden goodness of her friendly passion.

Edouardo did not raise the subject again, and their friendship continued in apparent serenity. In the spring of 1914, at any rate, he became too preoccupied with European rivalries to be troubled further over sexual inadequacies. He was deeply pessimistic about the outcome of what he now saw as inevitable war. On their long carriage rides by the river he spoke forebodingly of the might of Wilhelm II.

"People know the Kaiser is strong, Ivy, but they have no conception of how strong. His triumph will be the end of our way of life. We have had peace too long. We have cared too much about art and beauty and good manners. We are lost things. It is sad, for we are still better than those who will come after."

"I don't think the Kaiser could conquer this country. I'd like to see him try!"

"Oh, I don't mean your great nation," Edouardo replied with a smile. "No, I believe an army of Ivys could still drive back the Hohenzollerns. I was thinking of the gold-laden empires of Britain and France and of poor old Italy, with all her past and treasures."

"You forget Russia!"

"No, Ivy, I don't forget Russia. Promise me something. If I am called home, will you write to me?"

"Edouardo, you know I will!"

He returned to Italy in the war, and he wrote to her every month thereafter. Uncle Fred retired and went back to live in Auburn, and Ivy went with him and her aunt because it seemed unthinkable to do otherwise. It was there that, after the Armistice, she received the letter from Edouardo which asked her to come to Florence to be his bride.

"I have been ill," he wrote, "and I am not what I was, but I am still something. I have a few years, perhaps, and a bit of money and an old house to share with you. I think you might be amused. Of course, if something better has turned up for you I understand — from the bottom of my heart."

There was nobody to go with her — Aunt Amy and Uncle Fred were far too old — but Ivy never hesitated for a moment. She had more than ten years of savings. She bought herself a trousseau and a passage to Genoa and departed.

The train from Genoa to Rome paused for an hour in Florence, but Ivy was ready to get off the moment it stopped. A very tall woman, with a huge beak of a nose, frigidly fashionable in black furs, stepped forward to take her by the arm.

"My dear Miss Trask, I am Antonina de Selli, Edouardo's sister. He has sent me to talk to you. Could we go back into your compartment? Never fear. The train won't leave without our being warned. That has been arranged."

Ivy calculated afterward that she had been thirty-seven years, two months and three days old when her life was cut in two. For what she now learned, shivering in the cold, dusty compartment, looking at the photographs of the Forum and of the Villa d'Este over her interlocutor's grim face, was that Edouardo had changed his mind. He was too old, too ill, to marry her. He had cancer, which he had kept from her. His family had persuaded him that it was his duty to leave his diminished property intact to them. He had sent his sister to break the news, but he had armed her with a confirmatory letter and with a check that he hoped would be expended on a wonderful vacation in Italy. Antonina went on so long and in such detail, in her grave, grating phrases, that Ivy had more than the time she needed to prepare her answer.

"You are relieved, Contessa, to see how middle-aged and plain I am. I am also poor. You marvel that your brother could have contemplated so unequal a match. But let me tell you something. I could get off this train right now and go to Edouardo and make him change his mind. I could! And looking at me now, you know I could! But you needn't worry. I shall not do it. Because I know it would kill him. I can imagine what you've all been up to — hounding him, persecuting him. And even if I rescued him from you, he'd always wonder if I'd done the right thing. You see, I know him. I leave him to you because it's easier that way. Easier for *him*. And I'll take that check, only because I despise you so utterly that it would be overrating you to reject it!"

Ivy was never to forget the look of astonishment on the Contessa's face. Twenty minutes later she was on her way to Rome. In the dreary wilderness which choked her heart and mind she had yet the energy to face the fact that her disaster had not come wholly as a surprise. An expurgated *Jane Eyre* had become an expurgated *Portrait of a Lady*. That was all.

When Ivy disembarked in New York she decided that she would remain in the city. It was not that she did not wish to expose herself to the humiliation of family sympathy in Auburn, it was simply that nobody could make a life for her now but herself. She owed her job on *Tone* to the intervention of a cousin, but thereafter she owed little to her relatives except for an occasional dinner at a restaurant when one of them came to the city, and this she more than paid for with her services as a guide. Her rise at *Tone* was slow but steady. She learned each department fully and finally settled in fashion, where she became the editor. She was never ill, never missed an opening, went to Paris every fall and developed a pungent style of her own, which made sensible dressing attractive and available to middle-aged suburbanites. She also

intermixed her column with personal items about the best-
dressed ladies of Manhattan, so that a blend of gossip and
garments became her trademark. "Ivy not only tells you
what the ladies put on," Sam Gorman, the feature editor of
Tone used to say. "She also tells you when they take it
off."

Little by little she developed a social life. She drew an
allowance from the magazine to cover choice little dinners,
parties for eight, in her tiny but charming apartment at the
Althorpe, furnished with presents from firms which adver-
tised in *Tone*. People came because she did things well; they
loved the rapid talk over lively topics in the oval green-
paneled parlor hung with exotic oriental birds on satin. Ivy's
trick was always to have one important, unexpected guest, an
actress, a visiting designer, a popular woman novelist, and to
be sure that the other six would be the sort to amuse her star.
The efforts to which she went to procure the latter were as
laborious as they were carefully concealed. But nobody ever
heard her complain about the toil that went into the creation
of a social life which a pretty face or a bank account would
have made for her in a day.

Ivy's greatest success was with the Steins. Her value to
them was very much what it had been to her aunt and uncle:
an ability to straighten out a party as one would a sheet on a
bed, by giving it, all unobtrusively, little pulls and twitches.
When the Steins took her to Europe she was helpful with
timetables and accommodations; when they were ill she was as
good as a trained nurse. Once when they were in Mexico,
and David had been caught smoking at boarding school, they
delegated Ivy to go up to Connecticut to talk to the headmaster, a matter she handled so skillfully that the dreaded
suspension was avoided.

And yet all was not perfect. There were times when the
Steins seemed to forget about her altogether, when as many as
six weeks would pass without an invitation. And then, when

Clara did call, there would be only the cool formality of her usual overture: "Ivy, dear, would you by any chance be free on Friday? We're having some amusing people in." Irving even presumed to disinvite her if he saw fit. "Oh, Ivy, I know I needn't stand on ceremony with as old a friend as you. Nicolo has just given out, and I haven't a man to balance you. Ordinarily I wouldn't care a hoot about an uneven table — you know I'm above such trivia — I ask my friends to dine, not to mate — but we're having Clara's old aunt, Angeline Warren, and you know what a stickler she is . . ."

Ivy knew too much of human vanity to expect any gratitude for her social help, but she began to be afraid that if the Steins took her too much for granted, they would end by despising her. She was never allowed to forget that it was *their* home, their food, their children, their parties. Her proposal of Elesina Dart for a weekend at Broadlawns had been a deliberate effort to show Clara and Irving that she was capable of producing something of value herself. It had been impossible for her to imagine that everyone might not feel about her young friend as she did.

She had met Elesina at Sam Gorman's. Sam was the bright, funny, effervescent arbiter elegantiarum of *Tone*. He was small, and bald on top, and had the big sad eyes of a lemur, but he never stopped joking and laughing. His apartment was an ever-changing warehouse of the household gadgets which he promoted, and his guests were as frequently varied as the decorations. Visiting Sam's rooms was like flipping the pages of *Tone*. He was constantly amused by Ivy, who used him, he claimed, as her social retriever and whom he professed to find "deep and dangerous." "I act as her screen," he would tell people; "the old spider selects the flies she wants from my net." Sam was also an occasional guest at the Steins', but he was apt to irritate Irving with jovial references to their shared Jewish background.

"Be nice to my friend Elesina Dart," he told Ivy one night.

"She's just lost her part in *Rosmersholm* for cutting rehearsals. If she doesn't beat the bottle, she's finished. It's too bad, for she has a very nice little talent."

It was not uncommon at Sam's buffets for two guests, even of the same sex, to eat their supper together in a corner, and when Ivy took a seat by Elesina, the latter welcomed her with a casual friendliness and an air of vague melancholy that seemed to relegate any expectation of a male companion to the realm of nonserious things. "Oh, how pleasant, Miss Trask. Will you join me? I want to hear about your work. I've often wondered what it would be like to be an editor. It's one thing I haven't tried so far."

It was rare to meet a person of striking beauty who seemed so unconscious of her own effect. Elesina was not naive, or even modest; more probably she simply did not care. Her interest in Ivy's life on *Tone* was mild enough, yet it was stronger than her interest in anything else that the room seemed to offer. Did she realize, Ivy wondered, that anyone born a Dart was a bit déclassée at Sam's party? Yet it might have been precisely a part of Elesina's charm that she could throw away assets with scarcely a shrug — as her career, for example. Ivy protested when her new friend asked the waitress for more bourbon.

"Try the wine, dear. It's better for you."

Elesina's eyes slightly widened. "But what a remarkable thing to expect of wine: to be good for you. Very well. I'll try it."

Ivy proceeded to talk about her life on *Tone*, but she guessed correctly that she would not hold this young woman's interest for long without striking a more personal note, and her instinct prompted her to shift to the story of herself and Edouardo as the origin of her magazine career. Elesina heard it to the end without saying a word. She seemed moved.

"But my poor Miss Trask . . ."

"Do call me Ivy."

"Ivy. You should have got off that train and gone to him! You should have saved him from his atrocious family. You could have, too. You have the force. I feel it!"

"I know I could have. But would it have been worth it? He didn't really want me. For such men the status quo is always best. Edouardo would have hated what I had cost him. Whatever I could have given him wouldn't have been worth the family row."

"You're wise. Too wise for your own good."

Ivy asked Elesina to dinner in the week following. It was at this dinner that the mishap occurred which precipitated their intimacy. Elesina arrived in poor condition and was very silent during the meal. The evening was not a success, and the other guests left early. Ivy suggested that her new friend, now frankly drunk, should spend the night in her bed while she slept on a couch in the living room. At one in the morning she saw the light go on under her bedroom door and went in to find Elesina, quite sober again, shaking pills in what seemed an undue profusion out of a bottle. Ivy hurried in to snatch the bottle.

"Elesina! Don't be a fool!"

"Oh, Ivy, it's not what you think — it's not that at all. I'm simply tired, and I can't get to sleep. All right, then, I *won't*. But you'll have to give me a drink."

"Just one. A small one. With a cup of hot milk."

"Very well. But you'll have to sit up and talk to me."

When Ivy had brought her a small bourbon and a large milk, Elesina seemed to take heart again. She came into the living room and reclined on the chaise longue, puffing a cigarette.

"No, Ivy, I wasn't trying to do myself in. I don't say the time won't come when I will, but it's not here yet. And when I do — *if* I do, that is — I'll be too much of a lady to do it in the home of a friend. How could you think I'd leave you with a mess like that to cope with? Think of the janitor and the police. Ugh!"

"Oh, my dear, do you think I could think of anything but you?" Ivy's instant tears made her image of Elesina blurred and wobbly. "How could you even contemplate doing such a thing? With all you have to live for? If you only knew how much less I started with!"

"Perhaps that's just it. I detest compromise. You see, Ivy, I was very greedy once. I wanted the whole world. Oh, I don't suppose there's anything wrong with that, any more than there's anything wrong with failing to get it. But it somehow seems ignoble to hang around indefinitely after one has failed."

"You can't talk about failure at your age."

"You can talk about failure at any age."

"Look at me. I was born a failure."

"That's why you're a success today."

"Some success." Ivy sniffed. "But if I'm not altogether a failure, it's because I don't admit it. Because I don't drink and take pills and carry on!"

Elesina took this in very good part. She laughed almost cheerfully. "Well, I shan't carry on, at any rate. As to the drinks and pills I make no promises. Not yet anyway." She sighed. "Oh, Ivy, I had it all! I had the looks and the ambition, perhaps even the talent. And what did I do with it? I threw it all away." Elesina described a long arc with her arm and shrugged at the futility of her own self-dramatization.

"How did you throw it away?"

"By not being satisfied. I once played Hedda Gabler. That should have been happiness for a lifetime. How much more can a woman ask than to play Hedda, Nora, Candida? Small wonder actresses have so little left over for their private lives. They've had enough — more than their share. There is no joy like theirs. Oh, yes, I've been near enough to it to know. Love — it can't compare. It's not in the running. But I had to have love, too. Yes, and motherhood. And parties and popularity. And money to scatter about. And drinks to drink. And things to pep me up and things to calm me down. God!"

"We live in a greedy world. That doesn't mean we can't learn not to be greedy."

"Oh, Ivy, how wise you are! Perhaps you can help me, after all. Can you take away my inner mirror so that I am not always seeing myself?"

"Seeing yourself how?"

"Seeing myself acting. Seeing myself making love. I could see my own Hedda, and it wasn't good enough. I could see the men who made love to me, and they weren't good enough. I could see my little girl, Ruth, and why she bored me. And I could see myself looking down on everybody, and I hated my own condescension. So I drank, but I saw myself drinking. I saw myself slipping — to the level of Sam Gorman's parties . . ."

"And Ivy Trask."

"Oh, Ivy. I'm sorry."

"Don't be. I was wondering if you did realize that you had slipped. If you do, you're all right. You can get back."

"Presuming I want to."

"Of course you want to! And you can get anywhere you want. I'll see to that. If you'll just let me be your coach. I think that's the word."

Elesina looked into her emptied glass for a long moment, but it was clear that Ivy was not going to refill it. At last she seemed to accept this, for she placed the glass carefully on the table. "Why do you care?" she asked.

"Will you really listen if I tell you?"

The two women stared at each other. Elesina, surprised, was the first who turned away. She lit another cigarette.

"We must be very frank if we are to work together," Ivy continued. "Have you ever seen a great star, one who has come up from the bottom, and thought how wonderful it

would have been to help her — before she made the grade?
Well, I won't be one who waits until it's too late."

"Great stars can be notoriously ungrateful."

"I'm not looking for gratitude."

"I see. You're Pygmalion. Must I go back to the stage?"

"When I say you'll be a star, I don't limit it to the stage."

"What then?"

"Anything!"

"A society leader? A millionaire's wife? A congress-
woman?"

"Anything!"

Elesina got up. "Ivy, you're an old fool. But you're a nice
old fool. I think I'll go home now."

"You'll stay right here. I won't have you going back to
that nasty hotel of yours at this time of night. And I think
you'd better get your things in the morning and move in here.
I'll take the maid's room. It's where I sleep in summer anyway, because it's cooler. And you needn't think I'm an old
lesbian, either. I have nothing to do with sex. I'm neuter!"
Elesina shrugged, as if questions of sex were irrelevant, boring. "And if I take you in hand, Elesina Dart, and help you
make something of yourself, you will owe me nothing. I shall
have done it all for the fun of it and nothing else!"

As Elesina turned to go back to the bedroom Ivy sensed
that she was accustomed to having people sacrifice themselves
for her. Good! It was the only way to start.

⋐ 4 ॐ

On a weekday after the weekend at Broadlawns which had
witnessed the unhappy events of the Schurman dinner, Clara
Stein sent Ivy a little pink note asking if she would come to
68th Street to discuss a "delicate matter." It was like Clara to
consider the telephone too public for private converse and to
assume that a working woman should always be able to find
the time in a busy day to call on a lady of leisure. Had she

not bought the services of Ivy Trask with a hundred dinners? The services? Had she not bought her soul?

"Mark my words," Ivy told Elesina. "She'll find some way to hang Irving's ugly outburst to Mrs. Schurman around *my* neck."

When she called on Clara, as early as she dared, on the excuse that it was on her way to work, she found the latter still in bed, reading a book in the great gilded Venetian shell that almost filled the room. Frescoes of angels and cupids against a blue sky and white clouds surrounded and covered her. On the half columns, in rococo style, sculptured cupids, who seemed to have flown out of the canvases, blew their horns.

"Ah, my dear Ivy, how good of you to come." Clara closed her volume slowly, as if she were doing her visitor a precious favor.

"I've only got a minute, I'm afraid, Clara. I have to get to the office."

"Of course. What I have to say won't take a minute. I simply wanted to make this observation. I'm dreadfully afraid that Miss Dart is not going to prove a true member of our little group. I didn't get the feeling that she liked us."

Ivy stared. "Maybe she can learn."

"Well, I don't know if that's necessary. It's not as if we were reduced to going into the highways and byways to compel guests to come in. Miss Dart is hardly indispensable."

"We must keep growing in this life, or we shrink."

"Dear me. You make me feel like a bad laundry. Perhaps we must agree to disagree. I think I should tell you that I have decided not to invite Miss Dart to our musicale on the thirteenth."

"But I've already asked her!"

Clara's expression became at once inscrutable. Faced with insurrection, she retired behind the silently closed doors of her impassivity. At the sound of the alarm small, dark heads would appear on the top of marble walls. Boiling water. Molten lead.

"You told me I might!" Ivy pursued hotly.

"I think your memory is at fault, dear. I told you *I* might. It did not occur to me that you would act as my delegate. I'm afraid that you will have to *décommander* Miss Dart."

"What has she done to you?"

"Nothing whatever to me. But Irving was most upset last Saturday night."

"That was hardly Elesina's fault."

"Your friend struck me as having an unsettling influence on the party. Maybe I'm being unfair, but even you will have to admit that she's a controversial character. She's been twice divorced, under decidedly unsavory circumstances. She abandoned her child. She is partial to stimulating drinks . . ."

"You've been investigating her!"

"The facts were not hard to come by."

"And I suppose nobody with those faults has ever been numbered among the guests at Broadlawns!"

"I don't think I like your tone, Ivy."

"How do you think I like yours?"

There was a moment of silence as they took each other in. The dark heads were lined up along the walls, the buckets poised. Then the drawbridge fell. The trumpet called for a parley.

"I suppose it's best to be candid," Clara said with a sigh. "Evidently you and I have been developing resentments against each other. I have imagined, for example, that you have been growing more worldly. More cynical. Indeed, it has struck me quite frequently in the past year."

"Worldly! This from the mistress of Broadlawns?"

"I don't judge worldliness by possessions. I judge it by character."

"And I'm too cynical for *your* parties? I and poor Elesina?" Ivy laughed. It was a hard, braying, mocking laugh.

The empress-commander paused, perhaps nonplused. What would they say on the ramparts? Would that laugh find an echo?

"At any rate, I shall expect neither of you at the musicale. I am sorry *you* will not be there, but the decision, you must admit, has not been mine."

It took Ivy until lunchtime to recognize that she had broken definitively with Clara Stein. All morning she half expected to pick up her telephone and hear Clara's voice assuring her that what had passed was simple madness. But that would not have been Clara's way. It would always be possible for Ivy to throw herself on Clara's mercy and beg forgiveness, after which she might expect to be reinstated in the Stein circle on a guarded provisional basis. But the first move would have to come from her. Clara did not need her. Clara did not need anyone. She expected to be surrounded by a tapestry of approving human faces, but whose they were at any particular time made little matter. In the month that followed no invitation came from 68th Street to the Althorpe. The break seemed final.

When Ivy heard from Fred Pemberton that Clara had gone to Florida for her annual visit to her old mother, she sent a note to Irving:

"I hear you're a bachelor. Could I break in on your busy liberty and claim you for one night — Wednesday dinner? I shall try to have some amusing people. Elesina Dart will be so happy to see you again. You made an immense impression there!"

She had assumed that Clara would not have mentioned the cause of the dispute to her husband. He accepted immediately, by telephone, stating gallantly that he was breaking an engagement to do so.

"I think I'll ask Sam Gorman," Ivy told Elesina. "He irritates Irving, it's true, but if he gets too fresh, you can slap him down, and Irving will be enchanted."

"Ivy, you old schemer! What makes you think I'd take the Judge's side against Sam?"

"Well, don't you want to help me get back into Clara's favor? It was you who lost it for me. If I can persuade Irving to intervene . . ."

"What must I do? Vamp the old boy?"

"Just be yourself. That should do nicely. He admires you so much. Besides, if you want an angel for your new comedy . . ."

"Ah, so that's it! Trust me!"

That was not it at all, but that would do for the moment. Ivy was pleased with her friend's progress in the past month. Elesina had moved into her apartment and had accepted her ministrations quite as if they were her due. She kept insisting that she would stay only a few days, but her departure was continually put off. She drank less now and went regularly to see her agent. She was even learning a part in a comedy by a young unproduced playwright.

"I shan't let Irving talk to you at cocktails," Ivy continued thoughtfully. "I shan't even put him next to you at dinner. By the time he gets you to himself, he'll be so frustrated he'll be ready to do anything you ask."

When Irving Stein arrived at the little party of eight the other guests were already assembled and Ivy was able to devote herself to him exclusively. She led him to a corner.

"I had a terrible tussle getting Elesina to let me ask you tonight," she confided in him.

"But why?" Irving's great bushy eyebrows were arcs of astonishment and sudden hurt. "Am I so objectionable?"

"Quite the contrary." Ivy permitted herself a smirk. "But you must know how actresses are. She's interested in a play, and she was afraid you'd think that she was looking for a backer."

Irving examined his hostess severely. Obviously he knew that he was dealing with a very clever woman. "And why should Miss Dart not regard me in that capacity? I have frequently put money into plays."

"That's just it. She has a horror of appearing to want anything from people. From people she likes, that is. You know how families like the Darts are. They can't bear to owe money to friends."

"You mean she considers me a friend?"

Ivy laughed roguishly. "There's no accounting for tastes, is there?"

"I suppose she sees me as a kind of avuncular figure."

Ivy pretended to give it up. "Yes, that must be it."

"Or even a father?"

"More like a grandfather."

Irving's look of disappointment was comic. "I must expect that sort of attitude at my age!"

She slapped his wrist. "Oh, Irving, don't be such an ass. I said she *liked* you. That means she's attracted to you. Do I have to cross all the t's in 'attracted'?"

"You mean she's the type that likes older men?"

"Well, I don't say she likes you *because* you're an older man. Both her husbands were rather callow youths. Perhaps they taught her to appreciate judgment and maturity. And you're still very good looking, Irving. Don't pretend you don't know it. I used to have a bit of a thing about you myself!"

She watched the Judge narrowly. But his vanity was proof against all suspicions. The lull in their argument was now interrupted by a livelier one between Sam Gorman and Fred Pemberton. It was, of course, Shakespeare again.

"It is one of the rare situations in which the bard seems dated," Pemberton was explaining. "He shared the morbid Elizabethan belief that a woman should never give herself to more than one man. How they loved to rant about this! Their faith in God would be lost, their sun and moon eclipsed, their universe degraded to an unweeded garden, if some poor female chose to exercise the simple human prerogative of sleeping around."

"But surely a man's compulsion to keep a woman to himself is not restricted to the Elizabethans," Irving interposed. "What about the Arab world? What about those harems guarded by eunuchs?"

Ivy looked about the pleasant little green-paneled room where the eight were assembled so cozily. Pemberton was doing just what she had wanted. His chatter was creating the same pedantic-erotic atmosphere of the disastrous night at Broadlawns. A fire crackled in the small grate under the marble Victorian mantel; Tiffany lampshades sparkled with iridescent hues. Elesina in black velvet looked creamy and elegant, as in a Sargent portrait. The other two women, magazine editors, were decorative without being competitive, and Irving, large, leonine, gravel-voiced, made a splendid guest of honor.

"Trust the Judge to assert the rights of the great proprietors," Sam Gorman chuckled. "I can just see you, Irving, as the master of a harem, striding through it, like Rembrandt's Grand Turk."

"And I can see you, too, Gorman. Perhaps in a different capacity."

"That should teach you to cross swords with Irving, Sam!"

"But, Elesina, if he's a Grand Turk and I'm a eunuch, what do you think that makes *you?*" Sam retorted. He appealed to the others. "Don't you think Elesina's an odalisque? I find her decidedly an odalisque!"

"Then look after your charges," Elesina told him, handing him her glass. "Get me a drink. I want to hear Fred's reply to Irving's interesting observation."

"Orientals are not relevant to the issue," Pemberton responded dogmatically. "The pashas simply strangled naughty wives; they did not become suicidal over them. They were realists. The stout walls of the harem indicated a healthy awareness that the weaker sex might be expected to bolt at the first opportunity. But somewhere along the line Christian society went off the tracks. It may have had to do with the deification of the Virgin. A man raised to believe that there was something holy in virginity could only forgive the woman who surrendered hers to himself. But I admit that the aberration produced some of the most beautiful poetry in the world. Art often flourishes on a denial of nature."

"I confess I have always been something of a medievalist," Irving observed. "Like Henry Adams, I am inclined to Mariolatry."

"Ah, one can see that in the divine Clara," Gorman exclaimed impertinently. "You have enshrined her at Broadlawns. It is your Chartres!"

Ivy was a bit uneasy at this, though Irving appeared to take it as a compliment. She decided it was time to move her guests in to dinner, where she placed Irving, to his barely contained displeasure, at the opposite end of the table from Elesina. Her plan cost her his cooperation during the meal, for he remained for the most part rather sullenly silent, but she knew that she could count on Fred Pemberton to keep things going, and her reward came later when they returned to the living room and Irving pressed angrily close behind her.

"I trust I shall be allowed two words with Miss Dart before I go home?"

Ivy stared with affected surprise. "Why, Irving, you old darling, of course! What *can* I have been thinking of?"

At midnight, when the guests were gone, Elesina, glass in hand, stared moodily into the dying fire.

Ivy, back from locking the front door, asked: "Well?"

"I feel like a whore. And what do you think that makes *you?*"

"Our customers didn't pay anything. We must be novices in the business."

"Novices! Everything went just as you planned. I shall have no trouble raising the money for the play. No trouble, that is, other than we anticipated."

"And what did we anticipate?"

Elesina turned now to look at her scornfully. "I shall have to sleep with him, of course."

"Did he say so?"

"What do you take him for? He's a gentleman. But we know what these understandings are."

"The madam doesn't."

"Oh, Ivy, stop being funny."

Ivy came over to take an opposite seat by the fire. "All right, I'll be serious. If you become Irving Stein's mistress, I shall never have anything to do with you again."

Elesina seemed only mildly surprised. "You wish me to lead him on?"

"Certainly not. I want you to be perfectly direct and perfectly honest. I want you to marry him." Elesina continued to contemplate the embers. "Fred Pemberton is not altogether the ass he seems. He has some shrewd insights. We women have been unjustly treated. Oh, I'm not talking about the political side," she added as she saw Elesina's shrug. "I'm no militant. I can make do with things as they are. But men have to be jockeyed a bit. There is no reason why Irving should not make up for what his sex has done to you. Particularly when he will find a new life and a new happiness in doing so."

"What about Clara?"

"You find me disloyal?"

"I find you . . . interesting."

"Clara has had quite enough out of life. She has had a lot more than she needs or even wants. She doesn't care for Irving physically anymore. I doubt she ever did. It's only right that she should give him up to a younger woman. She will have money, and the devotion of children and grandchildren. She should not complain."

"Ivy Trask, you're a very wicked woman!" Elesina exclaimed with a sudden laugh. "I see now I was right to be afraid of you from the start."

"I take the world as I find it," Ivy retorted. "I have had to maneuver and scheme for every bone that's been flung at me in the yard. Clara has only had to sit on her ass and receive the bounties of the world. It's all very well for her to hold up her moral titles and cry: 'Hands off!' But the only laws I obey are the laws of the land. I never subscribed to any others. I never benefited from any others. So let Clara watch out! There is no law against divorce."

Elesina said nothing more, and Ivy, who always knew when to stop, rose and bade her good night.

☙ 5 ☙

When Elesina was sixteen, she played Shylock in *The Merchant of Venice*. It was the custom of Miss Dixon's Classes, as her school was named, to produce one Shakespeare play a winter, and the dramatics coach had assumed that Elesina Dart, who had made such a hit the year before as Juliet, would seek the role of Portia. Great had been the astonishment in Miss Dixon's "green room" when Elesina had not only insisted on the role of the Jew, but had performed it with such fire and spitting venom that some of the mothers had complained about the choice of play. Where on earth had Elesina Dart, so admirably reared, learned to impersonate an oleaginous Hebrew moneylender? Surely not from anyone in the guarded circle of Mr. and Mrs. Amos Dart.

Mrs. Dart made no secret of her distaste, either for her daughter's role or for her success in it.

"I don't approve of girls acting in any case," she remarked to Elesina after briefly watching the closing minutes of a rehearsal. "And I certainly don't approve of the attitudinizing required by a character part. It brings out the worst social characteristics. Don't forget, my dear: the greatest clown on the stage can be the biggest bore at a dinner party."

But the value of her role to Elesina was precisely that it taught her for the first time to question her mother's social judgments and to wonder if she wanted a life whose supreme sacrament was the evening meal. Until then her parents had seemed so strong, so well attired, so correct of speech and coordinated of movement, so in control of their bodies and tempers, whether on the golf course or at the bridge table, like improbable aristocrats in luxury advertisements, that she had been forced to assume the existence of some kind of true faith behind such impressive orthodoxy. But now she began to wonder if it were not all a front. She began to question the rule at home and the rule at school. Shylock became her protest against three hundred incipient female anti-Semites clad in the bulging green bloomers, plain green blouses, black cotton stockings and low-heeled shoes which Miss Dixon required as the uniform necessary to mortify the vanity of her sex in preparation for a lifetime devoted to its gratification.

But Elesina dwelt only passingly on the ethnic aspects of the play. It was in Shylock's passion that she found her balm for the sore inflicted on her soul by the aridity of her world. As she scuffled about the stage, clutching her cloak around her neck and snarling at Antonio, she had a gleeful sense of corrected vision, of being able, in the few short hours devoted to a rehearsal for what would be the mere two of performance, to glimpse a greater reality of hate, of indignation and of joy, pure joy, at creating a little nugget of beauty out of the spit and sediment of her inheritance. For the trouble with all the world, she could see now, was just that it was not a stage, or even a decent replica of one. The most one could do with it, if one had any gift at all, was to turn it into an audience.

Amos and Linda Dart were the kind of doves whose life-long satisfaction was to perch and coo on the tiptop rung of the social ladder. They differed from more ordinary social aspirants in that they never felt the smallest urge to impress others with their achievement. One could have taken a cruise around the world with the Darts without hearing them once drop the name of Grace Vanderbilt or Mona Williams. Nor had they anything in common with those little brothers of the rich who, constantly in debt, cadge loans and scant tips. Their income from a modest Dart trust, however exiguous for their milieu, was never overspent. They had just enough, with careful planning, to equip themselves smartly, to keep a little jewel of an apartment in Manhattan, to send Billy and Elesina to private schools and to travel in first-class accommodations to the various country houses where their presence was regularly sought.

In summertime the Darts often enjoyed the loan of an unoccupied villa by the sea or of a comfortable gatehouse, but they were always careful not to place themselves too much under even moral obligations, and any benefactor was apt to regard himself more in their debt than they in his. "Think of my luck," he would exclaim to friends. "Amos and Linda are going to be in Far Hills all of August in our guest cottage!" For the Darts not only played games with skill and perfect sportsmanship, they talked well; they were never sick, late, drunk or ill tempered, and they could be counted on to be charming even to poor relatives. It was also a source of gratification that they were happily married and much in love, which not only removed them from the suspicious probings of jealous spouses, but gave them a rather stylish little air of independence from the social pattern in which they were otherwise so deeply enmeshed. Only a stupid observer could have failed to see that Amos and Linda would have given up anything for a dinner party but each other.

Amos as a husband was more led than leading, not because he was weak, but because Linda had the clearer eye, the sharper mind. He in turn had the greater sex appeal, being gentle and affable, with sunny blue eyes and curly hair, while her Grecian nose and erect posture suggested an armature under her handsome figure. Had Linda's motto, "Nothing in

excess," been applied to her domestic life, her children might
have grown up in the pattern of their parents, but nature
betrayed her to a single exaggeration: a passion for her sullen,
delicate, brooding, dark-eyed son. She did not neglect Elesina; no mother could have been more correct in her attentions, but the girl was never under the smallest illusion that
Billy was not the favorite child.

Obviously, it was up to Amos to correct this imbalance of
family emotion by making a particular thing of his relationship with his daughter, and being a gentleman he did what
was expected, but Elesina from childhood had a suspicion,
murky at first, clearing later and at length bathed in laughter,
that both were playing parts. When she flung her arms about
his neck and cried: "Oh, Papa, my beloved Papa, swear you'll
never leave me!" and he cried back: "Liebchen, I'll shoot the
man who tries to take you from me!" they would smile
broadly enough at the benignity of their performance, but
behind that smile there was always, at least on her part, the
suspicion of tears, tears that their reality was not what they
played, could not be what they played, because reality could
never be art, because truth could never be more than the
mirror of aspiration.

In the two years that followed her success in *The Merchant*
Elesina became even less emotionally involved with her family. She was occupied now in a love affair with herself,
intoxicated with the discovery of her own dark beauty. She
would spend hours before her mirror, making herself up,
doing her hair in different ways, posing as Nazimova, as Pola
Negri, as Natasha Rambova. She formed passionate, brief
attachments to girls in her class; she wrote a whole novel
about a debutante who was abducted by a bootlegger; she
was even suspended from Miss Dixon's Classes for smoking.
Only her mother's threat to send her to a strict boarding
school in the South induced her to come back to graduate.
Her classmates voted her most likely to succeed — in all
matters not pertaining to domesticity.

But all of this mattered little enough; the time had come for boys. Linda Dart had to give up some of her own social activities to supervise and chaperone her giddy daughter through the fever of her debutante year, and that Elesina was still a virgin when she eloped with Bill Nolte a month before her coming-out party was attributable entirely to the indefatigable maternal endeavors. But the elopement was to cost Elesina more than she had reckoned. It was to cost her a large portion of her mother's interest and care. From now on she was on her own. Linda, to be sure, was available for consultation, for advice, but Elesina had heard the splash of washed hands. Bitterly in her mind she accused her mother of having objected more to her elopement than to her marriage. Had it not mortally offended Linda's very grandest friend, Mrs. Emory, whose ball in Elesina's honor, the product of the subtlest Dart planning, had had to be called off after the invitations were out?

Nolte was a cipher. In later years Elesina found it difficult to recall even what he had looked like. He was one of those pretty boys who went to every party and knew every debutante without having any clearly identifiable family or even friends. In fact, he had attended Columbia and was a customers' man in a small brokerage house. He was also endowed with a dull but respectable widowed mother who lived in Orange, New Jersey, and who detested Elesina on sight. With marriage Nolte rushed to domestic dullness as if it were a heaven of limited seats and lost his looks, as it seemed, overnight. Who was this chubby, pompous little bore to whom Elesina now found herself bound? In less than a year she was home again.

Alas, it was not the same home. Amos had cancer, and in the bleak months that were left to him his despairing wife had little time for her troublesome daughter. Elesina turned to the stage and obtained two walk-on parts. Then she had a break. A season in summer stock in Westchester resulted in a Broadway role that she was uniquely fitted to play: the bored heiress who yearns for a "real" experience and becomes the willing tool of a cynical but charming jewel robber. The play was trash, but Percy Hammond noted in his review: "Miss Dart brings to her part the authenticity of a lady and the *sans-gêne* of a flapper — a fine job of balance. One wonders where she will go from here."

The good luck of this part was largely canceled by its bringing Elesina into the orbit of Ted Everett, who played her brother in the play. He was the son of a Wall Street banker, and his real reason for being on the stage was to irritate his father, though he fancied that his loud, shrill voice and morbid temperament might one day make him a distinguished Hamlet. He was good looking, in a weak, blond, attenuated way, and he made an excellent first impression when he wished to, knowing how to endow his interlocutor with the flattering conviction that he was one of the few who were capable of responding to Ted Everett's intense vibrations. Elesina, like many who fancy that they wish to escape from society, was enchanted to discover a fellow refugee in her new milieu, and soon she and Ted were having supper together every night after the show, drinking whiskey and exchanging horror stories about their families. Ted was amusing, until one realized that his only true interest was in himself and his imagined grievances, but Elesina did not know this until after they had gone down to that lavender chamber in City Hall and exchanged their vows. The very next morning Ted made a terrible scene because the newspaper item about their union described Elesina as a rising actress and himself as merely the son of Lawson Everett.

The marriage, like Ted's acting career, seemed to draw its principal support from paternal disapproval. Mr. Everett, a Southern Baptist who did not recognize divorce and would not countenance actresses, refused even to meet Elesina, which gave Ted a saturnine satisfaction. But what little chance of happiness the young couple might have had was eliminated by Ted's failure, when the run of their play was over, to find another part. He expected that Elesina would share his idleness so long as their bit of money lasted, but she was offered a role in a new comedy and accepted it. Only then did she discover the full depths of her husband's egotism. For ten days he did not address a single word to her. Then she received a telephone call from his father asking her to come downtown to lunch.

"Everything that my son Theodore does is designed to thwart me," this large bland disciplined man of money explained to her over an omelette and a glass of claret. "His marriage to a divorced actress is merely the most recent example of this. Don't take offense, my dear. You're too intelligent. Face the fact that you've married a weakling, and leave him to me. When he is finally convinced that he cannot anger me, he will become manageable, and I may be able to make something at least respectable of him. But while he is married to you and fooling about theaters, I can't do a thing. Give him up. I cannot believe that your emotions are deeply involved. Give him up, and I'll make it worth your while."

"Why do you assume he'll come back to you if I give him up?"

"Because he has no place else to go. After all, you're paying the rent now. You see, I'm well informed."

"But do you really want him to come back?"

"I want to do my duty. There's nothing you can do for him. There's something I might."

"Poor Ted." Elesina reflected for a moment. "The trouble is that I'm pregnant. I'm afraid we'll have to go on with what we've started."

It was like Elesina to be able to take in the little scene as it was being enacted. She saw just what would have been wrong with it on the stage: none of the three persons involved really cared about either of the others. It wouldn't play. Nor did it, in the ensuing two years. Little Ruth was born; Ted took minor jobs in advertising, in publishing, in radio; he and Elesina gave periodic drinking parties for a motley group of actors, writers and publicists whose common denominator was a disposition to failure. For Ted had an instinct which always recognized in others his own particular weakness. Only Elesina, of all his group, seemed bound for better things, and even her career seemed to have reached its top when she joined the Columbus Circle Repertory, an institution as applauded by the liberal press as it was neglected by the general public.

Nor had life been kind to the Darts. Amos Dart was dead, and Elesina's brother, Billy, had become an interior decorator in partnership with the man who was his lover. Linda Dart's passion for her son did not survive his choice of a career and mate. She passed through what was to her a tunnel of the blackest humiliation and emerged as contained and uncomplaining as before, but colder and even more reserved. She lunched with her two children now at regular intervals, and she was always civil, amusing, interested, but both knew that they had disappointed her beyond the possibility of redemption. Linda now devoted all of her time to her rich friends, and she found herself in greater demand than ever. Her arrival in a drawing room, erect, cheerful, crisply neat, with the right greeting for everyone and the latest gossip strained through a sieve of worldly wisdom, gave a cachet to a party. The astute climber would know that he had arrived when he heard his neighbor say: "Ah, there's Linda Dart. I always know I'm in for a good evening when I see her. Would you believe she's sixty-five?"

Elesina was surprised at her own reaction to her mother's cooling toward Billy. There was not the least hint of sibling jealousy in it. She was simply shocked. Somehow it did not seem to matter which child their mother loved so long as she loved *one*. That Linda Dart should turn from Billy showed a hollow in the very core of a family love that Elesina had somehow regarded as basic to her environment even if it did not wholly include herself. It taught her to face the shabby fact that her indifference to little Ruth was something more than the "horror of babies" that she had, with a show of the charming actress' easily forgiven capriciousness, affected for the benefit of herself and others. Ted was more and more boring; he listened to her now only in discussions directed to some aspect of his own self-pity. He drank more, and Elesina began to drink with him.

Theater life is conducive to love. Not only is romance the usual subject of the drama, with all the accompaniment of public strutting and public embraces, but a humid atmosphere of lubricity invades even its technical conversations. Everyone is "darling" or "sweetie"; hands are held; arms are stroked; even hostility is expressed erogenously. Elesina drifted into the habit of casual affairs, usually with other actors, vaguely hoping that a great passion would come her way, but never much surprised that it failed to. Ted, furnished with information and money by his father, who had remained Elesina's implacable opponent, sued her at last for divorce for adultery and claimed sole custody of their daughter. Elesina did not bother to defend the suit, and she found herself, with her thirtieth birthday already well retreating into a disordered past, in the midst of a world depression, childless, husbandless, homeless and penniless, except for the precarious income derived from her repertory company. Even this ceased when, drunk, she failed for a third time to appear for a rehearsal of *Rosmersholm*.

Linda Dart was as kind as could be expected. She took Elesina into her apartment and kept her as long as either could stand it. Elesina found the order in her mother's life a daily reproach, and Linda in turn was disgusted by her daughter's carelessness as to hours and engagements. Eventually it was agreed that Elesina should live in a small hotel around the corner at her mother's expense and come home for certain meals. This was still their arrangement when Elesina announced her proposed move to Ivy Trask's.

"I've inquired about Miss Trask," Linda told her daughter

dryly. "She seems to come of a respectable upstate background. I believe there was even an uncle in TR's cabinet.
But she's identified now with that slick, rather sleazy fashion
world, and she's intimate with the Steins. I should think you
could do better. Is she a lesbian?"

"No. At least I don't think so. She says not."

"Did you ask her? Anyway, I wouldn't be sure. But I
don't expect my advice to be followed by my children. Isn't
it funny? All my friends come to me for guidance."

"You pick your friends. You didn't pick your children."

"That's true enough. Speaking of which, what do you hear
of little Ruth?"

If Elesina had had any further doubts about the wisdom of
her move, the tone of her mother's question would have
convinced her. "Little Ruth is very well, I believe. I shall be
glad to have a place where she can visit me without disturbing
anyone."

⤙§ 6 §⤚

Elesina had to admit that Irving Stein's attentions came at an
opportune time. The author of her new comedy had with-
drawn it from production under a charge of plagiarism, and
she found herself without a prospect. It was an occupation in
her idleness to study her new friend's procedure. Both she
and Ivy were surprised at the Judge's conservatism. He took
them to dine at a restaurant and then to hear Flagstad as
Isolde. He took them to a private viewing of Leonardo drawings, to a Lunt-Fontanne matinee, to a lecture at the Bar
Association by Justice Cardozo. On these occasions he devoted his attention exclusively to Elesina, treating Ivy with
the perfunctory courtesy that is accorded by the tenor in
Italian opera to the duenna contralto. But it was interesting
to both women that he made no effort to drop the chaperone.

"Maybe he's afraid to be alone with me," Elesina suggested.
"Maybe he thinks *I'm* the schemer."

"No, he has a plan. I've known Irving a long time. He's a very deliberating man."

"What does the divine Clara think of our excursions? Surely, she must be back from Florida."

"Oh, she's long back. She's just being her Sphinx-like self. You're not, after all, my dear, Irving's first illicit passion. Even if it does happen to be my theory that you'll be his last. Clara gives him a lot of rein."

At last came the invitation for Elesina alone. It was formal, by letter, and entirely proper. Could she lunch with Irving at the 21 Club and discuss a business matter? When she arrived, strictly on the hour as became the nature of such an engagement, she found him, regal at a corner table, discussing wines with the proprietor. He had already ordered for her. They discussed no business over the soup or fish. Irving was in an expansive mood: he held forth on the economic inequities of the modern world and of the warnings to public figures that he had issued in vain. He had said this to Franklin Roosevelt, that to Alfred Landon. He was a bit pompous, to be sure, but there was a touch of majestic gravity, of senatorial dignity in his measured tones and gesticulating hands, in the great nodding head, the plump, rigid figure. Irving was at least the portrait of a statesman.

When he turned at last to business, the change was marked by a pause, a muffled cough. "Have you ever read *Les Corbeaux*, or *The Vultures*, by Henry Becque?"

"No."

"Well, you must do so now. I am planning to underwrite its revival by the Columbus Circle Repertory. On condition that you play the part of Marie Vigneron."

"Are you aware that I have blotted my copybook with that company?"

"Oh, yes, we've discussed all that. They are quite ready to forget those missed rehearsals. I told them it had been a difficult period in your life."

She might have been an erring student before an amiable,

omnipotent headmaster, but there was sympathy and even humor in the reddish pupils of his solemn gray eyes.

"Tell me about the play."

"The scene is laid in Paris, in eighteen eighty-one. We are in the happy domestic interior of Monsieur and Madame Vigneron, prosperous burghers. They have three daughters and a little boy. All is love and good will. One daughter is engaged to a young noble, a big social step forward. But at the end of the first act the father suddenly collapses and dies. Instant ruin. His lawyer, his architect, his business partner, all combine to cheat and destroy the widow and children. These are the major vultures; the minor ones are tradesmen who dun the poor women for already paid bills. The young count withdraws from his engagement, and his fiancée goes mad. You see, there was no way for untrained women in that time to earn any effective income; they were perfectly helpless. At last Marie Vigneron decides to accept the offer of marriage of Teissier, her father's old business partner and the worst vulture of all."

"And that's all?"

"That's all. The family are saved. Teissier is strong enough to drive off the other vultures."

"So Marie really likes him?"

"Oh, no, not at all."

"Not even a tiny bit?"

"He absolutely repels her. That's the point. She does the only thing she *can* so. It's a terrific play."

Elesina reflected. "Because it's true? Or because it was true back then? But is it true today? Would a girl like Marie have to marry a vulture?"

"Hardly. Today a girl could support herself. You know that. But there are still such problems. *And* such remedies. Becque is not as far back as the Dark Ages. Besides, it's a wonderful part. Marie is cold, still, even a trifle grim."

"Is that how you see me?"

"Don't be coy, dear. That is how an actress of your stature

would play her. And yet at the same time convey a sense of the ache and passion within."

"Does Marie have a lover she gives up for the vulture?"

"No, she has nothing. Nothing, that is, but a whole inner life throbbing with thwarted emotion. That is why it is such a rich part. I see Marie in mourning, in simple black, very pale, businesslike, tense, allowing the family sympathy to be lavished on her giddy younger sister, not caring if people think she's giving up nothing because they find her cold, yet all the while feeling a burning pain at the senseless cruelty of the world, at the bleak smothering of her natural ardor . . ."

"Why, Irving, you should have been an actor yourself!"

"Oh, my dear, as a young man, I had many ambitions. I wanted to be an opera singer. A pianist. A poet. My father was a clever man as well as a humane one. He humored me in all my dreams. And when I began to realize the paucity of my histrionic and artistic talents, he eased me into the ancient compromise of law. I believe that all the while he knew that I would one day come back to his banking business."

"But you don't regret that, do you? Aren't you happy, being rich and important, buying beautiful things and . . ."

"Trying to buy beautiful people?" he interrupted with a chuckle. "Is that where you come out, Elesina?"

"We'll get to that later. Answer my question first. Do you regret your banking career?"

"Yes and no." Irving took a sip of white wine, almost as if it were a medicine. Certainly he was not a drinker. He coughed and fixed his eyes glassily at a point across the room. "I once told a young man in our office that the person whose career I most coveted was Judge Learned B. Hand, my old Harvard Law School classmate. He is now the great legal philosopher of the second federal circuit, and would have been, but for our New Deal president — you needn't rise — the greatest luminary of the Supreme Court today. Well, it so happened, unbeknownst to me, that this same young man was related to the judge, and the next time he dined there, he was careful to relay my compliment. "B" Hand pounded angrily on the table and roared out: 'Irving Stein envies me my career, does he? Did he tell you that, as he strutted before his Rembrandts? Or as he sank, knee-deep, in Persian carpet? Well, go back to Irving Stein and tell the old robber I'd give my career for a paltry one of his millions!' "

Irving hit the table as he simulated the angry, self-dramatizing jurist. Elesina smiled. "I like that," she said. "I think I'd like Judge Hand."

"Of course, he didn't mean it. At least not all of it. It goes to show that only a fool is satisfied that he's led just the life he should have led. How do we know? As you say, I've been able to buy beautiful things, and that is a solace. And now I can produce a beautiful play. That is another."

"But you need solace?"

"Who doesn't? I hate *not* having done so many things. And I hate growing old."

"Oh, Irving, you're not really . . ."

"Don't say it, dear." He put his hand over hers, and gave it a squeeze. But it was a friendly, almost fraternal squeeze. The acceptance of it committed her to nothing. "Let us think about the part. Does it attract you?"

"I don't know." She paused. "Of course, I'm immensely flattered that you think I can do it. Obviously, it's a very difficult one."

"It's a challenge. But you deserve a challenge."

"Is it just a challenge?" She was a bit ashamed of the arch that she felt it was now time for her eyebrows to assume.

"What do you mean?"

"Well, isn't it taken for granted, in sophisticated circles, that wealthy bankers don't invest in plays for actresses without a certain recompense in mind?"

Irving nodded, his lips pursed, grave. "I'm glad you made the point. Of course, what I'm doing would bear that look to the world. But I promise you, Elesina, that I shall never expect anything that is not accorded of your own free will and inclination. I make no secret of the fact that I am attracted to you. How could that not be? You are young and beautiful, and I am still a man. But what of it? I was never one to buy love, nor do I esteem you so little as to suppose that you would sell it. Let there be an end to such talk between us. You and I are friends. The best of friends. Why not? If our relationship should ever change, it would be only because *you* wished it to. And as that is hardly likely, you can put the matter out of your mind. Why should we care what other people say?"

"Well, I don't, certainly, but then I'm free."

"And so am I, where my friends are concerned. Mrs. Stein does not trouble herself with such matters."

Elesina hardly believed this, but then she hardly cared what Clara Stein thought of her husband's friendships. She suspected that Irving's seeming candor might be part of a scheme to seduce her through her gratitude on some night when she had drunk too much. But what if it were? Could she not handle herself? And so long as she purported to take him at his word, how could he possibly complain?

"Well, then, it's a bargain," she agreed with a sealing smile. "I'll read the play this afternoon."

During the rehearsal and short run of *The Vultures* Elesina was happier than she had ever been before. The play was too bleak to be popular, but the notices were good, and her performance as Marie Vigneron established her, in the eyes of professionals, as at least a contender for high rank. As one critic said:

Miss Dart puts one in mind of some abandoned princess on a reef about to be engulfed by a rising tide. There is nothing in the closing waters of which she has the least dread; they will simply free her from the scurrying, malignant crustacean life about her. She makes one feel that her real tragedy is not her abandonment, but her rescue.

The role gave Elesina her first sense of creative accomplishment. Her Hedda Gabler she had modeled from Nazimova's, but she had never seen *The Vultures* performed. There she was, on the boards, Marie Vigneron, something independent of Elesina Dart, something that had not existed before, a tiny piece of reality, something "done." Oh, yes, she saw all the things of her own that she had put into it: her self-pity, her identification of her failures with Marie's plight, her half-bitter, half-amused dependence on Irving. And she never fooled herself that there was anything in common between the heroic Marie and the self-indulgent Elesina. But none of this made any difference. Was not everything grist to an artist's mill? *King Lear* could have been made up out of Shakespeare's vanity; *Hamlet,* out of his resentment. Art was a process of conversion, a machine that could turn even garbage into something clean and glistening. Had Irving seen this? Had he seen that Marie was the image of her own ego touched up?

She lunched with him now twice a week. He was willing to leave his office at her least suggestion. Walking down the street to their rendezvous, she would enjoy a pleasant sense of power when she saw the big blue Isotta pull up beside the restaurant and Irving leaning forward to wave at her. She had learned to savor the sweep of his conversation and the breadth of his ideas. She was merely amused now by the persistent little vanity that provided a plaintive chorus to larger themes. She had become humbler with her own small success, humble enough, anyway, to recognize that the friendship of Irving Stein might turn out to be the most interesting thing that had ever happened to her.

Sometimes they would spend an afternoon in galleries, for he maintained his relentless pursuit of beautiful objects. They would pass into the back chamber where the tactful proprietor would leave the great collector and his friend alone to contemplate a selected number of rarities. Irving would sit silent before a canvas or a statue for as many as fifteen minutes at a time, and Elesina loved the peace of such periods. It seemed to her that she was witnessing a kind of draining, as if whatever was finest in the masterpiece were somehow passing into the silent, crouching acquisitor. She began to see what Irving meant when he said that art was only communication, that if the recipient could take in the beauty in its totality, he might become the equal of the creator.

On an afternoon of particular peace and pleasureableness Elesina sat with Irving in a mauve-curtained show room before five French eighteenth-century paintings: two Bouchers, a Fragonard, a Greuze and a Charpentier. The sexuality of the scenes was intense: alabaster nymphs with large exposed thighs and breasts clutched ineffectively at silken undergarments to excite or frustrate peeking gallants; a wife in nightdress sent a flying kiss to a departing husband as a lover concealed behind her bed clutched her free hand in anticipation; a naked girl on a red couch contemplated her painted cheeks in a mirror held in one hand while the other fingered her crotch; a panting Leda submitted to the violent attentions of a huge lusting swan against the background of a riverbank which provided an audience of leering flowers.

"The Frenchwoman of that era was your sex at its most superb," Irving commented placidly. "Woman was at her most feminine: every chateau, every piece of furniture or porcelain, every medallion, every bit of drapery, every fan, every loop and tassel bespoke the charming, the worshiped female. Not for those girls was the law degree, the medical career. Ah, no! They knew that the way to power was to be irresistible to men. And the century was theirs! Marie Antoinette, Sophie Arnould, the Du Barry, Catherine of Russia. It is hard to point to a statesman except Frederick of Prussia — and he liked the boys — who was not under petticoat influence."

"Until we come to America."

"Exactly. Martha Washington. What aridity! What puri-

tanism! That was a man's world, of business and of politics.
And in the nineteenth century men reduced it to business
alone. What could the poor women do but strut around in
diamonds and Irish lace and give balls? Compare the Mrs.
Astor with Madame de Pompadour!"

Elesina was filled with a sense of ease and laughter. Laughter at herself and laughter at him. How beautifully he had
planned it all! The champagne that she had drunk at lunch
made her pleasantly drowsy; the pink and white flesh tints in
the sexy French scenes titillated her. There were no nude
males in any of the canvases to offer an unlovely contrast to
Irving's own plump figure or gray hairs. The lusting swan
was all there was to suggest the copulating male. Nothing in
Irving's words or his demeanor betrayed the amorous old
man, the ludicrous Pantaloon of comedy. He preserved his
dignity, nay, he preserved his superiority — the superiority of
his greater years and experience and wealth, of his venerable
old bull maleness — without the least remission. He was like
some eminent doctor, the last authority in his field, whose
diagnosis she had sought and for an appointment with whom
she had waited anxious hours in a crowded anteroom. Now
she was in his office, the holy of holies; she had stripped off
her last stitch behind a scanty curtain at his gruff instruction
and was about to step forth, shivering, to expose herself to his
grave contemplation.

"And where does that leave the poor twentieth-century
female?" she demanded.

"With everything before her. There is nothing women did
in the past they cannot do in the present."

"Oh, pooh, Irving, you know that isn't so. You speak of
women giving men an ideal. What woman ever gave you
yours? Your ideal was to create a temple of beauty at Broadlawns, and you've done it. You could have done it as a
bachelor."

"No, my dear, I needed a priestess for the shrine."

"And that was Clara?"

"Certainly. Clara played an immense role in the conception of Broadlawns."

Elesina noted the use of the past participle. It was as near as he would come to denying the continuing function of Clara. Really, he was almost too tactful. She closed her eyes in sudden giddiness, and she was back in the doctor's chamber, now lying on the examining table. In her fantasy she raised her knees, and his clinical fingers deftly searched.

"Irving!" she exclaimed in a rasping tone as she opened her eyes. "Do you have any place that we could go? I loathe hotels." He reached at once to take her hand, but she drew it quickly back. "Please, no preliminaries. But we'd better go now. I might change my mind."

"I don't think you're going to regret this." She rose, and he helped her into her coat. "I have a house in the West Fifties. It's empty, but furnished. They clean it every morning. I use it to store things I haven't room for at home. It's a bit heterogeneous but entirely comfortable."

After that he had the sense to be silent until they arrived at his house. It was in a huge Louix XIV canopied bed, in a chamber filled with baroque armoires and tapestried bergères, with the fading winter sunlight filtered through silk curtains, that Elesina tested the identity of her fantasy doctor with Irving Stein. Like all her other experiments it had its elements of disappointment. But it was not as bad as she had feared it might be in the renewed sobriety of the taxi ride from the art gallery.

❧ 7 ❧

Irving Stein sat in his office, thirty floors above Broad Street, turning the illuminated pages of a fourteenth-century book of hours, made for a king's brother. No matter what his perturbation of mind, he could usually find consolation in the primitive figures of saints in golden orbs, equally at peace whether feeding birds on tiny emerald lawns under fairy-castle towers or lying prone on flaming braziers. "Everything can be made to fit," he would say, "if only one sees the whole."

His office was appropriate to the contemplation of a book of hours. It was a Burgundian library, with gray panels interspersed in checkerboard design with painted boards, representing crude but charming landscapes, a green blob for a bush, a silver cord for a stream, a gray stone for a castle. The ceiling was arched into a cupola with a fresco of the Last Judgment; the walls contained cupboards with dark grilled doors to protect the gold gleaming folios. But Irving rose now, restless, unable to read, and walked to the window.

The week that had followed his afternoon with Elesina in the empty brownstone had been one of a strange sustained exhilaration. At the office, at his club, at home, his mood had been vague, detached, inattentive. He was like a mystic who had penetrated to a finer realm of truth; for those less privileged he had only a remote pity which merged with a faint impatience when they forced themselves between him and his vision.

It had always been his habit of mind to fit each new event into an aesthetic pattern. He liked to match the successful underwriting of an issue of municipal sewer bonds to the discovery, after months of seeking, of the twin of a Cellini dolphin, completing a gold centerpiece. He liked to think of Cicero when he addressed a stockholders' meeting, and he had even gone so far as to try to identify the furtive handpressings and clutchings of his later years with a lifelong pursuit of beauty. Everything could be made to fit if only one saw the whole.

In his youth he had agonized his Orthodox parents by what had seemed to them his casual abandonment of their faith. They had even taken his interest in collecting reliquaries as a threat that he might become a Catholic convert. They had never been able to comprehend that the search for beauty was bound to take him across religious and even moral lines. If

Irving had any faith at all, it was that an assemblage of the finest objects, heaped up before the eyes of the supreme critic and offered as the ultimate tribute of man, might induce that deity to forgive, or at least to overlook, the crimes that lay behind art: the Inquisition behind the Gothic cathedral, the gladiatorial combat behind the Roman temple, the slave ship behind the porticoed Southern mansion. Certainly, in his cultivation of rich Episcopalian bankers, the type of American most distrusted by his parents, Irving had been more apt to see the art-loving trustee of the Metropolitan Museum than the anti-Semitic trustee of the Metropolitan Club. But then he had always found it hard to see evil in any soul that shared his passion.

As a young man he had been dedicated to literature and had purchased the great Shakespeare quartos for his library, but as he had grown older his tastes had become more sensual. It was not that he abandoned poetry and philosophy and other pleasures of the mind, but rather that he came more to value the aesthetic experience that involved the senses: the ear, the eye, even the touch. It seemed to Irving that the act of love must be the closest that a human could come to the comprehension of perfect beauty, and he would play over and over his discs of the second act of *Tristan*, sensing in its rhythms the finest interpretation in any art of the movement of lovers in sexual intercourse. He had even gone so far as to play the scene while he and Clara were in bed, hoping to give her some faint conception of the joys locked in her fine body, but the experiment had been a shaming failure.

Everyone, he had always been aware, both in the Stein and Clarkson worlds, had taken for granted that he had married Clara for social advantage, and in a sense this was true, though it seemed less crude to a bridegroom who filtered it through the tints of a hyperactive imagination. For Irving had seen in Clara a sort of Roman princess, tall, beautiful, proud, chaste, a Julia or Honoria, garbed in white, last daughter of a dying race, a final chapter of a mighty history, and in himself an

Attila, splendid in energy, savage in sensuality, yet redeemed in the eyes of the captive princess by his vision of the glory of Rome. Their union might have been the saving of two worlds! He had had splendid plans for a Clara-Honoria who would condescend to him, attracted, for all her high birth, by his vitality, by his very lowness, and had seen already in his mind's eye the palace of beauty that he would construct for her when love had softened her features and transformed her into the Venus of his ideals. But this fantasy, although vivid enough to keep his sexual urge for Clara alive for years after their marriage, was never shared, and after David's birth they slept in separate bedrooms.

The long succession of mistresses in his middle and later years had usually been drawn from among the houseguests at Broadlawns, pretty young wives of impecunious artists or musicians who needed financial help for their husbands and lovers or pin money for themselves from the rich patron. The commercial aspect of such affairs, combined with the icy contempt of Clara, who always seemed to discover them, had kept Irving in a state of perennial apprehension, and when, at the age of sixty, he failed to function with a young opera ballerina whose reputation for sexual agility may have unduly alarmed him, he decided that he was old and impotent and should confine himself in the future to sugared compliments and hand stroking. It thus happened that he had been continent for six years when Ivy brought Elesina to Broadlawns. But the first time that his knee touched hers under the dining room table he knew that he had greatly exaggerated his incapacity.

He had been perfectly honest when he had told Elesina that any change in their relationship would have to be proposed by her, and equally honest in assuring her that he did not anticipate any. He had allowed himself to dream that it might come, but he had also resolved to content himself with her conversation and career. When, therefore, she had gone with him to the brownstone and given him some indication that she might have received pleasure there, he had felt that the great gold curtains of his imagined opera house had opened at last on his own second act. In that unbelievable afternoon he had almost lost consciousness in bliss.

But the very next day had brought a shock. When he had telephoned Elesina, Ivy's voice had answered with the barking news that she had left on a Caribbean cruise with her mother.

"One of Mrs. Dart's rich friends had a cabin that she suddenly couldn't use because of illness. It was the chance of a lifetime. But Lord, how we had to rush the packing! They'll be gone a month."

"A month! How did Elesina seem?"

"Why do you ask that? Didn't you see her yesterday?"

"I just wondered."

"Actually, she seemed upset about something. What were you and she up to, Irving?"

"What kind of upset? Not unhappy, I hope?"

"No. Not exactly. It was as if something had happened that had, well . . . bewildered her."

"Such as?"

"Such as being molested by an old satyr!"

Irving felt as if his heart had stopped. "And she hated it?"

"I didn't say that."

Whereupon Ivy had cackled in her ugly way and hung up. But beyond the strident sound of that laugh Irving had seemed to hear the chorus of angels. She hadn't hated it! He could face now even the prospect that Ivy Trask would be part of his future life. For maybe she would be useful. The future was going to take a lot of planning. One thing he promised himself was that Elesina was not going to be like the others. Elesina was going to have everything!

That had been a week ago, and since then he had not heard from Ivy. Nor had he dared to telephone her, for fear that the wicked little woman would say something, in sheer malice, to disillusion him. Standing now by the window of his office he looked out over the misty harbor and made great plans for the apartment that he would furnish for Elesina. Her boudoir would be hung with Bouchers and Fragonards; her drawing room with examples of the Pont-Aven school which he had purchased only last year and which were still in storage, and her dining room . . .

The telephone rang. "A Miss Trask" was waiting to see him. A minute later Ivy was seated, somehow insinuatingly, in the chair opposite him, her elbows on the black, baroque table that served for a desk, her green eyes popping.

"Have you heard from Elesina?" he asked anxiously.

"No. That's not what I've come about. I've come on my own. I want you to tell me what you plan to do about Elesina. Don't turn away from me like that, Irving."

"I can't imagine why I should be accountable to *you*."

"Because I consider myself responsible. She is my dearest friend. She lives in my apartment. It was I who introduced you to her. Of course, you can call me an old meddler and kick me out of here. That's your right. But I doubt that you will find it improves your relations with Elesina. She is very loyal to her friends."

"Friends? Aren't you and I friends, Ivy? Older friends by many years than you and Elesina?"

"Well, I hope we are, Irving. But I was put off by your tone."

Irving kept silent now until he felt sure of his temper. After all, there was no reason he should not cope with Ivy. All he had to do was change her category. He had classified her among the extras who swelled the chorus of his and Clara's dinners, like the guests in *Tannhäuser*, or *Lucia*, who arrive in a unit and leave in a unit and exclaim with uplifted arms over the heroine's madness or the hero's presumption. But now she was singing her own aria; she was part of the plot.

"You ask me what I plan to do about Elesina. Let me

assure you that she shall have everything her heart desires."

"Everything? Are you talking about money, Irving?"

"I am talking about whatever she wants."

"Do you mean that you intend to treat Elesina as a kept woman? It will do you no good to look disgusted, Irving. I am determined to dot my i's."

Was there no way to burn this witch? The pain around Irving's heart became acute. "What reason is there for you to use such vulgar terms? I am a married man, Ivy. I offer Elesina everything that it is in my power to offer her."

"Except what she wants."

"And what is that?"

"What does any woman want but the chance to marry the man she loves?"

"Loves?" The library seemed to spin under its cupola.

"You heard me. Elesina loves you, you old fool!"

"Did she tell you that?"

"No. I don't know if she even knows it herself. But I know how upset she was when she came home after that afternoon with you. And it was hardly like her to rush off on that cruise with her mother. Who, by the way, is totally unsympathetic to you."

"Why did she go then?"

"Because she doesn't know where she's at. She's never had an experience like this before. She doesn't understand that a woman *can* be in love over such a gap in years. And then she doesn't want to be a homebreaker. She doesn't want people to say she's after your money. Can't you see it, Irving? On one side there is this mysterious new feeling, this unexplored country into which you have led her, and outside, in the big world, are sneers and giggles and low interpretations of her motives . . ."

It was as if all the little panels of the Burgundian landscape had turned into open windows on a cool, early spring day. Irving felt a moistness in his eyes and a soothing fullness about his heart. The shrieking old gypsy, the malevolent

Azucena, was now a melodious Brangaene, chanting from the watchtower. He saw Elesina suddenly, not in a West Side brownstone, but as mistress of Broadlawns, standing in the swimming pool by the yellow Spanish patio, splendidly naked, the surface of the water playing about her alabaster thighs, her hands stroking her low hanging breasts, her eyes mistily seeking his, where he stood, clad in a red velvet robe, smiling benignly, possessively, adoringly . . .

"But there's Clara, Ivy!" he cried in a choked voice.

"Do you think I'm forgetting her? Clara has had you for thirty years. Isn't that enough for any woman? You men are so vain. You think Clara will be lost without you. Give her a trust fund. She's never cared about anything but herself. Be frank with me, Irving. When did you and Clara last sleep together?"

He turned away again, in horror. "We needn't go into that," he muttered. "Surely you will admit that divorce at my time of life, after so many years of marriage, with grown children, is something of an undertaking?"

"And so is Elesina an undertaking!" Ivy exclaimed indignantly. "Do you know what you are gambling with? Her very life. Oh, she has suffered, that poor girl. With an indifferent mother, with two beastly husbands, with a child torn from her arms, with the distractions of gin and whiskey . . . I tell you, Irving Stein, if you let this girl down, now that she believes in you, now that she thinks she's found something at last to cling to, you'll be responsible for anything that happens."

"And what may happen?"

"Who knows? She might go out the window. She's threatened to."

"Oh, Ivy, no!"

"Oh, Ivy, yes! That girl can stand so much and no more. And why do I have to talk as if I were begging a favor? Do you know what a pearl you've got hold of? Do you know what she could do for you? She could make you *happy,*

Irving. Happy as you've never dreamed of in your play-acting life with Clara."

"You think she really wants to marry me?"

"I tell you, she doesn't know what she wants. She doesn't want to bust up a home. But I do! Because I know it's a sham home, a sham marriage. If you leave Clara now, if you take the blame on yourself, if you persuade Elesina that it's a fait accompli, irreversible, and that you've done it all for her, she'll probably fall on her knees and bless God for you!"

"It's not you who'll have to face Clara," he murmured.

"Do you want me to? I will."

"Oh, no. No." He shuddered. "But I have to talk to Elesina. Where is she?"

"I don't know."

"Will she call you?"

"Possibly."

"Then will you tell her . . ."

"That you'll do as I say? I won't tell her anything else."

"Oh, Ivy, you're impossible," he groaned.

"It's up to you, Irving. Whether you and Elesina are to be happy, or whether you and Elesina are to be miserable. You know that old hymn that Clara's always playing: 'Once to every man and nation, comes the moment to decide.' Well, this is yours. Every day that Elesina spends with her mother will take her further away from you."

"Why?"

"Because Mrs. Dart would rather have her daughter called your mistress than Mrs. Stein!"

The appalling creature let out an impudent cackle. Irving rose, trying to shake off some of his fury in motion, and turned his back to her.

"Go now, Ivy. I've had all I can take."

Alone, he telephoned his secretary to order his car. Leaning back on the cushions of the Isotta's rear compartment as they sped uptown, he felt himself return to reality. He saw the Hudson River and not a Burgundian landscape. How was it possible that he could have contemplated even for a moment the dissolution of a union as venerable as his and Clara's? Were not the Steins an integral part of the culture of the city? Were they not old, respected, important? Important, he explained to himself, as being part of reality, to the extent that an Irving without a Clara and a Clara without an Irving would somehow be a fantasy, even if that fantasy had its titillating, throat-filling aspect? And Lionel and Peter and David, what would they say to such an impossibility?

He had planned to spend the afternoon in the music room in 68th Street playing the harpsichord, but as soon as he let himself into the dark front hall through the grilled glass door he heard the sound of that instrument. Stepping to the door of the long narrow chamber, all yellow curtains and smoked glass and ballroom chairs, which he had built into the old yard in back, he saw Clara playing one of her hymns. As he stood there, listening to the plaintive tinkle of the old evangelist strain, so evocative of the desperate emotional faith of rustic American communities, he had a surge of sympathy for that upright figure. Clara's air of pale integrity seemed to stand for some primitive American concept of honor against the luxury of a wicked old Europe. She might have been Elizabeth, struggling with Venus for Tannhäuser. But after a few moments the impression passed.

Clara stopped playing and turned around. She did not seem surprised to find him there.

"I saw Ivy Trask in the street yesterday," she said in a matter-of-fact tone. "I did not speak to her. In fact, I rather hurried past. I was afraid that she might ask me to invite her friend, Miss Dart, for a weekend. Apparently, she told Fred Pemberton that it was very odd that we had never asked Miss Dart a second time."

Irving was dazed by the suddenness of the attack. "And why should we not?" he asked blankly.

"Because I dislike her. I dislike her intensely."

"You only met her once."

"It was quite enough."

Clara had risen now and was standing before the harpsichord with an air of cool defiance that was certainly premeditated. Of all things that he had not predicted, this would have seemed the least likely — that *she* should take the offensive.

"Of course, you are aware that Miss Dart is not only my protégée. She is a friend."

"A friend." Clara weighed the word. "Of course, I know that. Just as I have known of all the others." She paused to let him consider this. "You are wondering what leads me to speak now, when I have so long and tactfully held my tongue. I shall tell you. I am speaking now because this woman is different. Or rather *you* are different. You're getting old, Irving. You're getting soft and sentimental. You're making too much of this last fancy. You're making a public fool of yourself. It is time for your friends to speak up and bring you back to your senses. And you have no truer friend than I."

"You see me as an old fool, Clara. That is clear enough. But do you suppose that everyone sees me in that light?"

"Everyone does not have my insights."

"Or your prejudices. It is impossible for you to believe that a woman might find something in me that you miss, that she might . . ."

"Like Miss Dart, I suppose," Clara broke in contemptuously. "Are you really going to try to persuade me that that woman loves you, Irving? Can't you see that she's nothing but a juicy bait that Ivy Trask has dangled before you? And that you swallowed, hook, line and sinker, like the old carp you are!"

The shocking crudity of her language, so unusual for Clara, seemed to obliterate the very room with its yellow hangings and smoky mirrors, to dissipate the dim, golden air, so that he and she were somehow standing, in tatters, amid rubble, like two survivors of an air raid in a cartoon. But it was this, was

it not, that Clara had always wanted, to pull him down, to
tear down his tapestries and pictures and statues, to isolate him
from all his attributes, so that, naked, he would have nothing
to contemplate but the ostensible superiority of *her* naked-
ness? He seemed even to make out, in that cool blue gray
stare, the scorn of a Nazi storm trooper. He had a shivering sense of huddled bare bodies summoned to a dawn reveille on a freezing morning in a prison camp that stank of
feces.

"How do you suppose it feels to be married to someone
who despises you?" he shouted at her. "Who looks down on
you as a dirty Jew?"

"I only look down on your weaknesses. I have never looked
down on you for being a Jew. The accusation is absurd."

Even in his anger he had to concede this. But might it not
still be true that for all her chilly tolerance she yet despised
the great Jewish gifts: the imagination, the love of color, the
love of life? Could he not pick up the suggestion of a sneer in
the tinkle of her arid nineteenth-century hymns? He lost all
control.

"You have been against me from the beginning! All your
life you have pretended to be above the attitudes of your
family. But you haven't! The Clarksons have always domi-
nated your soul. Except for your father, they all sneered at
art and beauty." He had to pause for a moment because of his
pounding heart. "And so what do you do about that besotted
vulgarian Irving Stein? You spend your life sneering at his
excrescences, his showoffs, his parvenu display, with little
shrugs, little smiles. The great Clara, whose head is in the
clouds and stars! Do you wonder that I want a wife, for the
few years that may remain, who has some sympathy with my
aspirations?" The last sentence he brought out in a kind of
bellow. "Who knows I have the soul of an artist?"

And now what had happened to her? There was a fissure
in the marble wall. It stood, but it had been shaken. Proud,
firm, controlled, Clara might have received an arrow under

the heart. It was she now who answered reveille on the biting morn, clutching an old wrapper around her trembling frame, terrible in her vulnerability, in her unyieldingness, in her hopelessness.

"Is this what you want, Irving? To marry her?"

The pain was wracking. He had to do something, for his pain, for hers. He had to find a club; he had to strike her, crush her skull, end her, end it.

"Yes!"

"And you want me to agree to a divorce?"

"Isn't it more realistic? You can have this house. You can have anything you want."

She seemed to tremble for a moment; then she resumed her seat on the stool. "The boys warned me about this," she said with a slight quaver. "I did not credit them. So it has come to this. At last. But I know what I have to do." She was looking away from him now, staring at her music. "I shall not see a lawyer. I shall not consent to anything. If you wish to go to Reno, that is your decision. I shall never go to law with you. Here I am. Here I stay. And I think that is going to be my last word on this impossible subject."

"Clara, you must listen to me. Let us not cross Rubicons and burn bridges. Let us be rational."

But for answer she simply resumed the playing of her hymn, and after a few moments of consternation he could only leave the room.

✺ᶂ 8 ᶂ✺

When Clara was fifteen she had a religious experience before the western portal of Amiens Cathedral. Her father, an amateur student of Gothic art who had even written a private monograph on apsidal chapels, was in the habit of taking his large family with him on French ecclesiastical tours, and Clara at an early age had learned the names of all the saints who appeared in the niches and the symbols of their martyrdom and could even identify those apostles supposed to be grand-sons of Saint Anne. But on that sunny afternoon before Amiens, waiting outside in the square while her indefatigable father paid a second visit to the crypt, it occurred to her that she had gone through Europe seeing more of guidebooks than of churches, and, looking up, she took in the cathedral for the first time.

What she noted was something that she was later to recognize in Monet's studies of Rouen. The towering façade was high, cluttered, complicated, formidable, a looming, terrifying mass, like a mammoth breaker about to crash at sea. But then, even as she caught her breath in near terror, she saw that it was not about to crash. On the contrary, it might stand forever. Why was the edifice so much greater than its individual parts? Why did it speak to her now? Was it possible that the faith of the toiling, believing multitudes who had constructed it, stone by stone, had actually entered into the walls, the soaring tower, the sweeping voussoirs, the pointed arches? Or was it simply that God was there?

Religion for her now began to have color and vividness. She loved to read about the martyrdom of the saints whose images covered the dark walls and portals of the cathedrals or were emblazoned on glass or tapestry within. It seemed to Clara that it might be a very glorious thing to die in torment, one's eyes fixed on the heavens, confident of salvation and bliss. Was it not possible that with adequate faith there would be no torment? It was said of some of the early martyrs that they seemed to feel no pain, and Saint John and the Virgin were believed to have ascended directly to Paradise without the mortal experience of death. Clara did not feel that it was necessary for her to become a Roman Catholic. The great sky-thrusting cathedrals seemed to transcend the small arbitrary creeds of the little men who had built them. She felt herself a part of a vast spiritual cosmos of which the planet earth was only one tiny natural aspect.

By eighteen she had succeeded, at least in her own estimate, in reconciling her spirituality with the demands of a Clarkson world. She continued to derive comfort from her elevated thoughts and feelings, but she was able to care for her family and friends and to enjoy her reading and music. She had grown into a tall, fine-looking woman who dressed with a flair for simplicity. What more did people want? But people were unreasonable. "Clara is remote," they said. "Clara is never quite with us." "What is Clara dreaming about?" Never mind, her parents' bland faces seemed to reply. A man will come along, a fine man, the right man, who will be attracted to Clara's noble looks and character. And then you'll see her change fast enough!

But Clara thought something else might happen, although she did not know what. A clarion message from the sky? A command to go to the Antipodes and wash the feet of savages? To be boiled in oil? To prepare herself for every eventuality she practiced a rigid humility. She accepted only such invitations as her mother regarded as mandatory. She studied Latin and Greek and church history. She taught literature to a class of aspiring stenographers; she played the piano for Sunday services in a settlement house. People began to say that she would never marry, that she was too devoted to good works, "a saint, you know." Unmarriageable girls of that era were either "horsy" or saints. Clara continued to wait, but she began to consider that the age of miracles might be past. The Clarksons remained complacent about the scheme of things, and New York in 1908 seemed the capital of a prosperous world at peace forever and ever.

Irving Stein came to the larger Clarkson dinners. He was what Clara's brother called "Daddy's pet Jew." He was a rather splendid man, with flowing black hair and penetrating, unflinching gray eyes, who affected velvet suits and diamond cuff links, a bit of a dandy, with a touch of Disraeli and a fine stentorian voice. If Irving was a "pet Jew," it was only in the eyes of one snotty young Clarkson. He was highly cultivated and immensely well informed: in politics, in finance and in art. And he was rich. When he held forth at the Clarkson board, whether on trustbusting or the glass in Chartres, he spoke with authority and was listened to with respect.

From the beginning he paid a marked attention to Clara. She had only to mention a current book, and a copy, with a box of roses, was delivered at the door, or a play, and an evening would be arranged with tickets in the first row. And he professed great interest in her charitable activities. He insisted on inspecting her settlement house and auditing her literary class, and his check to the former endowed her there with an embarrassing prestige. But, best of all, he loved to talk about the problems of the world; he impressed her with the gravity of his concern for human misery. At last, when his attentions began to show themselves as romantic, she wondered if this might not be what she had been waiting for: the opportunity to share with another noble soul the task of using imagination and money for the glory of God. The fact that she felt no passion did not have to concern her. She was quite sure that she cared for Irving as much as she would ever care for a man. Besides, he seemed perfectly content with her coolness.

Her family were neither pleased nor displeased. They evidently thought it was as good as she could do. They declined to have anything to do with Irving's relatives, but they always treated Irving himself as a member of the family. Clara's first hint of how things were going to be was when Irving failed to support her request that his parents be asked for a weekend to the Clarksons in Southampton. He made it very clear that in matters of race and religion he was not going to rock the boat.

And so it was that the decades of smooth sailing in unrocked boats began. Clara never came wholly to understand the complicated personality of her interesting husband, for the simple reason that she lost her desire to do so at an early

date. She knew soon enough that he was not what she had
been foolish enough to suppose. Was it his fault that she had
been a dreamer? He was a good man, and she owed him her
respect and affection. If her failure to respond to his ardor
only inflamed him the more, this was something that had to be
endured. Time was bound to make her nights more peaceful,
and as for her days, they could be devoted to the task of
keeping up the appearances of a religion that had suddenly
collapsed. For Clara no longer thought of Gothic cathedrals,
of Reims or of Amiens. She thought of a ruined abbey by
moonlight, beautiful even if its glass and roof and choir and
altar were gone and grass filled the stately nave. She began to
develop the curious faith that was to dominate her middle
years: a faith in the form and appearances which survived the
substance.

This new tranquillity, however, was shattered by Irving's
infidelities. Clara was shocked at the vulnerable femininity of
her own nature. It seemed unworthy of her to notice such
low things, but notice them she did. That her husband should
care too much for Clarksons and works of art she could
tolerate. She could disdain but overlook his near unctuosity
with the older members of her family and his tactile affection
for porcelains, ivory and gold. But when it came to a reten-
tion and pawing of pretty hands, a silly chuckling over silly
female jokes, a walking aside with younger guests to garden
limits and beyond, she began to see in the splendid Oriental
who had courted her a sentimental Western burgher in fancy
dress, like one of those Rembrandt models arrayed in a war-
like finery that his countinghouse nose makes ridiculous. And
then she would have moments of silent fury.

Lionel and Peter were always more Irving's sons than hers.
They were big noisy boys, friendly enough, without a shred
of their father's distinction but with some of his shrewdness,
who treated Clara with an affectionate but rather awed respect and never seemed to have much to say to her. They took
Irving's side in everything, because he gave them lavish pres-

ents and wished to chastise little David, a mother's boy, when David was impudent to his father. But the last time that this occurred was when Clara first learned of it. Irving had announced at a Sunday lunch that he had lost his wristwatch, and David, aged twelve, had shrilly demanded to know if he had looked in the bed of Madame Vibert, a pretty French actress who was staying in the house and whose knee Irving at that very moment was squeezing under the table. Lionel and Peter had jumped on David that afternoon by the swimming pool, but Clara, hearing his yells, had hurried to the rescue. Alone with David she had tried to reason.

"You must learn, my darling, that even if I love having a champion, it is sometimes better if we look the other way."

"But, Mother, I *saw* Dad go into that lady's room!"

"Your father, my love, is a very fine and good man, but he has a little weakness. You will understand it some day."

"Never!"

"I do not mean that you will share it, but that you will understand it. Now if you really want to help me — *really* — you will not notice what he does in that way."

"Not *notice?*"

"Not show you notice."

She finally convinced the angry boy, and he gave her his word and kept it, but he was always sarcastic afterward in family discussions which touched on the subject of romance. In time David came to like and, a bit grudgingly, even to admire a father whose affection it was difficult to resist, but he remained Clara's champion at heart. What kept her from becoming too close to this intense, beautiful son was a species of timidity, or austerity, or perhaps even something akin to fear. She had never in her life surrendered herself to another human being, and there was a fire in David that might have singed her. She would kiss him on the forehead or the cheek, but she would never fondle him or hug him. She kept him under a slight restraint — as she might have a too demonstrative dog. Sometimes she wondered if David were not perhaps the adventure that she had been waiting for as a young woman. But if he were, what on earth could she do with him?

Certainly, it was of David that she most constantly thought in the week after Irving moved out. David was coming down for the weekend from law school, and she would have to tell him then. Should she do it in such a way as to induce him to break altogether with his father? Something fierce and pounding in her head urged her to it. Was it not time, after years of equivocation, to strike, to be free, to take David with her? Had there not been a sick weakness in the passivity with which she had so long accepted a life that had offered little but disillusionment?

On the afternoon when David was expected Clara had an unexpected caller at 68th Street. Had she ever imagined that Ivy Trask would have the nerve to present herself, she would have left word in the hall that she be denied. As it was, the maid who answered the door, recognizing in the brisk little caller an old family friend, ushered her at once upstairs.

"I know you don't want to see me, Clara, but I have terms from Irving that you can't afford not to consider."

"You don't really believe that I will discuss my affairs with you?"

"When I'm authorized to offer what I am? Don't be a fool, Clara. Nothing in the world can bring Irving back to you now. Give him what he wants, and he'll give you what you want. Everybody's face is saved. Everybody's rich!"

"Nothing is lost but honor," Clara quoted grimly.

"We'll even leave you that! You'll get the divorce on any terms you wish. If it's blood you want, blood you'll have."

"I think you'd better go."

"You won't even hear what he'll do for you? And for the boys?"

"Go!"

"Very well." Ivy wagged her head from side to side. She

had not seated herself, nor had Clara risen. She seemed to be contemplating her hostess with the final misgiving of a disappointed schoolmistress retreating before a recalcitrant pupil. "I guess you're hopeless, Clara. Like most women of your age and class. Hopeless and useless. Has the world ever struck you as anything but faintly ridiculous?"

"Isn't it?"

"No, it's *hugely* ridiculous! If you'd ever thrown back that haughty head of yours and let yourself go in a horse laugh, you might have lived."

"I think I prefer my death to your laugh."

But Ivy's words were still written like the smoke letters of an airplane announcing a public event across the pale sky of Clara's calm when, an hour later, she told David of his father's move. In her desperate need for an ally she had almost been looking forward to this, but now her mind seemed full of small jumping figures.

"He wants to marry this woman?" David shouted. "He must be mad!"

"Your father always knows what he's doing."

"Then he's wicked. How can he throw you off — like an old shoe?"

"I suppose there will be some legal difficulties."

"Let him go!" David jumped up and stamped about the room. "We don't need him. I'll look after you. Who wants his filthy money, anyway?"

"Is it really a question of that? Your father has already settled money on me. Long ago."

"Let's give it back then. Let's fling it in his face!"

"I don't think we can. It's in trust."

"We needn't take the income!"

Clara began to see that things were not going to be at all as she had imagined. She and David were not going to build a citadel against the world, not because he didn't want to, but precisely because he did. For how could she allow a young man with everything in life before him to tie himself down to a penniless old woman maintaining a futile stand against a husband's philandering?

"My God, is it Ivy Trask's world, after all?" she muttered.

"What has Ivy to do with it?"

"Nothing." Clara shook herself, as if to shake off the image of Ivy. "Or rather I mean everything. It was she who plotted the whole thing. She wants to put her creature in Broadlawns. Well, as you say, let her. But don't make things harder for me, darling, by asking me to be poor."

"I thought it would make them easier! Wouldn't you be happier owing Dad nothing?"

Clara closed her eyes for a moment in silent recognition of how well he knew her. Then she arrayed her forces to assist her with the needed lie. "One changes, dearest, with age. I am used to my creature comforts. It would be difficult for me now to do without them. And you mustn't break with your father. He's going to need you now. More than ever before."

"Need *me!*" David snorted in disgust. "When he has his Elesina? I'll wait, thank you very much, until she bleeds him and fools him and leaves him. And *then* maybe the poor old besotted fool will crawl home to me for comfort!"

"David! He's still your father!"

"What do Lionel and Peter say about it?"

"Oh, they're horrified, of course. For the moment they won't speak to him. But they'll come around. You'll see."

"Of course," David sneered bitterly. "They're in business with him, aren't they? They won't want Elesina made senior partner."

"Oh, my child, I'm sorry about the way the world is. But we didn't make it, did we?"

"We certainly didn't!"

And Clara realized sadly that there was more love in David's bitterness, even for his erring father, than in all of Lionel's and Peter's shrugs. Once again life had refused her an adventure. Once again her way would be remorselessly smoothed.

❧ 9 ☙

When the world of Irving and Clara Stein learned that he had actually moved out of the 68th Street house and was living alone in one of his brownstones, the furor was immense. Not a voice was raised in Irving's behalf; everyone who had ever been to Broadlawns, it seemed, came to reaffirm their allegiance to Clara. One would have thought that Irving had invented the idea of divorce, that it was somehow essential for the security of their own marriages that they drag him to trial, crown him with a heretic's cap, burn him at the stake. Clara, usually so calm, so serene, seemed for the first time a bit flustered, perhaps a bit annoyed, as if she were inclined to resent so marked a disturbance of her customary detachment. She was still the gray-robed priestess chanting at the altar of the chaste goddess, but now she had occasionally to turn her head, interrupted by the murmuring of the congregation behind her, and to frown, or at least to pucker her brow, as if to remind the disrespectful throng that to those who exist in the divine presence the rantings and infidelities of mere males are to be brushed aside.

Ivy Trask was very discreet when she encountered members of the Stein court. She refused to condemn Irving's conduct, but neither did she condone it, simply nodding her head as one too well informed by high sources to indulge in idle chatter. She was quick to perceive that the new social vacuum in Irving's life had better be filled by herself before the sons, temporarily not on speaking terms with their father, should deem it prudent to resume relations. She filled the ears of the dazed Irving with accounts of the scathing denunciations issuing from his offspring, magnifying their threats and warning him that if he failed to be firm he would be sold back into conjugal slavery and made to stand, a domestic dunce in a stale domestic corner, at the beck and call of an eternally aggrieved, never pacified wife.

"Your sons seem to have forgotten one of the commandments," she observed to Irving tartly. "I hope you will find occasion to remind them of it. Don't Lionel and Peter depend on you in the firm?"

"They're partners. I can hardly fire a partner."

"But I'm sure you have a voice in their percentages. Be strong, Irving. Let them know who's boss."

"But everyone seems so against me, Ivy. I feel bewildered. Not myself."

"Just hang on. Things will straighten out. I've observed the institution of marriage for a long time, and I have the advantage of being single. People don't really object to divorce any longer. They just think they do. Things change so fast today that our moral posturings have to scamper to keep up with the facts. Everyone's on Clara's side now, but Clara's a bore. She'll never hold them. It is the rising star that will lure them all."

"The rising star?"

"I mean Elesina Stein!"

"Ivy, you're being ridiculous. I told you that Clara would never give me a divorce."

"Get one yourself in Reno. Marry Elesina out there! What can Clara do but sue you? And what can she get but the money you're already willing to give her?"

Ivy even proceeded to redecorate Irving's brownstone. The house was filled all day with painters and plasterers, and she hoped that the hammering would symbolize to the distracted owner the driving of nails into the coffin of his union to Clara. But she had had no communication, not even a postcard, from Elesina, and when she went down to the Hudson pier to meet the returning cruise ship she was ignorant of the mood in which she would find her friend.

Elesina and Mrs. Dart were still on board, but Ivy had a pass that admitted her to the vessel. She found them in the large first-class suite that had been given to Mrs. Dart by her ill friend. Linda, in tweeds, packed and ready to disembark, was sitting smoking while Elesina hung garments listlessly in a tall trunk. Both greeted Ivy casually, without the smallest expression of surprise or pleasure at the pains which she must have taken to meet them so far from her office in the middle of a working day.

"I was less than pleased, Miss Trask, at what I heard from friends in Nassau about this distressing Stein affair." Mrs. Dart's tone was contained, cool, faintly hostile. "I gather that Elesina's name has been bandied about in it. Of course, it's all nonsense, but I hate to have her involved with that kind of thing and that kind of people."

"Irving Stein is a very distinguished man, Mrs. Dart."

"Spare me such distinction! Of course, people know that he backed Elesina's play, and I suppose malicious minds will always draw odious conclusions from that."

"I grant it's all very distressing."

"I understand that you have some acquaintances in the Stein world. Perhaps, if you ever have the opportunity, you will be good enough to deny Elesina's involvement."

Ivy glanced at her friend, but the latter seemed interested only in her packing. She looked back at Mrs. Dart and took her measure. Should she take issue with her? She knew that Elesina was inclined to discount the maternal influence, but she had observed enough of the world to be aware of the persistent tug of the umbilical cord. No matter how frayed and chafed, it had a way of suddenly tightening and throwing the most seemingly independent child off balance. Linda Dart's contempt for Steins and Trasks, her well-bred scorn of all that was at once public and disorderly, might still affect Elesina.

"I already have denied it, Mrs. Dart. Nobody has more

concern in the matter than I. But would you mind if I took Elesina out on deck, just for a minute? There's a question I have to ask her."

"Of course." Mrs. Dart rose at once. "Please stay here. I have to see the purser, in any event."

When she was gone, Ivy hurried over to her friend.

"Elesina!" she exclaimed. "What's going on? Don't you care?"

"About what?"

"Don't you care that he's left his wife, that he's ditched himself with all his friends, with his own children, just for *you?*"

"Oh, Ivy, don't be dramatic."

"It's true! How can you treat him so?"

Elesina left the trunk now to light a cigarette. She seemed bored, impatient, but Ivy noted nonetheless that the hand which held the match trembled slightly. "I'm not treating anybody any way."

"You mean you won't marry him?"

"Ivy, you're out of your mind! He hasn't even asked me. And how could he, in his position?"

"As if his position couldn't be changed! Elesina, don't you care about him at all? Don't you care about yourself? What *do* you care about?"

"Isn't it a question of what *you* care about, Ivy?" Elesina seemed now to draw herself up. Her listlessness had been the costume for a scene that was now finished. "Isn't it a question of the restoration of Ivy Trask to her beloved Broadlawns? Don't you see yourself there as a triumphant Catherine de Medici with a puppet king and queen under your sway? Hasn't it been your scheme all along to undo poor Clara Stein and replace her with a creature of your own?"

Ivy smiled at the absurdity of the misconception. She walked over to Elesina deliberately and reached up to place a firm hand on each of her shoulders. "Don't you know that I love you more than anyone or anything in the world? More

than anyone has ever loved you? Or *could* love you? Don't
you know that you're my child? Don't you know that I am
never going to rest until I see you rich and famous, one of the
greatest women in the world? And happy, too, Elesina.
Happy!"

When Elesina turned her head at last to gaze back with
something between alarm and curiosity into her friend's burning green eyes, Ivy burst into a shrill laugh. She knew that
she had won!

PART
TWO

❧ ❦

DAVID

E LIOT CLARKSON was not only David Stein's cousin and closest friend, he had been his classmate through the Sheldon School, Yale and Harvard Law. In most friendships there is a cultivator and a cultivated, and Eliot occupied the former role. David's feelings were composed of respect, affection and gratitude; those of his friend came closer to a restrained adoration. To Eliot, a thin, dark, cerebral man, in marked contrast to the shorter, stockier, blond David, the latter was a Romantic hero. Eliot admired David's impulsiveness, his easy generosity, his independence, his courage. It was not that he himself lacked such qualities. But Eliot was one of those who, though possessed of many virtues, missed the fire to make his engine race. His sustained attitude of judicious reserve implied the choice, early made, of a secondary position from which he might watch and perhaps coach contenders for the first. But he had never had more than one candidate: David.

Although they were second cousins, and both of New York families, they did not meet until their sixteenth year, when David was sent to Sheldon, a boarding school in northwestern Connecticut where Eliot had been enrolled for a year. Large New York clans like the Clarksons tended to spread out and lose sight of each other, and the Stein connection had not been one to induce a reversal of this process. Eliot's parents were amiable, easygoing persons who liked Irving and Clara Stein, but they were true to their philistine type in finding Irving's artistic and social pretensions a bit ridiculous. In New York Eliot had gone to the conservative Buckley School, and David to the more liberal Bovee. There had been little occasion for the boys to meet.

It certainly never occurred to Irving Stein that Sheldon would prove an ordeal for his son. He was well aware that it

was a Protestant church school with hardly any boys of
acknowledged Jewish origin, but he was determined that
questions of race and religion should not bar David from
social advancement. He had been privately disappointed that
Peter and Lionel, whom he had sent to Grover Academy, a
school supported by the New York German Jewish community, should have become so enthusiastically Jewish in their
looks and associations. Secretly, he hoped for a different
future for his youngest son. Being eminently a man of reason,
he did not believe that a social prejudice which he regarded as
basically superficial would persist long enough to spoil the
school life of an intelligent child. And indeed it might not
have, but for two factors that he failed to take into account:
David's own passionate nature and the violence of his cousin
Eliot's support.

Eliot took an immediate interest in his new form mate,
appointing himself as a guardian "old kid" over the affairs of
the "new kid." He was a serious boy, tall and very thin, with
a long, lean, nobbly, slightly pockmarked, intellectual face,
short black scrubby hair and large, evasive, sensitive eyes. His
air of standing off, of waiting to see how you would take his
approaches — *if* he approached — suggested, or might have
been meant to suggest, that if one broke through, one would
find a loyalty more intense than that provided by less special
souls. He appeared in David's cubicle while the latter was
unpacking and introduced himself.

"We are second cousins, I believe. That means that out of
eight great-grandparents we share two. At home it is de
rigeur to see one's first cousins, at least while one is young,
but with seconds one may pick and choose. I suggest you
pick and choose me, David. As an old kid, I may be able to
help."

David searched for sarcasm in the bland expression of his
caller. "Will I need help? Everything seems so pleasant
here."

"Appearances can be deceptive. And boys can be vile."

David turned back to his half-empty suitcase. As he did so his eyes took in the gentle green roll of the countryside. It was a beautiful site. He shrugged. "I guess I can take care of myself."

"But you won't reject my proffered assistance?"

"Oh, I reject nothing!"

Life started easily enough. The masters were kind, and the work was not difficult. The hazing of new kids had been reduced by a new and benevolent head to a mere handful of formalities. David's form mates observed each other critically, like leashed dogs in a park; their sniffs did not necessarily imply hostility. Some even made overtures of friendship. But the episode with Nelson Weed changed everything.

Weed, like Eliot, was an old kid, and the undisputed social leader of the form. His appearance was pleasant enough, and there was apt to be a little smile on his handsome, rounded face that suited his rounded figure and lolling gait, but he could be cruel if his authority was questioned. One day, between classes, accompanied by a group of his sidekicks, he paused before David, who was reading a letter from home.

"I hope all is well with the Steins, Stein."

David looked up in surprise. "Very well, thank you."

"Are your family enjoying their riches?"

David flushed. "What do you mean by that?"

"I thought it a simple question. I asked if your family were enjoying their riches. One asks if people are enjoying good health. Why shouldn't one ask if they are enjoying good wealth? Your parents *are* wealthy, are they not, Stein?"

"I don't know what you mean by wealthy."

"You don't? Dear me." Here Weed glanced about with a mocking eye at his fellows. "Then let me tell you precisely. I did not mean to imply that the Steins were Rockefellers. It is a banality for minor Croesuses to claim they are not rich because they are not as rich as Rockefeller. But I should be surprised if your old man couldn't lay his hands on ten million bucks. What do you think?"

"I don't think."

"You don't or you can't?"

"I don't care to discuss it."

Weed's tone became very mild at this. "I'm afraid you're being impertinent, Stein. Haven't you been told about new kids?"

"It's not my fault. You drove me to it. You have no right to make remarks about my family."

"Is it making remarks to say they are rich? I beg your pardon. I thought it was a compliment. At least in Jewish circles. Isn't it considered a great thing for a Jew to be rich?"

"No more so than a Christian!"

"Really? But again I beg your pardon. I forget that you're a Christian, too. It's quite a feat."

"My mother's Episcopalian. My father belongs to no church. I haven't decided what I want to be."

"Well, to me, Stein, you'll always be one thing." Here Weed's voice dropped almost to a whisper. "And would you like to know what that one thing is?"

David stared at his tormentor, hypnotized in spite of himself. "What?"

"A Jew boy. A fresh Jew boy."

David flew at him and blacked his eye. Such retaliation in a new kid was a scandal, and Weed's gang felt no compunction in proceeding to beat him up. It might have gone very badly indeed with him had Eliot Clarkson not intervened. He was not a strong boy, but his fury made up for the deficiency, and when the bell for the next class brought relief, he and David were in a corner, still holding the group off.

Weed, however, had no idea of letting the matter drop, and the sympathy of the form was on his side. Most of the boys came from families where social anti-Semitism was taken for granted, and they did not see why David Stein should get so excited at being called what he so evidently was. Besides, for a new kid to strike an old kid, no matter what the provocation, was intolerable insubordination. And for that new kid to be supported by an old kid was a compounding of the scandal. Was nothing sacred?

David and Eliot found themselves not only ostracized but subjected to myriad petty persecutions. Their desks would be messed up before inspection; their beds would be found soaking wet; the pockets of their overcoats would be filled with oozy mud. David wanted to write his parents to ask to be taken out of the school. He could not see the point of trying to survive the unpleasantness in order to be accepted by boys whom he did not like anyway. But Eliot saw the matter differently and persuaded him to endure it all. To Eliot the persecution was a glorious challenge. Nelson Weed and his cohorts were simply the forces of evil; to defeat them, to come out with one's heart and mind unscathed by their machinations, was to prove that decency was stronger than rottenness. There was a jubilance in the way he took up the crusade that at first fired but ultimately bewildered David.

"You really enjoy it, don't you, Eliot?" he asked him. "I wonder what you would have done if I had never come to Sheldon."

"Oh, there's always a lost cause knocking around somewhere," Eliot retorted with his harsh laugh. "I might have taken up the cause of that Chinese boy."

"Thanks!"

But the real trouble for Eliot was not that the cause was lost but that it wasn't. Schoolboys tire even of cruelty, and Nelson Weed was smart enough not to push things beyond their normal limit. When David made a touchdown in the last football game of the season, he publicly congratulated him, and the conflict was officially over.

"We might even be friends," Weed told him on their way back to the locker room. With the charm of a superficiality transcending cynicism he threw an arm around his former victim's shoulders.

"You want a Jew boy for a friend?" David retorted, pushing himself roughly free.

"Maybe I do, at that!" Weed exclaimed with a high laugh in which only Eliot could have detected malice.

David could not long resist such overtures. He was perfectly willing to be on good terms with the school, if peace was offered without dishonor. He knew that he would not soon forget the bitterness of being called a Jew boy, but he also knew that in a violent world one could not be always fighting. It was odd that it should be Eliot, a Gentile, who urged continued resistance. David suspected that his friend took a dusky pleasure in isolation, that he might create issues even where they did not exist in order to splash his dark dungeon with the gold spangles of romance and idealism. Was Nelson Weed anti-Semitic or was he just a horrid boy like other boys, ready to seize any aspect of a new kid's personality as a target for abuse — his race, his religion, his accent, his warts, his bad breath?

"Don't trust him," Eliot insisted.

"What can I lose?"

Eliot had to come around, for he had too much sense not to realize that he could never hold David unless he shared him with others. The vision of the two alone against a cruel world had been a pleasing one, but Eliot had learned early that pleasing things had short lives. David, after all, did not abandon him for his new friends; he always made it evident that Eliot had to be included. Nelson Weed and his friends became summer visitors at Broadlawns, and at Yale they borrowed considerable sums from David. Eliot wondered bitterly in time if his own intransigency had not done more for David's social career than all of Irving Stein's ambition.

Their relationship, however, was not always one-sided. It had elements of symbiosis. At Yale, if Eliot acted as a kind of tutor to keep David from an overdistraction in fleshpots, it was also true that David opened up a larger college life than would have been otherwise available to his monastically inclined relative. At law school they became almost equals; they reviewed courses together and made the law review. But their equality fell away again before the intrusion of sex. There Eliot's role was always that of a tactfully self-removing third.

In Ireland, when they went on a walking trip in the summer after their second year at law school, David fell in love with a beautiful undergraduate whom he met at a party at the University of Dublin. Noreen Leslie was a student of economics, a poet and a rebel, whose father had been shot by the British in 1920, and who was determined to dedicate herself to the liberation of the northern counties. She never had any intention of complicating her life by a permanent union with what she deridingly called the "spawn of a Yankee Jew banker," but she joined the American pair in their hike through Connemara, and Eliot spent lonely nights looking up at the stars while David and Noreen were more intensely engaged under a blanket in another part of the field. At the end of the trip, in Galway, there was a violent scene when Noreen refused either to marry David or to go to America with him. He became almost hysterical when she tried to persuade him that she was adamant about closing the episode. She had to take Eliot out to a pub for a private talk.

"Look after my blue-eyed boy," she told him. "He's taking it harder than I thought he would. Show him you love him, Eliot. Don't be scared of it. You're not what you're afraid you are. No, you're not, my dear, not a bit of it. Oh, I can always tell. One of these days you'll make some girl a fine lover. Though I suspect she'll have to marry you to find out! You're the connubial type. Like David. You Americans are altar mad. That's not my tea. David will get over me soon enough, never fear. But there'll always be something else. He doesn't know what he is or what he wants. His parents, I gather, live in a fantasy world. It's been hard on him. He needs you. He needs you badly."

"Well, I'll always be there. So long as he wants me."

Noreen gave him a kiss on the lips of which David would have been jealous. When she left the bar, she had made him agree to assume the burden of telling his friend that she was not going back to the hotel.

David got over his misery, though not so soon as Noreen had predicted. In his last year at law school he was a quieter and more industrious student, but his conversation at drinking parties was now larded with remarks indicative of acerbity or cynicism about women. Happily he found a new god in the New Deal and a prophet in Felix Frankfurter. On weekends at Broadlawns he delighted to hold forth on the iniquities of the old regime, and only Irving Stein's obvious bedazzlement at the brilliance of his last-born kept some of the banking brotherhood from leaving the table.

On one occasion David had serious words with his uncle, Percy Symes, who had married Clara's sister. Symes was a hard-drinking, red-complexioned stockbroker, a huntsman and sailor, a member of the Racquet Club, who had lost his money in the crash and found it bitter tea to live on the handouts of Irving Stein. After dinner on a Saturday night, half drunk, he sauntered over to David who was smoking a cigar by himself on the patio.

"You want it both ways, is that it, David?"

"Both ways, Uncle Percy?"

"You want all the shekels of the old world and all the liberal laurels of the new."

David abruptly threw away his cigar. "Why do you say shekels?"

"Well, isn't that your national coin? Isn't that the secret of the Jews: to play both sides? How can you lose? Communism, capitalism, what the hell? Don't get angry, young man. Maybe you're smart. Maybe we should all be like you."

"I think you'd better leave this house before I forget you're Mother's brother-in-law and punch you in the nose!"

David had a long talk with his father later that night.

Irving Stein had had a few words with the Symeses before their abrupt departure, but he had contained himself until the house was free of guests and Clara had gone to bed.

"I know you think I compromise too much, David, but you must try to understand that the attitudes of your elders may spring from experience as well as timidity. I did not invent anti-Semitism, but I have learned to live with it. To paraphrase a Gentile saying: 'Some of my best friends are anti-Semites.' Your uncle is a coarse and stupid man, but he is also a very unhappy one. He would rather blame my prosperity and his poverty on a Jewish conspiracy than on my greater brains. When he's sober, he has just sense enough to conceal what he suspects most people will rightly consider as a low prejudice. But when he's drunk, out it comes! To condemn a man for what he says when he's drunk is to condemn a man for what he's thinking. How can he help it?"

"By cultivating a little human decency."

"Ah, but how many people do that? You must take the world, David, as it is. I hoped that you had learned that at Sheldon. I have found it wiser not to push peoples' anti-Semitism in their faces. I try to ignore it, as I should ignore a hiccup or the breaking of wind. There are moments, when I deal with certain kinds of Jews, particularly in real estate transactions, that I feel almost anti-Semitic myself."

"But, Dad, don't we have to stand together? Won't Nazism otherwise spread all over the world and be the end of us?"

"I fail to see any necessary correlation between atrocities in Germany and anti-Jewish social feeling in New York. On the one hand you have a political campaign directed against a helpless minority, arbitrarily chosen as victims for the purpose of uniting a nation by blood lust. The thing was cynically, fiendishly planned. On the other, you have the snottiness of an Anglo-Saxon upper crust with no real animus behind it. People like your Uncle Percy don't even know what a Jew is. They don't dislike people for being Jewish; they call people Jewish whom they dislike. Percy claims that Franklin Roosevelt changed his name from Rosenfelt!"

David brooded. "I wonder if that same argument wasn't used in Berlin before Hitler."

"Possibly. I did not mean to imply that there was no anti-Semitism in Germany for him to work on. It's a question of degree. But now let me tell you something that will surprise you, David. *You* don't know what a Jew is any more than Uncle Percy. Because you're not really Jewish."

"I am so!"

"You are as much a Clarkson as a Stein. But none of that really matters. What really matters is that you should be first and foremost a human being. A free soul. A citizen of the world. That is what *I* have tried to be."

"It's easier for you, Dad." David shook his head. "You have no Clarkson blood to deny. When I heard Uncle Percy tonight, I was ashamed to think that any part of me might belong to his world."

Irving's eyes became misty as he gazed at his angry son. "That's you all over, my boy. To take the Jewish side if it's a liability. If you had lived in the glorious reign of King Solomon, you'd have sympathized with the Egyptians. But the first Hebrew reverse would have brought you back to the Temple!"

"I don't see it as a liability to be a Jew," David retorted. "Certainly it had not kept *you* from reaching the top."

Irving looked as if there were a great many things that he might have said to this. But after a few moments he simply sighed and changed the subject. "Try to spare your mother this. She cannot abide this issue between her family and us. I told her that Aunt Eve was taking Uncle Percy home because he'd had too much to drink. If she suspects the truth, she'll never have them in the house again. And you know you don't want to be the cause of that kind of a breach."

No, David did not. That was always the trouble. He could never bear to hurt his mother. This was made more difficult by the fact that he was never sure what hurt her and what did not. One could not tell by complaints, for Clara did not complain. Why should it be that he always suspected pain behind her stillness, her averted head, her pale stare? Lionel and Peter never had; they had hugged her and shouted at her and ignored her, just as if she had been an ordinary mother. They did not seem to have any sense of her priestess quality. But then there was little difference between such relationship as they had with her and the one supposed to exist in the average convivial American family of Sunday drives to crowded beaches. David wanted to think of his own relation with his mother as something more special. Secretly, half ashamedly, he liked to imagine that the fashionable mother-child portrait of the two of them, done in 1920 by a protégé of Irving's, had caught an essential element of their bond, contrasting as it did the look of coaxing curiosity in the curly haired youngster, dressed in red velvet and sprawled before a chaise longue, with the faraway gaze of the reclining, gray-robed parent. But how much did Clara really care, even about her baby? What could one do with a heroine who kept slipping off to the wings?

With the great crisis of his parents' separation David had hoped briefly to be his mother's effective champion at last. When she had declined to shut herself off altogether from the paternal resources and depend on his, his bitterness had reached a climax. At a bar with Eliot he had heaped scorn on what he called his mother's lassitude and had passionately indicted his father. But Eliot, to his shocked surprise, did not concur.

"I know it's hard to be objective about one's parents, but that doesn't mean one shouldn't try. Your father is getting on, David. He sees the imminent failure of his powers. If he wants a last fling with this girl, of course it's rough on your mother, but I'm damned if I can't understand. He sees himself dead, extinct, nothing. And then where will his virtue have got him?"

"But, Eliot, you could say that about anything! Should we give in to every temptation because some day we'll be dead?"

"I know it's not logical, but I want to make an exception for an old man and sex."

"But he could have had an affair with her! We wouldn't have minded that."

"I am assuming that marriage is her price."

David fell into an uncomfortable silence. He had an uneasy sense that he might be ridiculous. Absurdly, he wished that he were a child, for surely a child would have the right to resent the destruction of his home. But now even Eliot, the defender of lost causes, declined to pick up this one. Would there never be a clear-cut issue where a man could stand up and hurl down his glove and cry: "Here I stand!"

"I suppose you want me to act as his best man," he said sullenly.

"Don't be an ass."

⋅§ 2 §⋅

The Steins now proceeded to regroup themselves. David, on his graduation from law school, moved in with his mother on 68th Street, abandoning, in view of her loneliness, a plan to share a house in Greenwich Village with Eliot. Irving, on his return from Reno, where he had married Elesina, established her in Broadlawns and in a new Fifth Avenue apartment. Lionel and Peter agreed to see their father in the office and to dine with him and Elesina at the apartment, but, out of what David regarded as a rather technical sense of loyalty to Clara, they and their wives no longer went out to Rye.

"Why didn't I tell Noreen I'd become an Irishman?" David complained bitterly to Eliot. "She might have married me then, and I could have spent a useful life making bombs. Now I don't know where I'm at. When Mother's relatives come to dinner and commiserate with her, I have the funny feeling that I'm somehow on the wrong side. Not because of

Mother, God knows. But there's a faint stink of Nazism about the Clarksons, and Dad, for all his socializing in Gotham, is still at heart a Jew."

"You ought to take a job."

"That's the Clarkson in you, Eliot. Deep down, you can't really believe that writing a novel is a fit occupation for a gentleman." David, having rejected the job which he had earlier accepted in Schurman & Lister because they had represented his father in the divorce, was now writing a novel about a summer love affair between a young American tourist and an Irish girl.

"You can do both in half the time you spend brooding about your old man," Eliot retorted. "I suggest that you go to see mine. He may have a job for you. Remember, the great Frankfurter himself suggested that you start with a Wall Street firm."

Eliot's father, Eben Clarkson, was a partner in Tyler, Cobb & Tyson, but Eliot, because of their policy against employing sons, worked for another firm. David, who was fond of Cousin Eben, agreed at last to go downtown to lunch with him. The latter was immediately optimistic about David's chances for a job, despite his late application. Like his son, Eben Clarkson was not typical of the family. He was almost painfully good mannered; his bright clear Dickensian countenance under a halo of white hair beamed at David as if to assure him that it was a good world, a benignant world, that he, for example, wasn't really a Clarkson or a future boss or perhaps even a Wall Street lawyer at all, but just a simple, lovable being, full of sympathy and affection for his dear son's best friend. David remembered that Eliot had hinted once that his father had a neurosis about not being quite up to the standards of Tyler, Cobb, of owing his partnership to the intervention of a powerful client.

"I am sure we'll find a place for you, David. Having you here will be the next best thing to having Eliot. Not that he isn't perfectly happy where he is. But I know how close you two have always been. I'll feel that I have a bit of Eliot here if you're here. However, there is one delicate matter. You had been going with the Schurman firm. Naturally, I understand that there could be no idea of that while they represented your father in the recent unpleasantness, but now that is all out of the way, and we're settling down to new circumstances and letting bygones be bygones . . ."

"That's all very well for other people, Cousin Eben," David broke in, "but it won't do for me. For me some bygones can never be bygones."

"Ah, my dear boy, I'm so sorry!" Cousin Eben seemed as genuinely upset as if he had been personally involved. "I have always been so fond of your father, and I know that he feels about you as I feel about Eliot. I had so hoped that you might forgive him."

"It is not a question of forgiving him, Cousin Eben. I think a son who forgives his father is presumptuous. But I do not see how I can countenance a life which is a daily insult to my mother. He and Miss Dart are not married, you know."

"Indeed, I did *not* know. You astonish me, David. Surely, I read about it in the paper."

"You read about an alleged marriage. My father obtained a unilateral divorce in Nevada without my mother's consent or appearance. In New York she is still his wife. His union with Miss Dart is a bigamous one."

Clarkson regarded David with surprise and a faint embarrassment. "Ah, yes. Well, legally no doubt you're correct. But so long as your mother does not see fit to attack the situation . . ."

"In which course of action she chooses not to follow my advice."

"I see. But even so, society looks for guidance to the attitude of the wronged spouse. So long as she does not complain, how can others? Certainly the state would take no criminal action."

"It's hardly likely. But I draw a line between not filing a complaint and giving public approval to what my father has done."

"Oh, I don't suggest you do anything in public. If you could just see Irving, once in a while, in private, it would make such a difference to him."

"But, Cousin Eben, you should be on Mother's side!"

"I can never forget the times when your father has helped me out. And I know how I should feel were Eliot to cut *me* off."

When, ten days later, David received an embarrassed letter from Eben Clarkson, informing him that there had not, after all, been the vacancy in the firm which had been anticipated, he was more surprised than disappointed. Eliot came that evening for drinks on the top floor of the 68th Street house which David had converted to an apartment. He silently read the letter which David handed to him.

"Do you think your father has appointed himself a public censor of my moral position in Dad's divorce?" David demanded. "Surely, his attitude will cause surprise among the Clarksons. I should suppose they would have applauded my stand!"

"But that's not it, David. Your stand is not involved."

David took in now a gravity unusual even in Eliot. "Your father exceeded his authority in offering me the job? Is that it?"

"No, Father had the authority to offer you a job. What happened was that the firm overruled him. They decided not to depart from their old practice."

"You mean not to hire people in the middle of the year?"

Eliot's voice became very flat now. "I mean not to hire Jews."

David rose and walked to the window. In the darkened street below he could make out the shiny top of his mother's old Packard town car. She was going out for dinner. She was going out a little more now. He had encouraged that. Was she going to a "mixed" dinner? It surprised him to note that his fists were clenched.

"It's funny, you know. I've never been banned before. I've lived twenty-five years and never been banned. Even at Sheldon they took me in. Oh, of course, I've known there were clubs and schools and dances which excluded Jews, but somehow I always thought they were pompous and stuffy and faintly absurd, not dangerous. That was always Dad's attitude, anyway. They didn't want us — well, we didn't want them. Except whenever they changed their attitude, *he* was quick enough to change his." He turned around, too full of anger to utter another word. He had to swallow before he spoke again. "What a damnable world, Eliot!"

Eliot rose, as if his own pain had forced him to do so. "There are plenty of big Wall Street firms just as good, better, than Tyler, Cobb which don't take that attitude. Father told me that he would make out a list for you. He feels very strongly about the whole thing. After all, he betrayed the confidence of his partners in telling me. That's almost unthinkable for him."

"He needn't be concerned," David said bitingly. "They will never learn of it. And I shall not use his list."

"Why don't we start our own firm? There's nothing I'd rather do!"

David saw that Eliot was as much upset as he. He came over to put his hands on his cousin's shoulders and give him a quick friendly shake. "No, you're happy where you are, and I don't want to practice law. Not yet, anyway. There are too many things I have to think out first. What this Tyler, Cobb thing means to me. And what it *should* mean to me. And how it fits in with what's going on in Germany. And with what's going on in my own family. I don't think Dad ever really faced the basic issue. I've got to think, Eliot."

"You'll think too much, that's the trouble. You'll forget

your blessings. You may think of me as a privileged Clarkson, but I'd change shoes with you any day."

"Why?"

"Well, you're rich, to begin with."

"Oh, be serious."

"And you have lots of blond hair. Mine is getting thin already."

"Eliot!"

"And you have a devoted friend in me."

"That's better."

"And girls like you."

"I always wondered if Noreen didn't have a secret yen for you."

"Noreen had a not-so-secret yen for all the boys. But you were first choice. You'll always be first choice." Eliot hesitated. "What I really mean is that you have a bit of genius."

"For what, please?"

"I don't know. I really don't know. But I'd hate to see it wasted."

ట૭ 3 ટ૭

David saw a great deal of his mother during the following winter. She tried to dissuade him from dining at home so often, but he would insist that he had nothing better to do, and indeed it struck her that he was as antisocial as he was idle.

"You might have had a possessive mother," she protested. "So many people do. Why turn me into what you're lucky enough to have escaped?"

"Because I'm a possessive son! I've always wanted you all to myself, without Dad or Lionel or Peter, and now I've got you!"

In truth he was as worried about her as she about him. Various of the old faithful group at Broadlawns had con-

tinued to call on her at 68th Street, but as she did little for
their entertainment, they were beginning already to defect
and to slip over the border to Rye from where word came
back that the new Mrs. Stein was entertaining brilliantly.
David made out in his mother's sporadic and ineffectual
efforts to amuse her old friends a vague fear that if she should
be abandoned now, she would be abandoned permanently. It
was not, moreover, he saw, that she feared this result so much
for herself as that she was afraid that her solitary state would
shackle him in ever-strengthening bonds of pity to her side. It
was to free *him* that she had to seem busy and occupied, and
as she had no experience in the technique of giving parties, or
even of running a house — for Irving had always done everything — she became the least bit frantic, like someone in a
baffling dream where a happy party, an Easter egg hunt, begins to take on sinister forms, the bunnies presenting shark
jaws, the painted egg faces leering.

"Why don't we dine alone tonight, and you just play me
hymns?" he would ask her.

"Oh, my darling, let *me* dine alone. I'm so happy with my
hymns!"

Two of the most devoted to Clara's cause were the Shake-
speareans, Fred Pemberton and Erna Cranberry, who had
long since made up their little row. Yet the seeds of another
lay in the poetess' suspicions of Pemberton's fealty, and when
word finally came that the unriddler of the sonnets had been
seen at John Gielgud's *Hamlet* in the company of Elesina
Stein, Erna's wrathful denunciations filled the parlor at 68th
Street.

"He's like that idiotic George of Denmark, the husband of
Anne, who sat about the dwindling court of James II, crying:
'I can't believe it!' with the news of each defection to William
of Orange. And when Anne at last decamped herself, taking
George along by the ear, and word was brought to the poor
King, all he could say was: 'Has "I can't believe it!" gone,
too?'"

It began to seem that what was left of Clara's court was worse than what was gone. Erna was constantly with her, and her clamorous sympathy provided a strange chorus to Clara's hymns. One evening David invited Erna out to dinner with no other motive than to remove her from the house. The poetess, drinking freely and eating well at the expensive restaurant of her choice, became confidential. After she had given David a particularly long smiling look, he began almost to wonder if, despite her years and bulk, she were not planning a seduction.

"If you'll buy me another brandy, David, I'll tell you my secret project."

Gallantly, he signaled the waiter. "See how fast you can bring us a brandy."

"Shall I tell you, dear boy, what *I* would do if I were as young and handsome as you?"

"Make love to America's greatest poetess?"

"Make love, yes. But not to a poetess. To an actress. Or perhaps I should say, to an ex-actress. To the beautiful but unscrupulous woman who now styles herself Mrs. Irving Stein!"

David stared, astonished, at those small, pale, squinting eyes. Erna's lantern chin was thrust forward, and her head was slightly tilted back. She held her expectant pose.

"You wish me to reverse the roles of Hippolytus and Phaedra?"

"Elesina's not your father's wife. She's his concubine."

"But do nice boys make love to their fathers' concubines?"

"Why not? If it's for their good? Poor old Irving is having a bad time of it, I hear."

"You mean the concubine is unfaithful? Already?"

"Well, I don't know as I'd go that far. But I hear she leads him quite a dance. I shouldn't be surprised if he didn't begin to pine for the peace and calm of your mother's presence."

"And all those hymns?" David laughed, in sudden nervous irritability, provoked, for the moment, by the thought of both his parents. But he was nonetheless struck by the image of his father as a possibly pathetic figure. Did the old sultan hear giggles from the harem? "And do you think that courting the divine Elesina would help my relations with the august author of my being?"

"Could it make them any worse?" Erna became even more animated in her approach. "I'll tell you how I see it, David. If Elesina should respond to your advances, she would cease to be an issue between you and your father. For you would have proved to him that she was worthless! It would be like the wager between Posthumus and Iachimo in *Cymbeline*. If Imogen should reject Iachimo, he would have to fight her husband. But if she succumbed, she was not worth a duel. Oh, I go very far! I see my way! I'm not afraid of consequences. Not a bit."

"Erna, I begin to think you're serious."

"Of course, I'm serious!"

"You really believe I should attempt to seduce the woman my father calls his wife?"

"Seduction is a strong word. Elesina has always been — how do you call it? — easy. She's a very beautiful woman, and you're a healthy, handsome young male. You needn't play the prude with me, David Stein. I heard all about that walking trip in Ireland. Your father even boasted about it! And, anyway, if you had scruples, you wouldn't have to go all the way. A simple flirtation could do the trick. Once your father saw his pretty bride taken up with a younger man, he might regret the whole business."

"And Elesina? You think she'd throw over Broadlawns and a fortune for my *beaux yeux?* How little you know her."

"Oh, I don't say that Elesina isn't going to cost the old boy a pretty penny. Unless he catches her, as you lawyers say, in flagrante. But as he would catch you, too, under my hypothesis, we must forgo that amusing alternative. Would that you were more Elizabethan, David! But let us play the hand that is dealt us. I suggest that all you have to do is make your father homesick for his old home. The rest should be a simple cash transaction. Elesina will have her price, never fear. Ivy Trask will see to that!"

"It may be a stiff one."

"Well, we needn't pay it, need we? We can always bargain. The point is to get the thing started."

David in the days that followed found his mind returning in fantasies to Miss Cranberry's theory. He remembered Pemberton's statement that an old maid could never comprehend the Elizabethan male. Now it seemed to him that just the opposite was true, that the big, hulking, sandy-haired poetess might have the gusty realism and sharp nostrils of the Virgin Queen. His reflections were invaded with hot, foolish visions of rose red brick and brown gold paneling, of tapestried chambers with slits of windows, of a beruffed Elesina in a dress parted between her breasts to expose her front right down to the navel, smiling expectantly, confidently, at a David, scarlet-cloaked, bowing deeply. Suddenly he sprang forward to take her roughly against the paneled wall. Really! What rot!

When he told Eliot of Miss Cranberry's suggestion, his friend responded gruffly with a Shakespearean quotation:

" 'My only love sprung from my only hate!' "

"Love? Miss Cranberry didn't suggest that I had to love the iniquitous Elesina."

"Love, make love, what's the difference?"

"But *can* a man make love when he hates?"

"Of course! It might be even better that way. Look at animals. They're always angry and snarling in the mating season. Hunger and sex provide our greatest drives. Both are apt to be accompanied by nasty shows of temper."

"Are you saying that love *is* hate?"

"I'm saying it can be."

They were on their way to a cocktail party given by Sam Gorman. Sam, as feature editor of *Tone*, gave parties where he tried to mingle the world of fashion with those of society and finance. He had met David and Eliot at Broadlawns and had been indefatigable in his subsequent invitations. Neither much cared for Sam or his parties, but it seemed crude to decline them all. Certainly David would not have gone that day had he remembered whom he was likely to see there. He was immediately accosted by Ivy Trask.

"At last I catch you, David Stein! Now don't think you're going to escape. Haven't I loved you since you were a little boy? Didn't I keep you from being kicked out of school? Didn't you cry your heart out to me when Barbara Brannon told you she only cared for college men? Didn't I run interference with your mother that night at Broadlawns when you finished off the champagne in the pantry and were sick to your stomach? And . . ."

"For God's sake, Ivy!" he exclaimed, putting his hand to her mouth. "Be quiet. I surrender. What do you want?"

"I want you to come right over to that window seat and listen to me. Why have you been avoiding me? Why didn't you answer my letter?"

"I figured we were in different camps."

"Just because you're unreasonable and violent about your father and Elesina, is that a reason to cut me?"

"I'm not cutting you, Ivy. We're talking, aren't we?"

"I had to collar you first. And what's all this about your not taking a job? I hear you've been pouting because some stuffy firm didn't want a Jewish boy. Is that true?"

"Not really. I was just sore for a bit."

"As if it made any difference! You should know better. It's a great advantage to have a name like Stein. Elesina has found it so. She's becoming a great figure in Rye. I shouldn't be surprised if the day came when the women of Westchester would want her in the Assembly. You should come out and help her, David!"

It was difficult to know how to take Ivy. She was absurd, she was outrageous; at times she was almost sinister. David knew that his mother regarded her as the devil behind Elesina. But he could never forget the boyhood years in which he had poured out his heart in the lap of this taut, tense, avidly listening little woman who had known how to raise a shiny bridge between the shores of adults and of children. They had met in the middle and leaned over the side together to watch.

"Mrs. Stein is welcome to the name and to the money," he observed. "But she can't have all the family, too. I think I'm going to stay in my corner, Ivy."

"Lionel and Peter see her. So do their wives."

"Then she should be satisfied. She can let me off."

"But you're the one she wants! You're the one everyone wants. Oh, Elesina's doing very well, it's true. People are beginning to forget the unpleasantness and come to her parties. And she's a brilliant hostess. You should see her! But she minds that you won't go there. And it hurts your poor father terribly."

"He might have thought of that before he did what he did."

"Oh, David, I can't believe it's my old friend talking. When did you get this stuffy? Wake up! We're in nineteen thirty-eight!"

"I stand behind my mother, Ivy. She has not protested, and she has not sued. She has been as modern as you. But I cannot see that being modern obligates me to take by the hand the woman who has ruined her life."

"Life, fiddlesticks! And I suppose your father had nothing to do with it."

"I hold them both responsible."

"Now let me tell *you* something." Ivy's eyes moved quickly from side to side to make sure that nobody else could hear. "Your father has had an operation."

"I know. Peter told me. The prostate. But that's normal for his age."

"What Peter doesn't know is that it left him entirely impotent."

David looked away in anguish from those popping green eyes. What nightmare had overtaken his world that the paternal genitalia, the source of his being, the creator of *him*, should now be the sport of this dyed-haired witch's cocktail-party gossip?

"You can imagine what that does to a man of your father's vanity, married to a beautiful young bride!" Ivy continued relentlessly. "And you think you and your mother have troubles! What's the use of children if they abandon a parent just when they're needed most? Your father loves you, David, and it's a bloody shame if you don't go to him now."

David looked at her pleadingly. Please, Ivy, he wanted to implore her, go back to the way you were, be again the funny friend who was so good to a little boy! He felt he could not endure the other vision. "And Elesina?" He enunciated the name with difficulty. "Elesina minds? She makes it hard for him?"

"Elesina is an angel from heaven! All she wants from your father is love and affection. All she asks is to take care of him, to treasure him. *He's* the one who cannot reconcile himself to the situation."

"Poor Dad. How it must humiliate him."

"And *now* will you come, David Stein?"

He stared. "Where?"

"To Broadlawns. This weekend. Tomorrow!"

When David left the party with Eliot, he had not promised Ivy that he would come, but he had also not refused. Eliot, listening to his friend's version of the conversation, seemed amused.

"What do you suppose Elesina really does for Ivy in return for all her services?"

"Services?"

"Like getting you to Broadlawns."

"But Ivy was doing that for Dad."

"How much does Ivy worry about your old man? Isn't she Elesina's retriever? No, no, it's Elesina who has her eye on you. And what Elesina wants, Ivy delivers!"

"Eliot, you're absurd."

"Am I? My dear boy, you'll have to admit that so far I've been a shrewd observer. And I note that Erna Cranberry and Ivy Trask seem to have a trait in common: the desire, for one reason or another, to deliver you, a pretty blond bundle, to your beautiful stepmother's bed. Why don't they try me? They'd have much less trouble."

"Because they don't like silly asses. Where shall we dine? Twenty-One?"

⊷§ 4 §⊷

Irving had always supposed that he thought less about death than most people, but his immunity was now at an end. The prostate operation, beset with complications and studded with agony, had produced a near fatal heart attack. As he and Elesina had agreed in advance that he was to have no visitors, it had been possible to keep this from the family and business associates, but he had been dismissed from the hospital only with the severest injunctions that he not quit Broadlawns for three months. He passed long, slow, dressing-gowned days in his library and in the patio or, now that the spring weather had come, in a wheelchair in the rose garden. The household was devoted: the nurses efficient, Elesina consoling, tactful, perfect. Yet he read his own demise in the very smoothness of the ministrations that surrounded him.

It seemed to him that everything about him was young. The older servants, except for the butler, Arthur, had gone with Clara, and Broadlawns was full of neophytes. And what was not young, the trees, the works of art, seemed to promise to live forever. Irving likened himself to another dying collector, Cardinal Mazarin, who used to paddle down the corridors of his gorgeous palace, in slippers and bathrobe, past rows of great statues and walls of peerless paintings, murmuring tremulously: *"Le moyen de quitter tout ça?"*

Because he would never again be able to make love to Elesina, she had begun to take on some of the luster of a goddess in a dream. His thoughts about her seemed to defile her by their very helplessness. And when he considered with despondency the decay of his flesh, the approaching decomposition of the man Stein, it appeared to him that his reality was the dream, that the greater truth was in his vision of the new deity at Broadlawns. He seemed to have survived, in some curious fashion, his own extinction and was now witnessing the translation of his old domain to a female fashion. It was as if by the hubris of marrying a young woman he had brought about his own humiliation and at the same time the austere privilege of being audience to it.

All, however, was not young at Broadlawns. Elesina's mother, who had soon reconciled herself to the marriage, had her regular room for weekends. Irving surmised that her other invitations must have been diminished by the death and illness of her contemporaries and that she found Broadlawns, where nothing was expected of her, a pleasant substitute for visits to ailing friends where she was under the increasing burden of being cheerful. He had no objection to her presence, for she was quiet and self-sufficient, entertaining herself with reading and solitary walks. The person whom he really minded was Ivy Trask. Elesina was trying to persuade Ivy to give up her job at *Tone* and become her full-time house-keeper-secretary. As Irving was no longer able to manage the household, his wife insisted that she needed this additional help, and he felt sadly sure that it was only a matter of time before the terrible Trask was mistress of all. Ivy was living in the house, although she still commuted to New York. She hired and fired the servants, and Arthur, the one old retainer who had remained loyal to Irving, had already made his peace with her.

Social life, interrupted by Irving's illness, had now been resumed on a moderate scale, and Elesina had begun to put together little house parties. Nothing was asked of Irving but to have himself wheeled into the dining room for any meal that he chose, even at the very last moment, or to chat occasionally at cocktails in the patio. Nobody said a word if he suddenly beckoned his nurse and asked to be taken to his room or the library. Oh, yes, he had to admit that his confinement was beautifully handled, by Elesina, by Arthur, even by Ivy Trask — blast her! — but the trouble was that it was precisely a confinement, almost a captivity. He yearned for David, but dared not write him.

On a Friday afternoon as he was sitting alone with his *Wall Street Journal* in the Fragonard room, he turned at the sound of Elesina's quick, light step. She was standing by the doorway, and a shaft of sunlight cut across the middle of her face, just failing to illuminate her smile and making it, he suddenly and quixotically thought, faintly sinister. But it wasn't sinister. It was friendly, very friendly. Elesina's equanimity of temper, after six months, never ceased to astonish him. He remembered with a shudder the tart answer to the question he had rashly put to his mother-in-law:

"You ask me if Elesina can possibly be as contented as she looks? Don't you know there are two types of acquisitive women? Those, the great majority, who are still discontented after they get what they want, and those, the one percent, who are satisfied. You've had luck, my dear Irving!"

Elesina sat down by the table and placed a small unframed canvas before him. It was a French seventeenth-century painting, perhaps a design for a ceiling or overdoor. A naked woman was holding up an oval portrait of the young Louis XIV. On either side of her cherubs were heaping up shields, spears, sheafs of wheat, emblems of peace and victory. In the rear of the picture two other cherubs were chasing away a horned figure, a satyr, a symbol of war. The curtain that another cherub was holding back to permit the satyr to escape was of the same deep purple as Elesina's velvet suit. Irving pointed this out.

"Ah, but that isn't the reason I brought it to you," she replied. "No such vain thoughts occupy me now. I wanted you to see how I was progressing. That French dealer who was here last week told me it was a Le Brun. He based his opinion on the fact that the portrait of the King is a copy of a known Le Brun portrait. But if you will compare the lady with nudes by Watteau and Fragonard, you will see that she must be much later."

Irving smiled patiently at her enthusiasm. "Why do you say so, my darling?"

"Because she's sexy! Surely you can see that, Irving? You, of all men! A nymph or goddess in a Louis Quatorze painting would be a man in a woman's skin, an Amazon, a Michelangelo. This gal looks as if she'd been surprised in her bath."

"Then how do you explain the Le Brun?"

"Well, some noble in seventeen thirty or seventeen forty may have wanted a fresco to celebrate the military glory of a grandfather who fought under Louis Quatorze. We think of people in the past as being surrounded by things of their period. But they had pasts, too."

"My dear, I think you're on to something. It's astonishing how you see it. Now, I look at that little picture, it seems clear that it's eighteenth-century!"

Elesina was very pleased. There was no need for him to tell her that her deduction was obvious, and that the French dealer was an ass whom he tolerated only because of his connection with a museum in Marseilles which sometimes disposed of items in its collection. What was important was the speed with which Elesina was mastering a field that was new to her. She worked every day with his curator, Leon Feld, taking up the Stein possessions century by century, room by room. Irving had never forgotten the impression which she had made on him at their first meeting with her knowledge of Shakespeare's sonnets derived from a single role in a trashy play.

"And the nymph, or whatever she may be," Elesina pointed out, "doesn't give a hoot about the emblems heaped up beside her. She'd much rather sport in the shade with that satyr they're kicking out of the house!"

"Poor nymph," Irving sighed. "Perhaps I, too, find myself in the wrong century. I ought to be content with one of those marble Louis Quatorze heroines. We could talk of old wars and past glories. But you, my dear, are like the Fragonard nymph at whose feet the cherubs pile up unwanted treasures."

"Treasures, on the contrary, which I want very much!" Elesina retorted with a peal of laughter. She jumped up to kiss him on the forehead. "And you know you're naughty to talk that way. Haven't we agreed that subject is taboo?"

"You must forgive a bitter old man."

"But I shan't! You've got to get it through your silly old head that you have a happy woman on your hands."

"Ah, but for how long?" Suddenly he caught her hand and pressed it to his lips. "How long, my beautiful girl?"

"Just as long as you keep away from that subject." She withdrew her hand firmly and gave him an admonishing tap on the shoulder. "Just as long as you try to keep it off your mind. I mean it, Irving. You can try."

Was it possible? Did she mean it? He could suppose so, anyway. Did life have to be wretched? Was there any law that decreed misery? Was it not possible, at least conceivable, that she was one of those women — there were such, one knew, nuns, nurses, teachers — who could live in peace with their dormant senses? Irving closed his eyes in a sudden seizure of pain as another thought struck him: that she might have been actually relieved by his operation!

"Elesina, dearest," he exclaimed hurriedly, in a frantic need to obliterate the idea, "let me tell you something. Something I've been thinking about recently. I've never been sure what to do with the collection. My will directs my executors to turn Broadlawns into a museum. But will they do it right? Will they really care? Lionel and Peter know nothing about art, and David will be off on some tangent of his own. Suppose you and I take care of it? Why wait till I'm dead and gone? We could convert the place into an art center and open it in my lifetime."

He noted the way her lips parted and the way her eyes fixed themselves again on the little picture. She was obviously struck. How long would it take to catalogue the collection, to set up the project? Two years? Three? It would see him out.

"Irving, I think it might be a wonderful idea!"

"What would?" a voice demanded.

Irving turned with a half-suppressed snort of anger to face Ivy Trask, standing in the doorway. Behind her was Mrs. Dart.

Elesina, very excited now, proceeded to tell them of the plan. Ivy clapped her hands with instant enthusiasm, but Mrs. Dart was denigrating.

"Oh, come now, Irving. You've had your kicks putting it all together. Let other collectors have theirs."

"You mean I should sell it all?"

"Not you, your executors. Our body goes back to the eternal earth. Why shouldn't our things go back to the eternal market? To me a memorial museum is like a mummy."

"But think of the Frick, Mrs. Dart!" Ivy protested. "Think of the Wallace Collection. The Freer Gallery!"

"I do. To me they're simply smug tombs. I detest their air of complacency. All those fat-cat collectors putting themselves on a par with the beautiful things they've simply bought!"

"You just don't believe in museums, Linda," Irving said flatly.

"Oh, a few, yes. But we're going to have far too many of them. The only way to learn about art is to start with bad art. All those schoolchildren who are brought up on master-pieces — no wonder they never learn to discriminate!"

"Mother, you're being ridiculous." Elesina got up to end the discussion. "Come on out now. I want to show you where I'm going to put the begonias."

Ivy, left alone with Irving, bustled with plans. All she had to do was to hear an idea, and in two minutes she had made it her own.

"It would be just the thing to start Elesina's new career with a bang. We could make the announcement a sensation. Elesina has been asked to take the chairmanship of the benefit ball for Saint Joseph's Hospital in Rye. Suppose you have it here? You could get the governor. We might have a fashion show in the patio. I could arrange that. We might get it underwritten by Saks or Bonwits. Oh, Irving, I begin to *see* it!"

What was most galling of all to him was the assumption which seemed to underlie her officiousness that the old and impotent should make good their deficiency with full shovels of heavily minted coin.

"I'm afraid, Ivy, there is a lot of hard work to be done before we can even think of bringing the public in. Still, I imagine you could help in the meantime. Your experience as a magazine editor might be valuable. My library has a collection of eighteenth-century Colonial newspapers, completely uncatalogued. Now if you . . ."

"Oh, no you don't, Irving!" she interrupted. "I know you'd like to put me in a corner where I'd be silenced. But Ivy Trask was exploited for the last time in nineteen eighteen. She's been on her own since, and she's going to stay that way. But now let me spring a surprise on *you*. When you know who I've brought for the weekend, you'll forgive me for everything." She threw back her head and laughed. "You may even like me!"

He stared. "Who have you brought?"

"Guess."

"I can't."

"Who would you rather see come into this room right now than anyone in the whole world?"

He looked a bit wildly at the empty doorway. "Not David? Oh, my God!"

David, hearing his name, hurried into the room, and Irving rose, staggering, to throw his arms about him.

"Oh, my darling boy!"

Ivy beamed at both, and then, miraculously, had the tact to leave. Even in the hectic atmosphere of his excitement Irving was able to reflect that she was either more generous than he had expected or that there was an unknown price to be paid. David's expression was of shocked surprise.

"You look so down, Dad. I had no *idea* you'd been that ill. I'd have come sooner. Believe me."

"Oh, I do." Irving collapsed now in his chair and began suddenly, convulsively, to weep.

"Dad! I'm sorry!"

"It's all right, my boy. I'm so happy to see you, that's all."

"But this isn't like you. Is something wrong? Is Elesina . . . is she being difficult? I don't mean anything bad, but sometimes, with younger wives . . . well . . ."

"No, dear boy. Elesina is an angel." Irving pulled himself together with an effort. "She is wonderful to me. It's just that . . ." He sobbed again. "It's all so . . . so strange. Don't leave me, David."

David's hand gripped his shoulder until it hurt.

◆§ 5 §◆

There were to be a dozen guests for dinner at Broadlawns that evening, and David understood that if he was to have any private talk with Elesina it would have to be before the cocktail hour. When his father had gone to his room and Arthur had informed him that Mrs. Stein was in the rose garden, he sought her there. He was mildly surprised to find her reading a volume of poetry. She closed it and looked up with a friendly smile.

"Oh, David, I'm so glad you've come."

"I hadn't any notion that he was that sick. Lionel and Peter told me it was a routine prostate. But it was a coronary!"

"It was that, too. Your father didn't want anyone to know. I did as he told me."

The haggard, haunting look that he had remembered from their first meeting was quite gone now. She seemed younger, more filled out. The black hair had a touch of bronze; the large dark eyes seemed amused. Her skin was a healthier white. If she was less mysterious, she was even more beautiful. But what astonished him most was the ease of her manner. She seemed to take it quite for granted that she should be welcoming him to Broadlawns.

"Between us we'll bring him around, you'll see," she continued. "At the moment he's full of gloom and ideas of death. But that will pass. What we have to convince him of is that every minute of life is equally important, whether one's seven or seventy. It's living that counts, not one's age."

"You should be able to convince him of that," he replied, with reluctant admiration. "You seem alive enough."

"Oh, I've never been better. The country air agrees with me. I've spent too much of my life in town."

David thought now that he could identify what was upsetting him: it was her healthiness. He had been mentally exaggerating her pallor, her air of lugubrious fascination, transforming her with his hostile spirit into the caricature of the vampire lady in a Charles Addams cartoon. He had not been prepared for her cheerfulness, her animation. God only knew why he had not been better prepared, with all the sexual fantasies which had raged in his angry head! He started to ask a question and realized that he had forgotten it.

"What are we going to call each other?" he blurted out.

"I've already called you David. What can you possibly call

me but Elesina? 'Mrs. Stein' would be ridiculous, and I'm certainly not going to be 'aunt.' "

"How about 'stepmother'? Or more familiarly, 'step-ma'?"

"It sounds so hostile. The term has a bad reputation."

"Undeserved, of course."

"Undeserved so far."

"Well, I shall be a docile stepson. I shall join the chorus of your admirers."

Elesina looked at him suspiciously. "Your tone is bantering. You are playing with me. Tell me frankly what's on your mind. It's much better that way."

"Well, try to put yourself in my shoes." David turned away from her and took a few steps. "I come back to Broadlawns to find everything yours. Not that I really object. Dad can certainly do as he likes with his own. But it takes a bit of getting used to. As Fred Pemberton would put it: 'Thou has it now: king, Cawdor, Glamis, all.' "

"And you fear I played most foully for it?"

He laughed in spite of himself at her quickness. "No, no, I don't mean that. You mustn't think I meant that. It was just a quotation. We've always gone in for too many of them."

"Ah, but I *do* think you meant it. Let us be beautifully clear, David. You have come out here to see your father because you consider it your duty, and so it is. But at the same time you want to square your conscience about your mother. So you chatter innuendoes. I don't care for that. Let it all come out. If you think I'm a hussy and a gold digger, say so!"

David stared into the challenge of her direct gaze. He wondered if she would laugh or slap him if he took her up. "Very well. Why *did* you marry him?"

"Because we needed each other. Because I thought we could do something for each other. And that is precisely how it is working out. If you think you're going to hear an apology, you're sadly mistaken. I'm proud of having married your father. Prouder than of anything I've done in my life!"

He felt a sudden stab of anger. "I should have hoped it was more a question of love than of pride."

"It is both. I needn't discuss that with you. But be assured that I have the temerity to anticipate that I shall continue to make your father an excellent wife."

It was not merely that the mechanized divisions had now occupied the old kingdom. The civilian aides had penetrated to the heart of the citadel and donned the robes of the priests, assumed the headdresses of the old monarchs. The velvets and satins of David's past hung from the walls to celebrate the conquest. Elesina's very beauty repudiated him.

"I suppose that's easier now."

"What is?"

"To be a good wife."

"Why?"

"Well, you see I know the effects of my father's operation."

"You ought to have your mind washed out with soap, David Stein!" she exclaimed angrily. Then almost at once her indignation seemed to subside. "I hope at least you'll tell him I tried to be friendly."

Her tone was unassuming but firm, and she turned away to her garden with the air of resolution of one who has too many duties to perform to dissipate her time in losses already taken into account. David went indoors, where he found Ivy Trask working at a card table covered with papers which she had placed near the fountain in the patio. He sat down by her and told her of his tactlessness.

"What shall I do now? Go back to town?"

"Not because of Elesina," she replied at once. "Do you flatter yourself that your presence will embarrass her? She may not speak to you, except for the minimum civilities, but that will be simply because there is nothing to say. She doesn't bear grudges."

"Not even for what *I* said?"

Ivy shook her head. "The past has no importance for her. If it had, it would have crushed her long ago. She knows there's always a new deal coming up and that eventually her luck will change."

"Don't you think it has? Don't you think she's won now?"

Ivy considered this for a moment. "It's a game; it's not the rubber."

"And you want a grand slam!"

"Oh, I want the world for her, yes. You'd better get on our side, David."

"Do I strike you as an opportunist?"

"You strike me as a man who can learn to face facts. I know a bit about injustice. I've had my share. It taught me not to dwell on the bad moments. Keep looking ahead!"

"You forget that it is not only the past that nags me. It's the present. Mother's present."

"Your mother has no present. She lives in the past. How does it help her for you to make the same mistake?"

"I suppose nothing helps her," he confessed, throwing up his hands. "How would you suggest I make my peace with Elesina?"

"The way rude little boys always make peace with those whom they've offended. By saying they're sorry."

"And you think she'll accept my apology?"

"Try her."

Which David did, before dinner, as the house party assembled in the parlor. He went straight up to Elesina. "My conduct this afternoon was abominable. Ivy leads me to hope that I may be forgiven."

She did not even look at him. "Leave Ivy out of it."

"Will you forgive me?"

She turned to him suddenly at this, with a rather artificial brightness, and he was sure that Ivy had warned her. "I shall." She stuck out her hand, as if not caring who noted the gesture. "Or rather I *will*. As Fred Pemberton would say, it's more than simple future. It's determination. *Let* us be friends, David."

This was rather further than he had intended to go, but how was one to be so churlish as to reject her? The large dark limpid eyes laughed at him, took him in, like flooding water over a valley, filling up the flat basins of cracked mud. How did she make one's loyalty, one's faith, one's word seem quaint, rather dear, old-fashioned things? "Are you sure you want to give them up?" her smile, half mocking, half commanding, seemed to ask. "Don't do it just for me, you know. I'm not a bit sure I'm worth it. After all, it might be fun to be a crank, a *joli garçon* of a crank, like you."

He reached for her hand. "Yes — let us be friends, Elesina."

There was a flicker of withdrawal in her eyes, perhaps at the pressure of his grasp. "Your father will be so pleased," she said in a more perfunctory tone and turned to speak to Arthur, who already too obviously preferred her to his old mistress. It occurred to David, with an inward chuckle that helped to leash his conscience, that it might be Ivy's function to scare the servants, leaving Elesina free to be worshiped. What a pair!

"You make it all easier than I would have thought possible," he said when she turned back to him.

"Why should things not be easy? Is there a law against it? Anyway, you can do something for me if you wish. You can be nice to my little daughter."

"Oh, is she coming here?"

"I hope so. Things have changed. Her Grandpa Everett, like so many of the parsimonious, has proved a reckless gambler. He's lost his fortune in oil ventures. And now that my situation has changed, too, he seems to want to have Ruth off his hands."

"I'd like to meet my stepsister."

"But of course you will. Isn't this your home? Why don't you help us catalogue the collection? At least until you get a job. You could be the most immense help. Your father says you're the only member of the family who cares about his things."

This was her first reference to the museum project of which Ivy had told him, and he mused about it as the house party now moved toward the dining room. Elesina seemed perfectly serious, although it was a cliché in his mother's circle to lament the fate of the Stein collection, destined, it was always asserted, to be converted into jewels and furs and yachts for "that woman." At dinner he found himself next to Mrs. Dart, a large, stylish woman, with big bones and lanky brown-freckled arms. Her hair was a dyed chestnut, and she smoked constantly, even at table, puffing her cigarettes with thick, deeply rouged lips.

"We have an unusual relationship," she instructed him. "My daughter's stepson." She nodded, as if to accept the bond. "Let's see what we can make of it."

"I have made my peace with Elesina. Will the same treaty include you?"

"Certainly not. I don't need a treaty. I don't take sides. I'm too old, and besides, I don't care. I can perfectly imagine that you and your brothers would have been less than over-joyed by your father's marriage."

"Oh, if he's happy, that's all we care about."

"Really? In your case, I should have cared about the money."

David was taken aback. "But we don't," he protested. "Or at least *I* don't. If Father and Elesina really love each other . . ."

"Love? Why should love be involved?"

"Isn't it usual?"

"With the young it's desirable. Perhaps even essential. But your father's not young. Neither, for that matter, is Elesina. Between them there can be respect, congeniality, affection. But those things don't add up to love."

David studied her long, serious, brown countenance; then

his eyes dropped to the heavy gold bracelet on her wrist. Yet he felt sure that there was something softer in her that her exterior was designed to hide. "I should have thought you were more romantic, Mrs. Dart."

"Do I look romantic?"

"Not on the surface. But behind all that discipline, well . . . I wonder."

Mrs. Dart's pale blue eyes settled for a moment on her impudent interlocutor. He thought he could make out a friendly gleam in them. "You are right, David. I *am* romantic. And you're smart to have spotted it. Or are you a fellow romantic? But how can anyone born in the twentieth century know what passion is?"

"Nineteen hundred is the cutoff year?"

"One has to approximate. The climate today is more conducive to mating than to romance."

"And that, I take it, is a bad thing?"

Her attitude was milder than he had expected. "I don't suppose it is really good or bad. But like everything in life, it has to be paid for. I believe that sex is a constant. Everyone starts with more or less the same amount. If it's poured out, it gets thin. If it's bottled, it seasons. Different eras have different tastes."

"So the cloistered nun, dreaming of Galahad, may be as well off as Cleopatra?"

"Perhaps better off. I measure experience by intensity. I've loved only one man in my life, David, and I had the good fortune to be married to him. We were the lucky ones! Perhaps it will happen to you, despite your century."

"But supposing I've already loved?"

"Oh, with a man, that's all right. I don't say one can't love twice, or three times, in a lifetime. It's a question of when dilution begins. It may be different with different people."

"But I thought we all started with the same amount!"

"Well, some of us may be leakier than others."

"What about your daughter?" he demanded, emboldened

by her tone. "She's been married three times. Can she ever know passion?"

Mrs. Dart looked down the table to where Elesina was talking with Fred Pemberton. She shrugged. "No, I don't think Elesina will ever know passion. Elesina, God help her, is a child of her century. Or should I say: God help *you?*"

❧ 6 ❧

Elesina was very serious about the plans for Broadlawns, and she and Ivy were soon engaged in reducing them to paper. Two experts were retained to make an inventory of the collection; Irving's lawyers were consulted about the creation of a foundation, and a prominent architect was invited to inspect the house and grounds with a view to their conversion to a public purpose. David accepted a post as adviser, and his name appeared on the special stationery which Ivy designed for the future institute: "Broadlawns, the Irving Stein Foundation for the Arts." It was agreed that until he put his law career into some kind of order he would come out to Rye twice a week and help in the library. This resulted in a rather tense scene with his mother.

"First you were too much on my side of the boat," Clara observed dryly. "Now I wonder if your shifting seats won't capsize us."

"Don't you want me to have a hand in what happens to the collection?"

"Oh, that's the least of my worries."

"You think I will fall under the divine Elesina's spell?"

"Is it still a question of 'will'?"

"I'm afraid I'm not a sufficiently modern person," David retorted with some heat. "I was all for cutting Dad and his bride, but you and Lionel and Peter cried out that I was going too far. All right! So I made it up with them! Is there no pleasing you?"

"You know perfectly well what I'm talking about, David,

so you needn't take that injured attitude. It's a question of degree. I never meant that you were to *live* at Broadlawns."

He let the argument go by default. The vision of his father, so pale and frail, and the contrast which Clara offered of an unbreakable health and of a seemingly ineluctable complacency, had begun to alter his point of view. Of course, it was possible that his mother was not truly complacent; perhaps, deeply within, she suspected that if life at Broadlawns could go on so well without her, it might be that she had not contributed so much to it. Certainly David began to understand how totally the place was his father's creation. He remembered what Eliot had said: that Clara, like Eliot's own mother, belonged to a generation of New York ladies who did nothing with their hands or bodies — no cooking, cleaning or even sewing — and whose minds, like high white corridors, seemed too lofty and clean for ideas. But then he at once felt guilty for even thinking such thoughts.

"I'm sorry, Mom," he blurted out.

"Oh, it's all right, dear. It's quite all right."

Would he ever get over his own pity, pity at the pain which he very likely simply imagined behind her stiffly held head, her large troubled eyes? It was a relief now to leave 68th Street for Broadlawns.

He always spent his first half-hour there with his father. Irving slept a great deal, but he liked to hear David talk about the library or about Europe — Germany had just opened her campaign of propaganda for the Sudetenland. He would keep his eyes fastened on David's, a little half smile playing about his lips.

"My only regret, dear boy, is to see you in the role of curator rather than collector. I should love to think of you putting something together for yourself. Can't I help you?"

"With the world about to blow itself up?"

"Maybe it won't."

"Won't fight? Then it won't be worth blowing up."

David sought distraction from Hitler in Broadlawns. He

and Elesina worked in different rooms, he in the library, she in the parlor, but consultations were frequent. Was the Veronese genuine? Wasn't it possible that the Fragonard was really by Boucher? Were the acoustics in the patio adequate for a concert? The summer of 1938 moved sluggishly by. He gave up even thinking about a job.

"I'm turning myself into a catalogue," he told Eliot. "Perhaps that's all we can do for the moment: make records of what may be destroyed in Armageddon."

"*If* that's what you're doing" was the sarcastic reply.

Lunch for David and Elesina at Broadlawns in the smaller dining room paneled with Japanese screens, cool at least in contrast to the heat of the garden beyond the open french doors, was pleasanter than on the more crowded weekends. The whole great house and place, when Irving was in his room and Ivy Trask in town, seemed a counterpart to Elesina. It was as if, an actress in search of a setting, she had finally found the right one, and the servants had become stagehands or choruses dedicated to the enhancement of her exits and her entrances. Elesina's quick sharp step on the marble of the front hall, her dark head bending over the cutting table in the flower room, the smoke from her cigarette in the jade holder rising from the long Venetian sofa when she read, the sound of her sudden, gusty laughter all combined to make him feel an audience of one in the drama of the union of a place and a mistress that seemed to have been always destined for each other. It was as if Clara Stein had never lived there.

The unreality of the atmosphere was intensified by David's horror at the turn of events in Europe. He felt at moments in the hot morning in the big library, with the chirping of crickets outside, as if the top of his head were coming off. What in God's name did he think he was doing, checking the morocco-bound quartos of Webster, Massinger and Shakespeare with the inventory prepared by Swan's, turning the pages gingerly, reading the golden phrases in the quaint old print, while abroad the world crumbled and at home a new

Mrs. Stein eradicated his very sense of the family? When she came into the library to slip into the chair beside him, to share a joke about the poor young man who was having such trouble with the prints, to take a few quick puffs on a cigarette or simply to pick up one of the quartos and silently read for a few minutes, he had a curious feeling that *she* might be his reality, his only reality, that the rest of the world of mothers and law firms and Hitler might go away if he could only succeed in turning his back.

Elesina was more practical. She was practical in everything, even in foreign affairs. She refused to see the Nazi issue as one between simple right and wrong. She talked about the wrongs to Germany in 1919, about the perils of communism. She did not believe that Hitler's ambitions were limitless. She advocated American neutrality in the event of war. David tried to make excuses for such heresy.

"It's because you're not Jewish," he told her. "You can't be expected to feel as we do."

"But I'm married to a Jew," she insisted. "And anyway, it doesn't make that much difference. After all, you're in no more danger of being put in a concentration camp than I am. It's merely sentimental to get so upset about cruelties in faraway places that you can't prevent."

He wondered if this was philosophy or simple callousness. Her eyes were sympathetic, her tone warm, but she had a way of turning her attention suddenly to other subjects.

"I suppose my trouble is that I'm not sure I can't prevent those faraway cruelties," he said. "Or at least *do* something about them. In however small a way."

"How? Be practical."

"Well, I could be getting ready to be a soldier. Learning to fly, for example."

"Wait and see if there's going to be a war first. You'll still have plenty of time, don't worry. And in the meantime what is more important than the Stein collection? If we don't preserve our art and beauty, are we really worth saving?"

"Yes! But that's not the point. The point is you don't really need me to preserve the collection."

"Ah, but I do, David."

Whenever she touched an intimate note, she would quit him, or alter the topic, or do something abrupt, like closing a book. He wondered if she were trying to create a special kind of friendship in which to clothe their new relationship, something warm but elevated, flicked with romance but not devoid of dignity. What the French called an *amitié amoureuse?* No, less than that. But wasn't anything less than that simply the old platonic friendship of frustrated virgins and anemic bachelors, the butt of endless vulgar comedy? No, Elesina was better than that, bolder than that. What *was* it then? Did she know what herself?

She went into the city less often now. She had closed the apartment, she said, without the least regret. She explained her love of the country to David as a natural reaction to her own bringing-up.

"Like so many girls raised in Manhattan, I've a secret yen for the small town. All my life I've wanted to put down roots. Well, now I'm doing it! I'm going to become Mrs. Rye."

"Won't you miss the stage?"

"But I'm on it! Do you know Henry James's *The Tragic Muse?* It's the best novel ever written about an actress. A rising young diplomat asks the heroine to give up her career to become his wife and a future ambassadress. She won't even consider it! Ah, how James saw it, the idiocy of any man's thinking that a real actress could even consider balancing love against the stage! But now I begin to see something that James didn't see. She *might* have wanted to add the part of ambassadress — in diamonds — to her roles."

"So that's what you're doing now — acting a part?"

"Don't we always? I certainly was when we had the Girl Scouts here last week. And I loved it! Don't look at me with those sad eyes, David."

"I don't like to think you're not sincere."

"But actresses *are* sincere. I'm always sincere."

"I wonder if you're not playing with me." He was suddenly bitter at the idea that her charm was a matter of manipulation, as uninspired by himself as it could have been by any other man sitting in the dark beyond the footlights. He searched angrily about for a weapon. "The way you play with Ruth?" Elesina's daughter had arrived the week before, a block of a girl, looking closer to fourteen than eleven, and she already had a crush on David.

But Elesina only laughed, perhaps complimented by the feeling which such rudeness manifested. "So you've noticed that I play with Ruth? I guess I can't be such an actress, after all. But children, despite the old saying, are easy to fool. Ruth wants desperately to believe that she has a loving mother, and the least I can do is to provide her with the image of one."

David, to his own disgust, found himself preaching. "Mightn't it become a reality?"

"It might. But I'm not a maternal creature. That used to worry me, but one learns to accept oneself."

"I haven't."

"Why? You're a good person, David."

He flushed before the apparent sincerity of her gaze. "How can you tell that?"

"Oh, I always can. You're strong. You're honorable."

The quick, hot pleasure that he felt in his chest as quickly turned to resentment. Was he to be taken in by a performance even after he had been warned that it was one? "Ivy says you were a bad picker of husbands."

She laughed again, still without taking her eyes off his. "I suppose she meant only the first two. After all, she was responsible for the third. But I think I knew from the beginning that Bill and Ted were losers. Not that I exactly told myself so. On the contrary, I tried to persuade myself that they were great. Yet, deep down, I had a pretty good idea what they were like. My trouble, you see, was perversity, not stupidity. A desire to throw myself away. From that point of view, my choices showed definite perspicacity."

"But with Father it was different?" he asked roughly.

"I've told you all about that, David," she said in a soft voice, as she turned away. "I don't think I have to go into it again."

He was now the prey of an almost continual fantasy of sexual relations with her. Her smooth, hard side, her enameled exterior, her brisk stride, the quick way in which, at her desk, pushing back her long hair, she got right down to business seemed to suggest, by very contrast, a warmth within, a need for submission, a dedication to the ideal of love. In his thoughts David was a violent, a raping lover, Valentino in *The Sheik*. He tore off her robe by the swimming pool; he loomed in the door of her bedroom; he reached a hand under her dress in the dining room beneath the eyes, unseeing, of the somnolent Arthur. She was angered, but not for long. Her resistance was formal, her ultimate acquiescence enthusiastic. David, looking at his own silly, guilty expression in the mirror of his bathroom, felt the tears of shame that such maudlin dreams evoked. Yet his loins ached with frustration, and in New York he did something which he had not done since his last year at college. He went to a brothel.

He was less troubled now by disloyalty to his father. What he yearned for it was no longer Irving's privilege to take. On the contrary there was even a kind of fire around the fringes of his imagination kindled by the idea that a rape or taking of Elesina would be a fitting revenge for the youngest son, the dearest son, the Joseph, that only thus could the heavy score be balanced, that Erna Cranberry's idea of a Judgment Day in his father's own bed was the sole way to yank victory out of the roaring rumble of the Steins' defeat. But then he would extend his fantasy to magnanimity. After the guilty Elesina had been exposed in her alabaster nudity to camera lights, after she had been repudiated, divorced, flung back penniless on a sneering world, who would pick her up out of the street, console her, love her, marry her but the guilty David? Marry her and take her off to a new world, a new life . . .

"David, you haven't said a word in five minutes."

It was not, however, Elesina coming into the library, but Eliot at lunch with him in a cafeteria in New York.

"I'm sorry, Eliot. I'm preoccupied."

"So I observe. And I think I can imagine what preoccupies you." He smiled at David's startled look. "Never fear, we needn't discuss it. We both know what it is. You see how tactful I am. But I think you'd better take that job in the Schurman firm. You can hardly object *now* to their being your father's lawyers."

David had to accept the discussion as offered. He could never fool Eliot. "What makes you think the job's still open?"

"Mr. Schurman. I saw him at a closing yesterday, and he said I could tell you."

"He could have told me himself."

"You turned him down, old boy! It's up to you now to make the next move."

David mused. "You really think I ought?"

"I think damn well you ought!"

David looked at his friend narrowly, but Eliot remained inscrutable. "Very well, then. I'll go around this afternoon."

∾§ 7 §∾

Elesina liked to picture her life in scenes. She quarreled with Fred Pemberton because he saw each play of Shakespeare as a whole and not as an amalgam of acted episodes. The bard, she would argue, had been a total theater person — actor, producer, director as well as playwright. He would not have been in the least concerned by inconsistencies in characters which good performances could conceal. Readers? He *had* no readers, except for the few who might have got hold of a

pirated quarto. Elesina would cite with approval Mrs. Pritch-
ard, the eighteenth-century Lady Macbeth who had never
read act four because she did not appear in it.

Now that she was not on the stage, this feeling of life as
episodic was actually quickened. Off the boards, in fact, she
was more than ever on them in imagination. Broadlawns
seemed a stage, and she marveled at the roles that her prede-
cessor had eschewed. For the community was utterly prepared to be an audience. People were fascinated by the
beautiful new chatelaine of the principal estate in the neigh-
borhood. Scandal collapsed into curiosity; curiosity swelled to
enthusiasm. Mrs. Stein was "so gracious," "so human," "so
natural." She was not stiff and standoffish like the aristocratic
Clara. Elesina was delighted to have the Girl Scouts use the
grounds for their spring outing, or to open the pool on Friday
afternoons to boys' groups, or to invite the town band to give
a concert in the patio. It was rumored that only by her
tender administrations was the poor old Judge kept alive, and
this despite the fact that his death would vastly enrich her!
Ivy Trask had predicted that a year would make Elesina the
most popular woman in Rye. She now admitted that she had
overestimated the time by six months.

But what was a play without love? Elesina had no intention of playing in so bleak a drama. She had always, more or
less, been in love; she found it a comfortable state. Now that
she fancied herself in love with David, life at Broadlawns was
supplied with the needed extra dimension. It was delightful to
have him there, to watch him, to listen to him, to take in his
obvious interest in herself, even to sense the misery of what to
him must have been an agonizing disloyalty. Her own conscience was not even faintly troubled. She did not regard
either her heart or her body as the moral property of Irving
Stein, and she was actually proud of the way she had fulfilled
what she deemed her wifely duties. But at the same time she
had no intention of risking a scandal or of rocking her
smoothly sailing marital boat. She saw that David was going

to be more and more difficult to handle and that any translation of their relations to a physical plane might always be a
practical impossibility. She could handle such a change, but
could *he?* Yet the very fact that he was so intense, so guilty,
so fevered, added to her excitement.

Each day now offered a different scene. She would seek
him out in the library on the excuse that he was working too
hard and take him to the pool. They would sit there for an
hour, usually with Ruth, her dull, stout daughter, who had
converted her former resentment into a possessive passion for
"Mummie," and talk of other peoples' marriages and romances. Ruth's presence, however irksome to her, was necessary to keep David under control. His looks and tones were
always on the verge of indiscretion. He told her about Eliot
Clarkson, who had fallen in love at last, but with a much older
married woman, a vulgar, ridiculous creature, and they discussed at length what David's role in the matter should be.
Elesina told him about her first two husbands and he told her
about the Irish girl and read her some of his novel. Each
agreed that the other had had the worst possible luck.

One Thursday morning before lunch she was surprised to
find her mother's smart blue suitcases standing like two cadets
by the door in the front hall. Linda Dart, in a blue city suit,
was consulting a timetable.

"I thought you weren't going till tomorrow."

"I wasn't. But Agatha Gray telephoned to say she could
have me tonight, so I'm making it a long weekend. I leave
after lunch."

"Will you be back next week?"

"We'll see. I don't want the household to think me a
permanent encumbrance."

"Why not?" As her mother did not answer this, Elesina
pursued: "What's wrong, dear?"

"Shall we take a turn in the garden?"

Out of earshot of any servant, to the crunch on the fine
gravel of their high heels, Linda explained.

"I do not presume to lecture you, Elesina. You have long since passed out of the maternal orbit. But there are things that I need not countenance by being your houseguest. I tell you frankly that I do not approve of your relationship with David."

"Do you suppose I'm trying to seduce him?"

"I suppose nothing. What I see you doing is bad enough. I shall not remain a guest in the house of Irving Stein while you flirt with his son."

"Oh, Mother, flirt, what a term!"

"Use any you prefer. Or use none. We both know precisely what I mean."

"Don't you think David can take care of himself?"

"I think he might be hurt."

"Flirt, hurt, oh, those *terms!* They're so much your generation, Mother. When everyone was brought up to regard sex as a dangerous, lugubrious thing to be shackled by oath and sacrament. Sex should be as light as spring air!"

"That's all very well for you, my dear. I never suggested that *you'd* be hurt."

"Mother, how nasty of you!"

"Why nasty?"

"Because your tone implies that people who can't be hurt are shallow and hard."

"I don't judge them."

"Oh, but you do! You've always peered down at me scornfully from the peak of your blissful marriage with Daddy. It's not that I don't admire happy marriages. I do. But there are lives and lives. You shouldn't be so smug about yours."

"Nor you so confident."

Elesina became angry. "Did I make Bill Nolte unhappy? Or Ted Everett? Or any of my friends in the interim? You exaggerate my power, Mother. You flatter me unduly."

"You've changed," Linda replied in a grimmer tone. "You're more attractive rich than you were poor. Odd, how few people that's true of. And, anyway, David Stein bears no resemblance to either of your first two husbands. He's not only a man, he's a gentleman."

"But he bears a resemblance, I suppose, to my third?"

"Very well, my dear. I've had my little say. I shan't mention it again."

Elesina was thoroughly provoked. It struck her as most unfair that a parent who had shown as little maternal love as Linda had should still be able to upset her. There was a reproach to the daughter in the simple discipline of the mother's life that no amount of wishful thinking could ever quite dispel. Linda was utterly convinced that a love like hers and Amos's was the only reality in life, and anything short of it struck her as shabby. Elesina knew that nothing would ever convince her mother to the contrary. "Why can't I accept it?" she asked herself angrily. But she couldn't, and she stamped her foot as she walked away.

At the swimming pool she found David with Ruth. The poor girl looked unusually absurd in a red bathing suit decorated with knitted white bunny rabbits.

"Ruth, will you please go to the house and change into the new bathing suit I bought you? And throw that rag you have on away!"

"But, Mummie, I love the bunny suit! It was a present from Grandpa Everett."

"I don't care if it was a present from the Queen of Sheba. You're never to wear it while you're staying with me."

"All right, Mummie. I promise." But the girl made no move to go in to change.

"*Now*, Ruth."

Ruth jumped up to obey, but was diverted again by her need to communicate an item of seemingly passionate interest. "Oh, Mummie, the most wonderful thing has happened! David is going to tutor me in French."

"I have Mademoiselle Lannais coming out from New York to do that."

"But I don't like Mademoiselle Lannais! She makes everything so hard, and David makes it all so easy."

"Perhaps too easy." Elesina glanced skeptically from the pleading eyes of her daughter, who was now clasping David's hand, to the latter's sheepish countenance. She did not approve the liberality with which Ruth had distributed the confidence that in the first two weeks had seemed her mother's monopoly. Besides, was there not a criticism of herself implicit in this appeal to David? Should not she herself have been tutoring the child? "I think you'll do better, my girl, with a professional teacher."

"I've taught French before, Elesina," David explained hastily. "I tutored Lionel's little girl last summer when she had the mumps."

"What am I to tell Mademoiselle?"

"Tell her to stay home. Tell her you'll pay her anyway. After all, I won't charge." He winked at Elesina over the girl's head to communicate his sense of the importance of obliging the child.

"Oh, please, Mummie! I can't stand Mademoiselle!"

Elesina understood the very different plea in David's worried eyes. He was begging her to accede, not for Ruth's sake, but for his own. She could read in their nervous glimmer the message: "Be nice, for God's sake! Be the woman I can't help falling in love with. Don't be the bitch people say you are. Oh, please!" Elesina felt giddy with the sharpness of her conflict. She wanted, on one hand, to send the wretched Ruth packing to her room, but . . .

"Please, Mummie!"

It was too much! "I have told you, Ruth, never to make scenes in public. In our family we wash our dirty linen in private."

"But David's not public. He's my brother!"

Elesina moistened her lips, dry now with anger, and glanced again at David. His white skin and broad, rounded shoulders were those of a marble gladiator. No, this was madness.

"We'll see, darling," she said with a great effort. "Mademoiselle is coming out this afternoon, so we must go through with the first lesson. But as for the others . . . well, I'll talk to her. If David really has the time."

"Oh, I'll make the time, Elesina. On weekends, anyway. Okay, Ruth? Now go and change that suit. I quite agree with your mother it's hideous!"

Ruth padded away across the flagstones, and Elesina's anger dissolved as she saw the gratitude in his eyes.

Half an hour later, at lunch in the big dining room under the Romneys, Elesina recaptured her good humor. A mild scented breeze was wafted from the garden through the open french doors. Irving had been wheeled to his place opposite her and had ordered one of his finest white wines. David, dressed for the city, as he was going back with Linda Dart, was telling the table how he had lost his morning's work in the library by not having been able to take his nose out of a second quarto of *King Lear*. Fred Pemberton became jumpy, as he always did when others poached on his territory.

"I see that *Lear* is to be produced in town next fall," he called down the table. "But I shan't go. They're playing the fool as an old man." He glanced about, as if appealing for snorts of derision, which did not materialize. "Does that shock nobody? It has always seemed to me that the fool should be played as a brilliant, sensitive youth, of poor health and deep feeling, a bit effeminate perhaps, but precocious, bitter and loyal to the death."

"Why not a girl?" Elesina demanded, raising the wineglass to her lips. It was very cold, very dry, as she loved it, as Irving knew she loved it. She nodded down the table to him gratefully. "It could be played as a girl, you know. We were going to do it that way in Columbus Repertory, but we ran out of money and did *Charley's Aunt* instead." She could tell by the way David was looking at her that he did not want to leave that afternoon. Perhaps he would change his mind. But what did it matter? He would come back. She felt a tingle of exhilaration in her sides, her arms.

"Were you going to play the fool?" David asked.

"Yes! And Cordelia, too. There's a tradition that in Shakespeare's time the same boy played both parts."

"It's very likely," Pemberton asserted, anxious to regain the initiative. "The fool disappears from the play toward the end of act three with the famous line: 'And I'll go to bed at noon.' He and Cordelia are never on stage together, and his absence from the last two acts is not explained. Of course, some commentators have argued that Lear's remark at the end, 'And my poor fool is hang'd,' means that the fool was hanged by the soldiers who killed Cordelia. But why would they have done that? One didn't butcher clowns. No, the better view is that 'poor fool' is there used as a term of affection for Cordelia."

"But why should he call his favorite daughter a poor fool?" David asked.

"We had a different theory in Columbus Repertory," Elesina intervened, her mind suddenly aglow with a happy vision of that time. Why had she ever given up acting? "We claimed there was no fool, that he is really Cordelia in disguise. You see, she knows her father is going to have a bad time, and that's the only way she can stay at court and watch over him."

"And what in the meantime has happened to the real fool?" Irving asked, reacting with a wink to Pemberton's expression of disgust.

"He pined away, don't you remember?" Elesina replied. "He pined away when his lady went to France. Perhaps he died. Cordelia, artfully made up, could easily take them in. Who, after all, recognizes Kent or Edgar in disguise? It wasn't a very observing court. Besides, Lear is half senile."

"There I object!" cried Irving.

"Ladies and gentlemen!" protested Pemberton. "Surely this kind of levity is not fitting in a discussion of the bard."

"But why not, Fred?" Elesina insisted. "The quartos are corrupt. You can tell that from ours. A line might have been dropped that explained the whole thing. And don't Shakespeare's heroines frequently disguise themselves as boys?"

"As boys, to be sure. Not as clowns."

"But they do disguise their sex? How many?"

Pemberton was faintly appeased by this appeal to his scholarship. "Four. Julia, Viola, Rosalind, Portia." He paused. "And Imogen. Five."

"Very well. It was evidently a common stage trick. So Lear in his hour of tribulation on the heath is accompanied by his three truest friends, the three loyal characters of the play, Kent, Edgar and Cordelia, *all* in disguise! I suppose Cordelia confesses it to her father in prison. She would, wouldn't she? Of course, she would! And in the end the broken-hearted old man, leaning over her corpse, moans: 'And my poor fool is hang'd.' Why, it's terrific! Only Shakespeare could have thought of it!"

"I suppose I must take you seriously," the scholar responded now, with a desperate effort at self-control. "Let me see if I can quell this madness. Very well. How do you explain the change in Cordelia from a grave, literal, almost inarticulate character to the uninhibited fantasist that the fool is? Granted she could change her face. Could she change the very essence of her character?"

"She didn't have to!" Elesina fancied herself as Rosalind now, disguised as a boy, following David, a moody Orlando, receiving the confidences of his love, feeling his friendly arm about her shoulders, sensing in his tightening muscles that her attraction has bewildered him, caused him, the great wrestler, to doubt his own masculinity, until, to his joy inexpressible, as his fingers reach guiltily but irresistibly lower, he knows it is a woman he touches. "She's only grave and inarticulate because everyone knows she's Cordelia, because she's always been expected to be Cordelia, the princess. Once nobody knows who she is, she is liberated. The true Cordelia can now express herself in the fool. Can't you see it, Fred? If you were somewhere where nobody knew you were the great Professor Pemberton, mightn't we all have a surprise!"

And she, Elesina, might surprise herself. Why was it not possible to lead different lives? She caught Arthur's eye and glanced at her empty wineglass, which he hastened to refill. How different from her first meal at Broadlawns!

"May I ask my imaginative hostess why Cordelia, having shown such quixotic devotion to her ancient parent, should desert him in his hour of greatest need and allow him to find his own way, mad, to Dover?"

"But she doesn't!" Elesina exclaimed in triumph. "She leaves him when Gloster comes out to rescue him from the storm. She has no way of knowing that Gloster himself is about to be seized and blinded."

"All I can say," protested Pemberton, obviously shaken, "is that the blindness and madness conceived by the bard must have been contagious. Shakespeare has never been the same since Sarah Bernhardt, old and one-legged, insisted on playing Hamlet."

"Or since Charlotte Cushman and her sister played Romeo and Juliet," Irving supplied with a chuckle.

" 'The rest is silence.' "

After lunch, when Elesina, still in an exuberant mood, was pouring coffee for her guests in the patio, David approached her.

"Let me ask you something. In a minute I must go to the station with your mother."

"Yes, dear?"

"Will you have lunch in town with me next week?"

"But you're coming out here, aren't you?"

"No, there's something I haven't told you. I'm going to go to work with Schurman and Lister on Monday."

"David! Why? Oh, dear boy, not that you shouldn't go

to work whenever you want — of course, you should — the cataloguing was only a filler, I know — but why so suddenly and so mysteriously?"

"That's what I want to tell you. If you'll lunch with me."

She refused to acknowledge the implications of his penetrating stare. "Well, of course, I'll lunch with you. Why not? I ought to go to town more often anyway." She handed a cup of coffee to Fred Pemberton as he came up. "How about the Colony? Next Tuesday? At one?"

"No, it must be at a restaurant of my choosing."

She shrugged and turned her attention to the next guest. "Please, Elesina!"

"Of course, dear. Of course. Send me a card or telephone me where to meet you. Oh, Miss Beggs, would you ask the Judge if he wants coffee?"

When she looked up again, David was gone. Across the patio she saw her mother watching her. She smiled at her, very sweetly.

⊷§ 8 §⊷

When Elesina arrived at the West Side address which David had given her, she discovered a small and rather dirty French restaurant, obviously selected more for its obscurity than its cuisine. But the table in the back yard where David was waiting for her was shaded by an umbrella and isolated beside a pleasantly plopping fountain. Immediately she felt the happiness trying to push out of her, as if it were smothering. When her cocktail was placed before her, she looked at it doubtfully. Was it really necessary for her happiness? Couldn't she be happy without smoking and drinking? Did it matter? She took a sip.

"That's heavenly. I suppose I care too much for alcohol. You don't, do you, David?"

"Not really."

"I sometimes don't drink, but I'm always very much aware of it. In my less happy days I drank too much. But I'm happier now."

"Are you really, Elesina? So am I!"

"The job's going well then?"

"Oh, the job. I wasn't thinking of that. It's only my second day. I was thinking of real happiness."

"I thought you were too worried about things in Europe."

"That was before you. Think of it! You've blotted out Hitler."

Elesina looked into those somber, staring eyes. Their blue seemed oceanlike, ominous. He did not once blink. She shivered and looked away. She took a quick sip of her drink. God, he was what she had fantasized! Here it was, love.

"Where is this going to get us, David?"

"Where do we want to get?"

"We're not alone in the world, you know."

"All I know is that I want to make love to you. If you won't let me, I'll have to go away. I can't stand it."

"But where do we come out?"

"I don't care."

"You don't care about your father?"

He gave a little groan. "I don't care about anything the way I care about you. I'd take you away from here. He'd get over it. Mother could come back and look after him."

She looked at his tightly clenched fist that rested on the table and remembered what her own mother had said.

"Think of the scandal, David," she murmured. "It would kill him."

"No, no, he's tougher than you think. And he's old. Old people don't feel the way we do. I'd take you far away from the scandal, anywhere you want. We'd get married and . . ."

"Married!"

"Of course. You're not really married to him, you know. Not legally. Mother never consented to the divorce."

Elesina was shocked by the rapidity of her cooling off. She sat for a moment in silence, taking in the full impudence of his remark. Their positions seemed suddenly reversed. David was now the one to be generous, to be willing to wed his father's whore!

"I don't quite like your saying that," she said in a dryer tone.

"Well, it's true! Anyway, what does it matter? You can get a divorce if you think it looks better. The whole business of you and Dad was a ghastly mistake, a nightmare. You were lonely, grateful — oh, I can see it. But must our lives be ruined because of a moment's folly?"

"*Our* lives? I didn't know my life had been ruined."

"Elesina!"

"Well, I didn't, David."

"You mean you don't care?"

"You might have asked me that before."

"But I couldn't feel what I'm feeling if you didn't care!" he burst out. "I know that, Elesina! You wouldn't be here. A man *knows*. When it's as bad as this."

She smiled and just touched his clenched fist to show he was forgiven. Instantly her hand was seized in a grip that hurt.

"Please, David." He released her. "Of course, I care about you. I'm not going to be coy about it. But I can't tell you how much yet. I don't know myself. And when we leave here, I'm going in my own taxi. I need time to think this out."

"And what do I do in the interim?"

"That's going to be your affair."

"Will you expect me to come out to Broadlawns as I've been doing?"

"I shall hope so."

"Elesina — darling — how long do you think we can go on like that?"

"I don't know, David," she replied, almost with impatience. "But it's something I'm going to find out. No, don't do that." She withdrew her hand again from his. "Let me order our lunch. You've made your declaration. You've given me a lot to think about. And I shall think about it. Never fear. But until I have, let us talk about other things. Now tell me all about your job."

David protested furiously, but when he saw at last that she really meant it, he had to do as she wished, and for the rest of the meal they talked about his law firm, his prospects there, the possibility of war in Europe. When they parted it was agreed that he would come to Broadlawns for the weekend, but that he would not expect either an answer or even any further discussion of the subject.

Yet Elesina knew on Friday night, as soon as she saw the expression with which David greeted the unwelcome sight of a half-dozen weekend guests assembled in the patio, including the all-observing Ivy Trask, that he had nonetheless hoped for a quicker solution. As he leaned down to give her a family kiss on the cheek he murmured:

"You didn't tell me you were having a crowd."

"It was to make things more cheerful for you, dear," she responded in a normal voice that carried to Ivy's ears. "It would be so dull for a hardworking young man to come out from the city to an empty house." And she honored him with her most brilliant, her most defiantly artificial smile.

She did not exchange another word with him that evening, but she observed him covertly. He was sullen and silent and drank steadily. Ivy devoted herself to him, but with little result.

"If I were you, I'd lock my door tonight," she said to Elesina after dinner, when they were standing for a moment alone in the parlor. "I don't like David's mood."

Two hours later, in her nightgown, Elesina went to her door to implement Ivy's advice, but as her fingers touched the

key there was a soft knock. She opened, and was not surprised to find David standing before her. He was still in
evening clothes, but his tie was untied and his eyes had a
reddish gleam.

"I want to give you a kiss good night."

"David, go to bed!"

His toe was in the door. He stepped in now and seized her
shoulders. He kissed her lips, hard, too hard, painfully. Then
he started to pull her robe off.

"Elesina?"

It was Irving's voice! With all her strength she shoved
David off. "Get back!" she hissed as she went to the door.
"Yes, darling?"

The nurse was wheeling her husband's chair down the
corridor. "I just wanted to say good night," Irving's voice
quavered. He seemed very tired.

"Good night, my love. Sweet dreams!"

Closing the door, she turned on the still sullen David. "It's
like a French farce," she snarled. "Get out! And stay out!"

When he had gone and she had turned the key in the lock,
she stood by the window until her heart had resumed its
normal beat. The danger had been too great. The risk could
not be repeated. For what she had now learned was that
David *wanted* to precipitate a crisis. He wanted to force her
hand. Consciously or not, he was still revenging his old bitch
of a mother.

~§ 9 §~

Ivy Trask had agreed to take a six months' leave of absence
from *Tone* to try out Elesina's proposal. Irving, obliged to
recognize what now seemed to be turning into permanent
invalidism, had at last reluctantly consented, not only that she
should be housekeeper of Broadlawns, but managing secretary of the Stein Foundation as well. He was quite docile

now. Elesina was in charge of everything, and Ivy was Elesina's first minister.

Ivy was too accustomed, however, to the persistent irony of life to be surprised to discover a hard little lump in the core of her new apple of content. She might even have probed for it had it not so promptly made itself manifest. It was the sudden change in Elesina's mood. The year that had followed her marriage had been marked by an uninterrupted spell of good humor. Elesina had dazzled everybody with the easy charm of a manner that nothing seemed able to ruffle. It was true, of course, that little had occurred to ruffle it, but Ivy knew that a bad temper will never lack occasions to make a scene. Elesina appeared to have disposed of hers. But now she would let whole meals go by, uttering hardly a word. She was irritable with the servants and even snapped at old Arthur for being slow to replenish her wineglass. Ivy reproached her for this when he had hurried off to get the bottle.

"It shouldn't be that important to you to wait a minute for a sip of Vouvray. You've had a glass already."

"Which is why I want another. I can't agree with you, Ivy, that it's not important. I think it's most important. There are two kinds of people, the slaves and the free. The free, like you, don't smoke or drink or make love. But the rest of us are addicts; we're always hooked on nicotine or drugs or alcohol or sex or something."

"Rubbish! You can go for days without a drink. I've seen you."

"Only if I have something else."

"Aha! Suppose we talk about that. Why doesn't Mr. Something Else come out here anymore?"

"He's working, Ivy. You know that."

"On weekends, too?"

"Presumably."

Elesina now resumed a sullen silence. It was perfectly plain that David's absence was the cause of her bad humor, but it was not equally clear to Ivy what had caused his absence. She

surmised that he had been sent packing, but she did not know
why. She had hoped to provide a discreet little affair for
Elesina, and what could have been handier than a handsome
stepson already on the premises? It was possible, of course,
that Elesina did not trust David's discretion, but what, in that
case, was to prevent them from meeting in town? Ivy assumed, anyway, that her friend's fancy, and with it her irritability, would be short-lived, but she had to reconsider her
estimate when the weeks passed, bringing no change in Elesina's mood. The mistress of Broadlawns even began to
neglect her work on the collection and to pass her afternoons
strolling listlessly on the lawn and in the garden.

One evening Ivy sought her in the rose garden and forced
the issue.

"What is it between you and David? You had better tell
me, for I'm not going to shut up."

Elesina closed her book and seemed to study its spine. "Oh,
Ivy, it's all so ridiculous."

"What is?"

"To feel this way about a boy at my age."

"He's not a boy. He's twenty-six, or almost."

"But I'm years older, and . . ."

"Nine, to be exact. That might be a problem if you were
fifty, and he forty-one. But at your age it's nothing. And
who are you trying to kid, anyway? Since when have boys
not been dangerous? I find David sexy myself. There's something about all that blondness and blue-eyedness in a Jewish
boy that's irresistible. If I had half your looks and were
twenty years younger, I'd give you a tussle for him!"

"Ivy, you're really the worst old pimp!"

"Only for you, love."

"Do you make nothing of the fact that he's Irving's son?"

"Ah, you see? You didn't say, 'my stepson.' You don't
want to consider that too closely. Neither do I. Why should
we?"

"Because it may be wicked, that's why!"

"So long as you keep things in their proper compartments, there's no need for moral hysteria. If I spit on the American flag before a squadron of marines, I'd be beaten up, and rightly so! But if I spit on it in my own room, behind closed doors . . . well, that's my affair. It's neither moral nor immoral. It's just me."

"Oh, Ivy, of course, I agree with you." Elesina, suddenly friendly again, reached out impulsively to clasp her friend's hand. "I can't kid myself that I'm really concerned about being faithful to Irving. I wasn't faithful to Ted, and that never bothered me. It's true, I was faithful to my first husband, but that was only because I was still scared of Mother. No, what really bothers me is that for the first time that I can remember I don't seem to be in control of my life. I always was before. If I was going to the dogs, it was because I wanted to. Because barks and bites attracted me. If I pulled myself together and presented people with a decent Hedda Gabler, it was also because I wanted to. And men . . . well, I chose my men, for one bad reason or another. I wanted to hurt Ted, and I hurt him. I wanted Irving to admire me, and he did. I always had to be the piper, don't you see? I had to call the tune. And with the various men who were my lovers — don't stare so, Ivy, there weren't all that many — I never lost my independence. It was usually I who called the halt. And I never shirked the job of telling them either."

"That takes guts."

"Maybe I liked it." Elesina shrugged. "There's always been a streak of cruelty in me. When I was a child in Southampton and the little boys at the Beach Club cut up live crabs and the other girls ran away, I stayed. It's not attractive, but I face it. And of course I've been a lousy mother."

"Not now, dear."

"But now it's easy. Now it costs me nothing. Oh, let's be honest, Ivy. That's our one virtue, yours and mine. What really troubles me is that I seem to have lost my perspective.

This thing I have about David is different from what I've felt for other men. I actually want to *do* things for him. Now why should that be?"

"Maybe it's love."

"Of course it's love. But I've been in love before."

"I mean, real love."

"Ivy, you're simply proving that all pimps are sentimental! I've been examining things more dispassionately. At first, I thought it might be a premature change of life. But I'm too young for that, and, anyway, Dr. Birch says I'm fine. Then it occurred to me that I might be attracted to David *because* he's Irving's son. That I'm trying to pick mates exclusively out of the Stein family, using one for a husband, one for a lover . . ."

"Really, Elesina, must you be so complex?"

"Except it wasn't that. It was more as if I had married Irving because I was already in love with David. I wonder if that first day that I dined here, when I told Fred Pemberton that if Shakespeare were at the party, he'd go after David, I wasn't already snared."

"Then why did you send him away?"

"Because he was getting out of control. You warned me about that. And you were right. If he'd stayed on here, there would have been the most frightful scandal. And the worst of it is that I might not have minded!"

"I see." Ivy nodded slowly as she put together her plan. "It's more or less as I suspected. The sooner you go to bed with that young man, the better. Will you leave it to me?"

"I most certainly will not!"

"And do just as I say?"

"Don't be absurd."

"Good. I'll go into New York tomorrow."

"Ivy Trask, if you pretend to be my ambassador to David, I warn you, I shall repudiate every word you say!"

"That is the prerogative of every principal." Ivy turned to

the house. "I shall have to speak to Irving. I shall need an appointment with Mr. Schurman."

Waving aside Elesina's continued protestations, she went back in and up to Irving's room. She told him that she wanted to go to New York to make her will and asked him to introduce her to his lawyers. Irving, always delighted to get her out of the house, telephoned to Mr. Schurman and made an appointment for the very next day.

When Ivy was received by the attorney in his office, she asked if David Stein could be assigned to her.

"David is in litigation," Mr. Schurman demurred. "I should like you to go to Mr. Devlin, our partner in charge of estates."

"Mine is a very simple will. I'm sure it could be handled by a novice. I'd like to think that David was in charge of my small affairs."

So it was that she found herself, fifteen minutes later, facing David across a small desk as, smiling a bit grimly, she fabricated a long list of trivial bequests. Behind him was the single window of the narrow, whitewashed office which looked out, rather dramatically, on the spires of St. Patrick's Cathedral. David was courteous, friendly, even charming. He wrote down on a yellow legal pad, in his careful round handwriting, the names of Ivy's numerous legatees.

"I think I'm going to change my mind again about the mother-of-pearl lavaliere," she said, watching him carefully for the least hint of impatience. "Harriet Tremaine would like it, I know, but it belonged to Aunt Bessie Troop, who was only her aunt by marriage. I think I should leave it to Prudence Weston, who, of course, was Aunt Bessie's own niece."

"Very well." David drew a thick, neat line slowly through an earlier note. "Does Prudence Weston have a middle name?"

"Two. Charity Augusta. And come to think of it, I don't think the amethyst bracelet should go to Emily Trask. She always loses things. She lost Grandma's amber necklace, though some think she hocked it."

"Do you suppose, Ivy, that these gifts could be covered in a memorandum? It's much easier to alter than a will if you should change your mind about any of these bequests."

"But would a memorandum be binding?"

"No, but I'm sure your residuary legatee would honor it."

"How do you know that? We haven't got to my residuary legatee yet."

"No, but I'm sure you wouldn't leave your residuary estate to a person who couldn't be trusted."

"And, anyway, why would my residuary legatee care for my junky jewelry? Is that what you mean? I don't suppose the lot of it's worth five hundred bucks."

"I didn't mean that at all, Ivy." His face expressed a proper concern at such an imputation.

"Oh, I know you didn't, dear boy! I was testing you. To see if you could put up with the garrulity of an old maid fussing over buttons and thimbles. And you can! You'd be a wonderful estates lawyer, honey. Let's reduce my silly will to a simple sentence. Everything I own to the person I love best in the world." She paused, waiting.

"And who is that?"

"Can't you guess?"

"Me, I suppose."

"Conceited ass! Elesina, of course."

David looked at her pensively. Then he studied his pencil point. "Don't you think my father will adequately provide for Elesina?"

"Who knows? If he does, your family will probably contest it."

"You think we're so greedy?"

"I don't think *you* are."

Their eyes met, but he looked away. "Thanks."

"You'd be on Elesina's side, wouldn't you, David?"

He moved his shoulders impatiently. "I don't know about

sides. But so long as I have any money, Elesina can count on it."

"David, look at me. I know how you and Elesina feel about each other."

David's brow was puckered, and his staring eyes expressed something between fascination and repulsion. "What do you know about it?"

"I know she loves you."

"Loves me!"

"Yes. And that is why I came here today. Not for the stupid will, though you'll have to draw one up because I told Mr. Schurman about it. I want you and Elesina to be able to meet in town."

Ah, *now* his eyes were everything she had greedily anticipated! "Does Elesina know you're here?"

"Elesina has agreed to nothing."

"I see."

"I want to draw up a plan. And present it to her. Do you wish to know what that plan is?"

"I think I'd like to talk to Elesina myself."

"Look here, David. This thing will be done my way or not at all. Now do you want to know what my plan is?"

His answer was barely audible. "Yes."

"Elesina and I will take a course at NYU in the history of art. I have already arranged it. Your father thinks it will help us with the collection. The course will be on Mondays, Wednesdays and Fridays at eleven. We will attend the lectures and then lunch at my apartment in the Althorpe before going back to Rye. Except *I* shall not go to the apartment."

"I see." His voice was still a whisper. His cheeks were flushed, and his eyes were intent on the yellow memorandum.

"I suppose you can give up your lunch hour three times a week." Ivy decided that the moment had come to relieve the atmosphere. "There'll be something in the icebox in my apartment." She uttered a sharp little laugh. "Fred Pemberton would say I'm like that character in *Troilus and Cressida.*

Is it Pandarus? But people in your and Elesina's situation need help. I love her, and I know she's unhappy. I want that girl to have something out of life. And if it's David Stein the poor creature wants, then it's David Stein she'll get!"

Ivy had let emotion blot out the cynicism in her voice. The effect on David was immediate. His eyes were moist. He jumped up and went over to hug her.

"Ivy, you old darling! You're not Pandarus. You're Juliet's nurse!"

"That's better." She released herself firmly from his embrace and then stared at him with sudden fierceness. "But you'll have to promise me one thing, David."

"Anything!"

"You must promise to be ruled by me in this matter. It is going to be set up so that no human being but you and I and Elesina ever knows. Is that perfectly understood?"

For a moment he wavered. "I hate subterfuge."

"David Stein, if you don't give me your word, I walk out of this office, and you shan't see me again. Now! Do you promise?" Still he paused. "No answer? Is *that* what young men call love today?"

"I promise you, Ivy."

"Very well." She studied him severely for a moment, assessing the possibility of default. "If you expose her, David, if you cause a scandal, I really believe that I will kill you."

His laugh had a note of surprise. "Why, Ivy, I thought you liked me!"

"I love you, dear boy," she said grimly. "I always have. But Elesina is different. Elesina is my child. Elesina is my life!"

∾ 10 ∾

Elesina had never had an affair so exclusively physical. She and David now met only in Ivy's apartment, and there was time in their brief appointments for little else. David no longer came to Broadlawns, for reasons which they never discussed. Indeed, it was their tacit understanding, at least in the first weeks, never to mention his father at all. Elesina liked to think of her hours at the Althorpe as an enchanted existence having no relation to the actuality of Rye. Stepping out of the old grilled elevator and walking down the dark corridor to Ivy's door, she would feel like a nymph loved by a god or demigod in a legend. Or she might think of David's ivory-skinned, muscular body as a Greek statue come to life in a deserted studio for her alone. Their first encounter was quick and feverish. Not until the second or even third had they achieved the kind of union that she had read about and never really believed existed.

And yet she sometimes wondered, paradoxically, if their relationship were not more spiritual than any she had experienced. She was like Psyche, loved in the dark by a stranger. The affair was freed of the vulgarity of jealousy, of curiosity, of distraction. Orgasm with David was like the raising of a communion cup before an altar that knew no sacrament but love. There was no guilt, no adultery, no incest, no divorce, no settlements, no law, no Hitler in Ivy's darkened bedroom with this never tiring lover in her arms. God, if she could only die there! Or *had* she died there?

In time they began to talk before parting. She would put on a kimono and make herself a drink or nibble at a piece of fruit. David, at her request, remained naked. He would puff at a cigarette, unusual for him. He would never drink or eat.

"How can you come here so regularly?" she asked him. "I thought law firms were so demanding of their clerks."

"They are."

"Doesn't Mr. Schurman sometimes ask for you at this time?"

"He does."

"And what do you say?"

"I tell him I have an engagement which can't be broken. Which is no more than the truth."

"Does he accept that?"

"What can he do? I am perfectly willing to work at night or all weekend, and I frequently do. I even like it. Social life no longer interests me, and writing briefs keeps me from daydreaming about you."

"Darling. That's all I do at Broadlawns now. Daydream. But what would you do if Mr. Schurman absolutely insisted that you had to lunch with him and the firm's most important client next Friday?"

"I'd refuse."

"Even if he threatened to fire you?"

"Absolutely."

"But then he'd know you had a girl!"

"He wouldn't know who."

It was agreed that she should always be the first to go. Sometimes when she was dressed, combed, made up and ready to leave, he would embrace her, still naked, and then undress her, all over again, to make love once more. She began to sense that she was losing her dominance in the relationship. She also began to realize how far from satisfied he was with the status quo.

At last he started to discuss the future, a subject which she detested and feared.

"But how long can we go on this way?" he demanded. "How long can you stand it? How long can I?"

"But I want it to go on forever!"

"This deception? What will it do to us? I sometimes think there must be a portrait of me somewhere, like Dorian Gray's — perhaps the one Mother has of me in the velvet suit — that gets uglier every day."

"Oh, darling, what rot! And how like a man to have to spoil things. What we're doing isn't hurting anybody."

"Except us."

"Anyway, your poor father isn't going to last forever . . ."

She stopped, realizing his immediate horror. He had turned quite white, and he rose quickly to put a towel around his loins.

"It seems so dishonorable," he said in a tight voice. "To wait. To make love and wait."

"But, David, what else can we do?"

"We could tell him."

"Do you want to kill him?"

"Dad is a kind of great man in his way. He might take it all better than you think. And it would be so honest. Oh, Elesina! To think what it would be like to have you all to myself, all the time! Oh, of course, there would be shrieks and screams and horrors. It would be the worst scandal anyone had heard of in years. But it would die down eventually. People get used to anything in time. And we wouldn't stay here. We'd go away, far away, until it all blew over. Mother might go back to Dad, and everything would be basically the same as if I had proposed to you that Saturday night I met you at Broadlawns. Why the hell didn't I?"

Elesina felt giddy. In the car going back to Rye, sitting silently by Ivy, her mind tore backward and forward, peeking into this possibility, tearing lids off others. Was it not perfectly possible? Why should *she* mind scandal? Had she minded Ted Everett's divorcing her and naming Max Allerton as corespondent? And as for David . . . well, hadn't he proposed it? He had money, some money anyway. They could live in Paris or Rome until things quieted down. They could have a baby. David wanted one, she knew. It might make up to him for having to leave his job and go abroad.

"I think you'd better tell me," Ivy said at last, reaching forward to run her finger up the glass between them and the chauffeur to be sure that it was closed.

"Tell you what?"

"What's on your mind. Whatever it is you're hatching. I think I can guess. You and a certain party are finding life too restricted. You want to go off on a weekend together. I've been expecting that. I don't say it's impossible. But give me time. It'll take some working out."

"I guess he wants more than that, Ivy." And she told her of David's plan.

"What do you think you'd live on?" Ivy demanded at once.

"Me? It's not my idea."

"You wouldn't have told me if you weren't flirting with it. I suppose you'll tell me David has money of his own. But I'm sure it's peanuts compared to the expectations he'd be ruining. Not to speak of *yours!* Of course, neither of you would ever see another penny of Irving's money. And what would your life be? Do you think he could stay in New York, the boy who'd run off with his own stepmother? With all those shrieking Steins and Clarksons?"

"New York's not the whole world."

"The place where you can't live is always the whole world! At least it is for a man. But all right. So David will be gallant. So you'll live in some European watering place, where nobody will care. But David will be bored. Read *Anna Karenina!* And he's one of those boyish types who won't lose his youth until he's sixty. It'll be a long time to watch over him, Elesina!"

"Oh, Ivy, don't be vile."

"I'm being practical, dearest, and you know it. You have done pretty well under my guidance. Admit it. You have a fine husband, a great fortune, a social position and a pretty blue-eyed lover. But you could lose it all with one slip."

"What do I do, Ivy? David's the one who's rocking the boat, not I."

"If you can't induce David to keep his shirt on — no, I won't say that, for I suppose you like him to take it off!" Here Ivy indulged in one of her outrageous high cackles. "Well, then, you're not the siren I took you for. Have you no tears? Can you make no scenes?"

"I've always detested that sort of woman so."

"Well, borrow a leaf from their notebook just this once. Or skip one or two rendezvous at the Althorpe. I watched him coming in the other day. If ever I saw an eager young man . . ."

"Oh, Ivy, shut up!"

They were turning in the gates of Broadlawns. Elesina had always loved the gliding sound of the big car as it moved over the smooth blue gravel. Now she rested back in her seat and shivered. Was it greedy to take everything that life offered, even when life seemed to press it on one? She had not yet gone wrong following Ivy. Was it not simple good sense to keep on with a winning streak? Then she thought of the pain in David's eyes, and her own became moist.

❧ 11 ❦

Irving Stein had now accepted the fact that he was not going to recover. He was suffering multiple small heart attacks, coming at the rate of two a week, and it was fairly certain that a larger and more decisive one could not be far away. He rarely left his wheelchair except to go to his bed, and he found himself in a state of mild, but permanent exhaustion. Yet he was surprised at his own passivity. "This was bound to come one day," a small voice kept telling him. "Now it has come. That's all."

"Isn't it sad?" he would say aloud at times, even when his nurse was in the room. "But I've had a good life," he would always add. It was a longer life, too, he never failed to remind himself, than most human beings had enjoyed — certainly a better one. A good life and a not too uncomfortable death — how much more could one ask?

Elesina was wonderful. She had given up asking people to Broadlawns and hardly left his side now except for the trips to New York to attend her course. She would read aloud to him and listen to his reminiscences; she used Ivy Trask to collect all the gossip from the big city that might amuse him. Only once, when she brushed aside a reference to his own impending demise with some banality about his "living to bury us all," did he reproach her.

"My dear girl, let it be understood once and for all that I *want* to discuss it. Death is an interesting topic, and, besides, we have much to prepare for. I had thought I was going to have time to set up our foundation, but I may have to leave that to you. My idea is that it be arranged so that you may occupy Broadlawns and keep the collection for your lifetime. Jacob Schurman will tell you just how to do it. You must consult Jacob in everything."

When Jacob Schurman came out to discuss a new will, however, Irving asked Elesina to leave them alone.

The lawyer was a small man, potbellied, with a round bald head, large snapping black eyes and an aquiline nose. His good humor, his quick wit, even his merriment were fragile guards of a temper always ready to erupt over the hissing bubbles of his impatience. He was very nervous and always had to be handling something. In his office he would move objects of gold and glass to and fro over the broad surface of his desk. Sitting now in the armchair by Irving's couch, he yanked at his watchchain and placed and replaced the pince-nez on the thin ridge of his nose.

What Irving now had to say did not contribute to his calm. "I'm going to shock you, Jacob. I propose to leave my entire estate to Elesina."

"In trust, of course."

"No, outright. To deal properly with the collection she must have full control."

"And Clara, the children, the grandchildren? We'll just forget about them? Poof? Like that?"

"Now listen to me, Jacob. You know what I've done for Clara and the boys. Together they have as much as I have."

"I question that!"

"Leaving out the collection, they have."

"And why should we leave out the collection?"

"Because I don't regard it as money. If I die before it's set up in a foundation, I want Elesina to take care of it. So she's the one who's going to need my money. Peter and Lionel have large earned income in addition to their capital, and David's going to be a successful lawyer. As for Clara, she can't spend her income now."

The throb in Jacob's voice showed the depth of his outrage. "And what guarantee will you have that Elesina will carry out your wishes? That she won't cart the whole collection, lock, stock and barrel, down to Parke-Bernet and put it on the block?"

"I trust her. Obviously, you don't. But I'm the client."

"Even trusting her, suppose she dies right after you? What becomes of the collection then? It all goes to her daughter, I suppose."

"I've thought of that. I shall ask Elesina to sign a new will when I sign mine, leaving three quarters of what I've left her to my sons. But so long as she lives, I want her to feel at liberty to dispose of the property as she sees fit."

"And to tear up her will?"

"And to tear up her will. My confidence in Elesina is complete."

Jacob seemed about to say something and then to restrain himself, but only with the greatest difficulty. When he spoke at last, it was in a dryer tone. "Then you're determined to leave the boys nothing?"

"I tell you, Jacob, they're rich!"

"The term is a relative one."

"And they'll have Clara's trust when she dies."

"It's still bitter tea to be cut off by a father."

"Well, suppose I leave them each a painting? How's that? To Lionel the Holbein of Mary Tudor. To Peter the Botticelli. To David the big Tiepolo. Plus fifty thousand apiece?"

"Has it occurred to you that they may try to upset the will?"

"Of course it's occurred to me. And Clara, too, may have a good claim. She may even be able to establish that she's my widow."

"I'm glad you're aware of that."

"But that's the very beauty of my plan, don't you see, Jacob? Whatever I do for Elesina is bound to be attacked. Lionel and Peter will go after her like tigers the moment I'm under the sod. I'm not blaming them. I know how they are. My brother, Isadore, sued my father's estate. And they'll make their mother go along with them, too. Elesina will have to come to some kind of terms in the suit. Very well. Let's see that she has a strong hand to play. I want to give her as many trumps as I can."

Jacob shook his head somberly. "I don't know that in good conscience I can draft such a document."

Irving's tone now became brusque. "You will do what your client wishes! There is nothing unconscionable about a man's leaving his estate to his widow when he has already provided for his children. You know that, Jacob! The only thing that could properly deter you would be a doubt as to my testamentary capacity. Let me submit that to a doctor's examination. Furthermore, let us have two lawyers from your office come out here as witnesses to the will. And let them spend a whole day with me — or more if they need — to satisfy themselves, by asking me every kind of question, no matter how personal, that I am perfectly sane!"

Jacob sighed. "Oh, you're sane enough, Irving. I have no doubt about that. Your only trouble is that you're in love. And you're too old to be such an ass."

"That must be a matter of opinion. Now then. Will you do the will as I say?"

"I'll think about it."

"And will you defend it? Will you act as my executor? Will you help Elesina in the battle she faces?"

Jacob's brow was puckered at this, but he seemed moved. "Would you really trust me, Irving? After what I've said?"

"Perfectly. You're a true lawyer, Jacob. Once you've taken a case, you'll give it all you've got. And now tell me something else. I expected you to make more of a plea for David. How is he doing in your office?"

"Very well indeed."

"How does he get on with you?"

Jacob paused. "Well, I like to keep a certain distance with a client's son."

"Do you think he'll make a good lawyer?"

"Oh, yes."

Irving wondered what was being withheld. "Do you like him?"

"I don't feel I really know him yet, Irving. No doubt, I shall like him when I do."

"No doubt?"

"None."

"David charms so many people. I wonder that he hasn't charmed you."

"Perhaps I don't charm that easily."

"No, you sullen dog, that's so. But has he done anything to offend you?"

"Of course not. It's just that he seems . . . well, preoccupied. Impersonal, you might say. He'll never go out to lunch with any of us."

"Even you?"

"Even me. I've asked him two or three times. He's always tied up, which seems odd for a young man."

"That's the trouble with having your office in midtown. He's probably meeting some chick."

"I shouldn't be surprised. Some chick he doesn't want anyone to see. Some married chick."

"Well, Jacob, I suppose even you were young once."

"Yes, but I grew up — unlike some I know!"

The will, in due course, was prepared, and two lawyers spent a day and a half at Broadlawns to satisfy themselves that

Irving had the requisite testamentary capacity. When it was over, he had a strange sense of having died with the execution of the document and of being a ghostly witness to the administration of his own estate. Elesina, visiting his chamber, seemed now to him more intensely the mistress of Broadlawns; she might have been a kindly queen visiting an old pensioner in a turret of her castle.

"We're not providing enough social life for you," he protested on a rainy afternoon when she had finished an hour's reading of *Our Mutual Friend*. "Why don't you give a house party?"

"Because I don't want one. Society is only a drug, and I've kicked it. I could go on forever, just like this."

"But you used to love seeing people!"

"My past has been too crowded. I sometimes think of it as a subway ride in the rush hour. Now I love the peace of Broadlawns. I love to be with you. And with your things." She ran her fingers over the porcelain surface of the commode by her chair, a purple and scarlet theme of flowers. "I reflect that this was made for Madame de Pompadour. It brings her into the room."

"There's a great emphasis today on the value of getting on with other people," Irving said musingly. "Friendship, love, that's all some people can talk about. And the terror of loneliness. I suppose it's a defense against overpopulation. Turn your greatest liability into your greatest asset. The more people, the more love and friendship. Very smart! For not many can know the joy of living with Madame de Pompadour's commode. So we, the lucky few, fling love to the mob."

"Let 'em eat love!"

Irving placed his hand gently on hers. "But we have that, too."

"Oh, we have everything."

No, this was too much. He knew that Elesina was a truth-

ful woman, not so much because she loved truth as because
she despised falsehood. And this was a false note.

"If David would only come out here occasionally, I should
have everything. Why do you suppose he neglects us so?"

Her face was at once inscrutable. Why inscrutable? "He
works frightfully hard, you know," she replied.

"Doing Ivy's will?"

"Oh, that was just a favor. He's in the corporate department now, you know. He works night and day. It's a terrible sweatshop, that law firm of yours."

"How do you know? Have you seen him?"

"Oh, yes. We had lunch last week."

The great white liquid of his peace trembled with the
assault of one black drop. Appalled, he saw the cloud of
discoloration swell until the whole bowl was a dirty gray. So
much for happiness! Everything fell dismally into place: her
visits to the city, her willingness to be alone, David's absence,
Jacob Schurman's account.

"You can tell me now, Elesina," he said in a strangled voice.
"I can take it, and I'd much rather know. When did your
affair with David start?"

Her countenance was a frozen glass of conflict. But the
expression that at last predominated, curiously enough, was
one of admiration. Or was she simply glad that he had
guessed? "Three months ago. How long have you known?"

"Since just now."

"Just because I said I had lunch with him?"

"Yes. For otherwise you would have told me the same
day."

She paused to take in this simple truth. Then she nodded,
ruefully, to accept it. "Is it very painful for you?"

"Yes. But I may get used to it."

"Can you still believe that I love you?"

"I can believe it, yes. I can even admire your courage in
telling me the truth. You could have lied your way out, you
know."

"Perhaps if I'd had more time, I should have. The doctors say you mustn't be upset. But now that it's out, I'm glad. You're too big a man to be deceived."

Ah, she was thinking it was not really so hard for him! She was excusing herself with the facts of his impotence and illness. How could he really care? His lips were dry with exasperation. "There's a little devil in you, Elesina, that likes to court disaster. You see that third act where the wife tells all and loses all. Stripped, in a moment, of fortune and reputation!"

"So you *are* bitter. After all. Who could blame you?"

"How could I not be? A man can't be a rational animal at all times. But if I snarl at the actress in you, my dear, I also admire her." Irving stiffened. With stunning force the true pain of his situation had suddenly hit. He clutched the arms of his chair. Not David! "I think you'd better leave me for a bit. I am probably going to have some ugly moments, and it's better to be alone. Later on, we can pick up where we left off. Don't worry. I shan't discuss this again."

"Irving, dear husband, I . . ."

"Elesina! Please go!"

He sighed in quick relief as she closed the door softly behind her, and gave in almost greedily to the flash flood of his wrath. His own son and Elesina! The clutching, obscene pair, they could not wait for him to die! They had youth, they had beauty, they had health, but was all that enough for them? Never! They had to have his honor, too, his life. Well, they would see, they would find out! He would do such things . . .

"Mrs. Stein sent me in, sir. She said you might need one of your pills."

"Oh, yes, Miss Murphy. I do need one."

The shattering mood, the black driven thundercloud, passed. He took the pill, sipped the water and closed his eyes in the sudden relief of acceptance. What, after all, did it matter? There was no need to change his will. The cruelest thing he could do to David was to make Elesina rich. Poor David, how he must have been suffering, not to dare to visit his dying father. Poor David, how much more he had still to suffer . . .

"Miss Murphy, write out on a piece of paper, that I wish my executor to give each of my nurses a thousand dollars."

"Why, Judge Stein, that's very handsome of you, I'm sure. But there's no need to think about dying yet . . ."

"Write it down, please, and I'll sign it. I'm not feeling quite myself."

He smiled as he noted that her trip to the desk for paper and pencil was almost a discreet scurry.

⋖§ 12 §⋗

The death of a rich and important man generates so many ceremonies, so many communications and required observances, that the family hardly have time to reflect on what has happened and what changes in their life will be made. Elesina, from the middle of the night when Irving's nurse had awakened her to say that his breathing had stopped, to the moment, five days later, when the last of two hundred luncheon guests who had come out from New York for the funeral had departed, had been too occupied with plans and arrangements and telephone calls to be able to think out for herself whether or not her revelation to Irving might have caused his death.

The mind, however, needs little time. She would say to herself, as she hung up a receiver or turned to dictate to Irving's secretary: "It was *his* fault. He surprised me. I didn't have time to think. Anyway, he was doomed." But then, an hour later, she would feel a sudden sick chill of guilt and hastily review the same argument. When Jacob Schurman showed her a copy of the will, she could not restrain a little shriek.

"Oh, my God, how could he!"

She did not tell Ivy; she could not abide the prospect of her delight. She immersed herself in work, even more than was necessary. She insisted on speaking to every friend, every relative who called, holding them to longer visits than they had planned. She had no communication with David. At the service she sat with her mother and Ruth. The three Stein sons and two daughters-in-law occupied the bench behind her. She was grateful for her veil.

The service was held at a reformed temple. It was brief, as Irving had had no faith. The eulogy was read by Jacob Schurman. In the middle of it Elesina said firmly to herself: "Irving doesn't exist now, and I do. Therefore I must forgive myself. It's the only thing he would have wanted himself. It's the only thing that makes sense."

She felt better during the big lunch that followed the service and talked with animation. When the final guests had departed, and the family were huddled in groups about the house, she turned at last to David.

"We can go to the rose garden," she said briefly. She walked there, listening to his step on the gravel behind her. She sat on the marble bench and looked up to where he stood before her. He was very grave, so much so that she was suddenly afraid she might giggle.

"I've heard about the will," he said. "Jacob Schurman told me. It's a great tribute to you, of course. But the family doesn't know yet. I'm afraid they'll fight."

"And you, David? Will you join them?"

"Elesina! What do you think of me?"

All she could think was that he had never looked more beautiful. His black suit made his hair seem like a nimbus. "Darling," she murmured. "I've missed you so!"

"I don't want any part of Dad's money. I want to marry you. I want to marry you and look after you myself."

"Marry me? When?"

He shrugged, as if this were of little importance. "After some decent interval."

"Could any interval make it decent?"

"It would only be for the family's sake. We might have to wait a year. But we could still meet at Ivy's!"

There was a gardener working in the next plot. They had to keep apart. He was talking again. He was saying something about the estate. What was he saying?

"Give up?" she stammered. "Give up what?"

"Give up Dad's estate."

"All of it?"

"Every penny. Let Mother and Lionel and Peter have it."

"What about you?"

"I'd renounce my share. The only way I can take you, after what we've done, is without a cent of his money."

"David! We'd be paupers!"

"If only we might be! I could never live with Dad's money. It would soil everything we've done. Everything we've meant to each other. To make love and lie low until it's all over and then rake in the gold . . . oh, no, darling, we can't do that to ourselves. Don't be afraid. We won't be paupers. I have enough money. You just won't be rich the way you have been. And, oh, Elesina, we'd be clean. Clean! Think of it!"

"But I don't need to be clean. I am clean! I'm not ashamed of what we've done. Are you?"

"I would be, if I profited by it." He clasped his hands in a quaint but persuasive gesture of pleading. His eyes were tired, and she noted now the circles under them. "I've hardly slept since Dad died, trying to think this out. It's the only way, believe me, Elesina! The only way to make our love right and fine and valid."

"But what about the collection? I have responsibilities to it!"

"We can take care of that easily enough. If you give up the money, Lionel and Peter will come to terms about the collection."

"But you don't understand, David. Your father wanted me to play a role in the world. One doesn't walk out on a part!"

"Elesina! Will you never stop play-acting?"

She debated for a moment whether she should tell him about her last talk with his father. After all, Irving had known and still not torn up the will. But no. There could be no idea of that. Instinct told her that David would see her as a killer.

"I suppose I'll have to think it over."

"Think it over! Darling, don't you love me?"

"I'm sorry, David. I still must think it over."

"I swear to you that it's the only way! For you and me. The only way, Elesina!"

"You mean, for marriage?"

"I mean for — anything."

He turned with this and strode away. It was clear that it was an ultimatum and that he had planned it ahead of time. But if he had planned it ahead of time, it must have been because he had feared she might reject it. Elesina sat down dazed to find that her mind was already full of figures. Did he mean that she would have to give up what Irving had already settled on her? How much was in David's trust? Surely she could keep what she already had! Had not the gift preceded their affair? But then she recalled how stern David had looked. He would be impatient at any equivocation. He would sternly brush aside such arguments. But wasn't that precisely his charm? What was all of Broadlawns and its treasure compared to a lover like that? But how long would he love her like that?

She was still dazed an hour later when she consulted her mother in the library. There was no point talking to Ivy, for she knew what Ivy would say.

"Could you really give up all that money?" Linda asked in surprise.

"I'm thinking about it." Elesina looked away from her

mother as she said this, but hearing no response she looked back. Linda's eyes were taking her in with what struck her as a rather yellow stare. It was fixed, curious, distant.

"Don't you think you'd be biting off more than you could chew?"

"What couldn't I chew?"

"Love! That much love, anyway. You weren't made for it, my dear."

"How do you know?" Elesina demanded, stung. "You're so smug, Mother. You think that you and Father had all the pearls — that there are none left for David and me."

"I didn't say there were none left for David."

"Now you're being horrid! Why should love be a closed door for me? Why should you begrudge me the only worthwhile thing in life? You're jealous, that's what it is. You're envious of what David and I have together. You don't want your own daughter to be as happy as you were!"

"Elesina, pull yourself together. I don't say you don't love David. All I'm saying is that it's a bit late for you to give up all for love. For you to run off now and live on kisses would be grotesque."

"Mother!"

"I know it hurts, dear, but better have it hurt now than kill later. You have chosen to be the woman that Ivy Trask saw in you. Well, *be* that woman! Only make her into something bigger and better than Ivy Trask could ever visualize!"

Elesina looked at her mother with an astonishment that was greater than the pain. The woman that Ivy Trask had seen in her! Was *that* all her own parent could now see? Was it not what the dying Irving had seen? And even the departing, the ultimatum-giving David? How quick the world was to point its finger, to brand her with the mark of heartlessness, exulting all the while in the richness, the fullness, the genuineness of its own queasy soul. Hypocrites! But maybe she *would* be what Ivy had seen, maybe more!

She rose now to walk the length of the room. She paused

at the end to contemplate, in the big central panel between the two Shakespeare stacks, the Veronese *Venus and Adonis*. The youth, with his bow and arrow, clad in a leopard skin, two wolfhounds at his heels, seeking to evade the amorous clasping of the ivory-skinned goddess, had always reminded her of David.

"Mother, you took me away on a cruise when I needed it once. You had better do it again. Tonight even! Except this time I'll take *you*."

"Did you see something in that painting to make you change your mind?"

"I was thinking of what Irving told me about beautiful things. That they might make up for beautiful people. Doesn't Adonis, there, remind you of David?"

"Perhaps a bit."

"Good. Anyway, I'll always have the Veronese. Oh, that you can be sure of! Please leave me now, Mother. I think I'm going to weep, and it's most unseemly. Go look up cruises. The first to leave is the best!"

Alone, Elesina wrote one of the shortest but certainly one of the most important letters of her life.

Dearest David:

You're the only man I've ever loved. But for some persons love is not enough. I intend to accept your father's bequest, even at the cost of a lawsuit. You asked me if I was ever going to give up play-acting. I never am! I know now I'd be a fool to. Let there be peace between us.

Elesina.

ࣷ࣢ 13 ࣢ࣷ

Eliot Clarkson's life had been sliced in two by his marriage to Ailsa Murphy. After that event the tense tranquillity of his first twenty-seven years was gone for good. He had decided at last to act; he had clambered up from the comfortable dark of the auditorium and plunged himself into the brightly lit commotion of the stage — only to find that, garbed for *Hamlet*, he was acting in *The Merry Wives*. Every way that he twisted and turned produced a new uproar of hilarity from the pit.

For the mysterious Ailsa, the smiling Ailsa, the plucky little woman so admirably facing with amiable countenance a world determined to give her only knocks, was a hopeless drunk. At thirty-eight, this wide-eyed, wide-cheeked, pretty redhead had nothing left between herself and her need for alcohol but a habit of pert little sayings, expressive of her air of jaunty defiance against a large dark fate that was hardly a gentleman to have taken such advantage of a lady. This was the Andromeda that Perseus had come to rescue! Rescued and rescuer had ended up at a bar, treated by the genial sea monster who stood between them, his friendly claws encircling their shoulders.

But what really did the permanent damage to Eliot's personality was the humiliation of his error, not its duration. Actually, the marriage lasted less than six months. It was David who went to the nursing home where Ailsa was drying out and obtained her consent to an annulment. Eliot was the one who resisted. He was grimly determined that his friend would not find him easy to handle. He had made his bed, and by God he would lie in it!

"But it's the only way you can be saved," David protested.

"Saved from what?"

"From wasting your life trying to cure an incurable."

"Not all alcoholics are incurable. I believe even your revered stepmother overcame a problem of that nature. If you could help her, why can't I help Ailsa?"

It was his first overt reference to the affair, the existence of which he had long silently known. In the past trying months, he had hardly seen David at all, which had added to his bitterness. But now he was shocked by the green-whiteness of David's angry look.

"I've got to save you first, Eliot, even if I kill you later.

Elesina is *not* an alcoholic and never was. And if Ailsa really loved you, I wouldn't care so much about her drinking. But she can't love, you numbskull! It's not her fault. It's her illness. I told her it was no marriage, and she agreed. She was perfectly reasonable about it. She has no wish to make a victim of you. She only married you because you were so urgent. Give her your apartment and a year's rent, and she'll call it quits."

"With what *you've* secretly offered in addition, I suppose."

"I haven't offered her a cent. I swear it, Eliot. She's not mercenary. She's a generous, good woman with a problem she's got to face by herself. She doesn't want to ruin your life!"

"Suppose I love her?"

"You love a dream," David retorted.

This made Eliot think of an actual dream he had had the night before. He had been in a police station, held on a charge of hit and run driving, of having injured a child, perhaps fatally, and even as he denied the charge, with a throbbing sense of injured innocence, a ghastly memory had assailed him of a crumpled bicycle wheel and the pressure of his own foot on the accelerator. And then in the sullen hopeless misery of his unaccountable guilt came the news that the child was dead, and that he had not been responsible, had not even been on the same street. And his ecstasy had been such that he had laughed in the face of the child's bereaved mother!

"You don't seem to understand, David," he insisted tensely, "I'm married to Ailsa. Do you make nothing of the obligation I incurred?"

"I suggest that you face, as she faces, the fact that life is giving you an unbelievable second chance."

Eliot finally took his second chance; he really had no alternative. A failure to do so would have been a kind of suicide. But he was never sure that he had altogether obviated his bad luck. It seemed to him that the annulment, obtained on a trumpery ground of refusal of marital rights, had made him a different man and had placed him in a different world. The great law firm with which he was associated, the layers of Clarkson cousins, the clubs, the benefit balls, the methodical to and fro of weekends in Greenwich, in Westchester, all of which had previously seemed to him parts of a culture which if not high was at least decent now struck him as the arid pantomime of a dead bourgeois tradition. Before he had been cool but accepting, cynical but tolerant, independent but conservative. Now he began to consider that the basis of the society in which he lived might be false.

Why should his own folly, his own inanity in failing to perceive the gravity of Ailsa's problem, have caused such a convulsion in his philosophy? Why should the poor world, so to speak, have to pay for his own mistake? He asked himself this often, trying to reason himself out of deepening depression. But what he kept coming back to was that somehow the case of Ailsa Murphy seemed the case of his world. If he had been wrong about one, how did he know that he had not been wrong about the other? If he had sat in a mental gallery all his life, treating his fellow men, with the exception of David, as if they were objets d'art in lighted glass cabinets and if, coming to life at last, he had seen the Tanagra figurine of Ailsa Murphy metamorphose into a blowsy drunk, what became of the rest of his little collection?

But he was now to be brought into David's life as closely as David had been brought into his. Irving Stein died in the middle of August, and three weeks later Europe was at war. Eliot, having given his apartment to Ailsa, had moved back with his parents, and he was sitting in the black walnut library of their big Park Avenue flat, after they had gone to bed, late on a weekday night, when he heard the front doorbell. It was David, pale and grim.

"I had to see you! I'm going to Montreal tomorrow to enlist in the British army."

For most of the night they sat up in the library and drank

whiskey. David showed Eliot Elesina's letter and explained the circumstances which had led to it. He insisted over and over that he was through with her forever. He roamed the room, glass in hand.

"But, my God, Eliot, what a woman she was! You can't imagine. The sympathy, the warmth, the understanding . . . it's horrible! That when it came right down to brass tacks, the very brassiest, tackiest tacks, she hardly hesitated between father's money and me!"

"You were asking her to give up a lot."

"A fortune?" David's tone soared into a sneer. "What's a fortune? I could have looked after her. She'd never have wanted. What's so fantastic about being rich?"

"She hasn't been used to it, as you are."

"Oh, she'll never be used to it!" David's bitterness seemed now to encompass even his friend. He might have been an angry prosecuting attorney as he struck the surface of a table. "They talk about Jews caring for money. God! We don't even know the first principles of it compared to Elesina. Think of it, Eliot! She married Dad for his money, and then amused herself with me while she worked herself into the will!"

"Be fair, David. She would have shared it with you."

"If I married her! Oh, yes, she wanted me, too. The fortune, the collection, Broadlawns and little David — there was no limit to her greed. She wanted the moon! Love, money, art, sex, you name it, she wanted it."

Suddenly, David sat down in the high-backed Italian chair to which he had been clinging and flung his arms along the surface of the table beside it, dropping his head between them. For several minutes, as Eliot sat silent, he sobbed. The grief seemed to emanate from an actually physical agony; he twisted his shoulders violently, and once again his fists pounded the table. When the fit had passed, he rose quietly enough and poured himself a drink.

"I'm sorry, Eliot. What a baby I am."

Eliot ignored this. "What are your family doing about the will?"

"Oh, they're fighting it, of course. Lionel and Peter are up in arms. They were eating out of Elesina's hand only yesterday, and now she's the Whore of Babylon! They've retained Ephraim Bauer. If it's scandal they want, he should give them a feast!"

"They're not going to bring out . . ." Eliot stopped.

"My little matter? They don't know a thing about it. You're the only one who knows — besides Ivy Trask — and you only guessed. No, Lionel and Peter are furious with me for not joining their attack on the will. They think I'm an eccentric idealist."

"What did you tell them?"

"I told them the truth. That Dad's will may be inequitable, but that it was not obtained by undue influence. I am convinced that he knew what he was doing and that he had testamentary capacity. Therefore I cannot in good conscience contest the will. Mother's case is different."

"She doesn't have to attack it. She simply asserts her right of election?"

"Exactly. She never consented to the divorce, so she's entitled to a widow's third. So I advised her."

"And will she claim it?"

"She already has. And Schurman has already offered a compromise. We've even had a meeting."

"Of everybody?"

"Everybody!" David spread his arms wide as he laughed bitterly. "You should have seen us all, Eliot, in the big conference room of Schurman and Lister. Mother, looking very regal in dark gray — the black weeds of widowhood might have seemed an affectation. And beside her Bauer, as ugly and motionless as a great bulldog. And then Lionel and Peter with their wives, trying desperately to look unconcerned, faintly bored, with a couple of fussing attorneys from their own minor firms. Last and very much the least, David, in tweeds, having discarded his Hamlet role in favor of a more litigious costume. But where was Ophelia? *Ophelia?* Where was Cressida? Where was Lady Macbeth? In comes Jacob Schurman, rubbing his hands, apologizing for the delay, and at last, wonder of wonders, in she sweeps, the Queen of Tragedy herself, in black with a black beret and two long black ostrich plumes. Never have I seen her more beautiful!"

"Did she speak to you?"

"Oh, no. She knows her part too well. She spoke to none of us, but in scanning the long table she allowed her eyes to rest on mine for a moment, with the least hint of a smile. It was charming. She seemed to be saying: 'All right, if this is really the way you want it, David.' "

"But you said nothing to her?"

"Oh, nothing. What should I say? There is nothing more between us."

Eliot, taking in the set jaw and the dry tone, began to wonder if it might not be true. "And then what happened?"

"Jacob Schurman made his offer. He was very precise, very efficient. He said that he had advised his client that the will was incontestable. He described the circumstances of its preparation and execution. I must say, even Lionel and Peter were taken aback. He then spoke briefly on the facts of Dad's divorce and indicated the main arguments that could be used for and against it. He submitted memoranda, with a copy for each of us, showing what Dad had already settled on his family and what he had left. And then he came to the point. To avoid litigation and salvage the family name and reputation, the divine Elesina offered us twenty-five percent of the estate! She would not bargain, would not haggle. It was, strictly speaking, a take-it-or-leave-it proposition."

Eliot shrugged. "I think I'd take it, if I were you."

"Me? I have nothing to do with it. I just went because Mother asked me to. But I think very likely they will take it. That's not what concerns me. What concerns me is what I saw in the faces around that table. The moment Jacob began to talk, the moment they began to listen, there was no moral issue anymore. It was only a matter of figures. Elesina, Lionel, Peter, even Mother — all that mattered now was a division of the spoils. Was there so much as a mention of Dad's benevolent purposes? Did anyone care what the man who had put together that fortune and that collection really wanted?"

"But he's dead, David! And besides, he did all he could to confuse them. And how do you know that Elesina won't fulfill his idea of an art center?"

"Oh, she probably will. And do it in the way to give herself the most glory. And Lionel and Peter will make a point of becoming friends again to keep her money in the firm. They'll all end up thick as thieves!"

"And what about you? Won't you be in it, too? Isn't your money there? Won't you share in the settlement?"

"I don't know. I don't care. I shan't need it where I'm going."

"You're really going to enlist?"

"Certainly. It's all arranged. Harry Custis has organized a group."

"Harry Custis? That playboy? What have you to do with the likes of Harry Custis?"

"Well, war is a great equalizer, you know. Harry and his friends may be a bit too posh, a bit Racquet Club for a Stein, but they're willing to make an exception. If I fight well enough, maybe they'll even take me in, after the war. Like Swann in Proust, and the Jockey Club."

Eliot assessed his friend's biting tone. "I suppose you might be elected to the Racquet Club without having your head blown off. I could put you up."

"No. I want to be the first member elected with his head blown off! Brains have never been a qualification there."

Eliot's heart was beating fast. He knew that if he did not speak now, he might never do so. The idea might not survive a night's contemplation. He had tried to live once in marrying Ailsa. Could he live again? "Would Harry Custis take me? Even if I'm not a social-climbing Hebrew?"

"Eliot! Don't be crazy! You don't want to get into this war."

"Do you think you're the only man who's lost his illusions through a woman?"

David stared at him and then burst out laughing. "God, man, do you think that's my only motive?"

"No. But I think it's your real one."

"You don't believe I care about fighting for civilization?"

"Oh, yes. That, too."

"And you, Eliot? What do you care about?"

"I care about caring. I care about *your* enthusiasm. It's a light at the end of the tunnel. Don't try to stop me, David. I'm going with you. How can Harry not want me? Food for powder, man, food for powder."

"You're making me feel it's my duty to give the whole thing up!"

"Give up civilization for Eliot Clarkson? Poor thing that it is, it must be worth more than that."

David's face at this became very grave. Then abruptly he walked over to shake Eliot's hand. "I'll call you at eight tomorrow. If you feel the same way then, I'll speak to Harry."

"Be sure to tell him I'm *in* the Racquet Club. He may be too grand to remember me."

৵৵ 14 ৡ৯

David and Eliot were sent to England where they received their training on the Salisbury Plain and their commissions by January 1940. They were then separated, for Eliot, who spoke German, was assigned to an intelligence unit in London and David's infantry regiment became part of the British Expeditionary Force in France. Eliot was very bitter about their separation; he was convinced that they would never meet again. He felt a poor fool to have gone to war in order to be with a friend and to have lost him already. But he conceded to himself that there was no reason why a world that had lost all sense and meaning should retain any logical sequence on his account.

He and David exchanged letters regularly until the German invasion of the Lowlands. After that Eliot heard no more. He was so convinced that David had been killed that he was not even surprised when he learned that he had been. In his near suicidal despair he sought consolation in a parallel. What else could have happened to Rupert Brooke?

David had been killed by strafing from a low-flying plane while attempting to board one of the flotilla of small craft sent out from England to evacuate the B.E.F. A few pages of a journal were found on his body on the beach at Dunkirk. These were ultimately sent by Clara Stein to Eliot:

May 28. Thirty pale green planes with black crosses on their underwings have just roared down the beach. There is no effective shelter. I am sitting under a dune, faced away from the still, black sea. There are hours, perhaps days to wait. It is difficult to believe that the army can escape by water. Surely the Nazis can blow up everything in the Channel. But it's a chance. The only thing any of us seem to be afraid of is that Churchill might ask for an armistice to save the B.E.F. from annihilation. Don't let him do that, God!

I may as well write. I have nothing to read, and nobody is talking much. I suppose these words will never be read, but what does that matter? What is read is soon enough forgotten, and many of the finest things ever written have perhaps been seen only by their authors.

Not that what I have to write is so fine. But I feel clear, clear as I have not felt before. What I want to write down here is the simple fact that I have enjoyed myself. I have been exhilarated. I have been happy!

There. It is said. It is recorded. Despite all the horror of the incredible mess, the crushing defeat, despite my own probable impending extinction, I have still been happy. I was even happy at the killing, the very little for which I was responsible: those three men who were rash enough to be sitting on top of their tank when they entered what they believed to be the deserted village of Neuville. It was not that I exulted in the deaths of three poor German boys who probably believed they were fighting for a good cause and may never have even heard of the Nazi concentration camps. No, it was not blood lust. It was simply that it was good at last to be shooting, to be *doing* something about evil.

We have talked and talked. We have beaten our breasts and shouted about our own crimes. We have said this and that about the wrongs meted out to Germany. But nothing will do in the end but to take a gun and kill the people who, guiltily or innocently, are supporting this wickedness. It is even a relief to know that the Nazis may have to kill David Stein to get to England. My generation may not have found things worth living for, but it has certainly found things worth dying for. And maybe that is just as good. Maybe it's even the same thing.

As it looks now, there may be a Nazi victory. But it won't last. It can't last. For eventually people will not stand for it. Or if they do, they're not worth saving. I guess it's necessary for this scourge to come into the world every so often so that we may know that men can still be men. Unless we reach the point where the bombs become so big that we dare not fight anymore, even Hitler, and that is a world I do not care to think about. I am still glad that I have lived when I have lived. Eliot calls me a romantic. But then so is he. We are a romantic generation.

I still think of Elesina. I have never written to her, though she has written, regularly, once a month, to me. I have destroyed her letters unread. I hear from Mother that she is an isolationist and that people are speaking of her running for public office. She is quite the great lady now.

Suppose I had taken her aside after dinner on that first evening when Ivy brought her to Broadlawns and said: "You're the most beautiful and wonderful creature I have ever beheld! Will you marry me?" And suppose she had accepted? What would our life have been?

Perhaps a happy one. Elesina is very agreeable when she gets her own way. That is what Ivy has had the genius to see. Give that little girl one half the world, and she'll get the other on her own. Look out, Hitler!

I think that war has heightened the colors for me. I have always yearned for colors, and I imagine that in our century they have faded. Again, that must be the romantic in me. I have always deplored Dad's fondness for Gentiles. I thought he ought to stand out, magnificent in his Semitism, a prince of Judah! And perhaps I looked too eagerly for anti-Jewish feeling in New York. It could be exciting to be the victim of prejudice. A world where everybody was nice to everybody, where every club was open to everybody, seemed to me flabby and dull. Wasn't the love of Romeo and Juliet intensified by the feud between their families? Didn't the risks of my affair with Elesina make it more ecstatic? Maybe I was looking for a world of thrills, which war could satisfy better than peace.

If that were so, I have indeed lived at the right time, and I need not now deplore an otherwise lamentable finale. If I am wounded, if I suffer, if I die miserably, at least I shall be sharing some of the wretchedness of those whom Hitler has penned in his concentration camps. I am tired of my immunity from their sufferings.

What shall I miss? The invasion of England is too ghastly to contemplate. The most jaded appetite for thrills could hardly enjoy a Nazi occupation of London, or even the passionate last-ditch fight that will undoubtedly be put up. And then what? A compromise between two hemispheres: America leading one, Germany the other? Elesina will marry again, and we can be sure that this time it will not be a Jew. I seem to see her as ambassadress to Berlin, being charming to everybody. With victory there would be a relaxation of persecutions. It might even become fashionable in younger circles of the Berlin elite to whisper that Hitler had gone a bit too far, that now perhaps a few talented Jews could be helpful in the administration of so vast an empire. And the lovely American ambassadress, becoming confidential at dinner with the German Vice-Fuehrer of France-Belgium, might say:

"I had an affair with a Jew once. He was very dear, very sympathetic. Can you believe that?"

"Of course, dear madame. Who wouldn't be sympathetic with you?"

"He died fighting you at Dunkirk." Oh, how I see the benign sorrow of her glance! The dazzling thing about Elesina is that she is always perfectly sincere. "He believed that life would not have been worth living if you won."

"So many good men felt that way. It is sad, the deaths which history seems to require. He was English, your friend?"

"No, American."

"Ah, yes. It took your countrymen so long to learn who their true friends were. Well, half the martyrs of the world died for wrong causes."

That is enough. I turn my eyes from that future. Death has no sting for those who envision it. But let me suppose, on the contrary, that Britain survives, that Britain even wins, that with American help — will it ever come? — the Nazi beast is beaten back in his lair, exterminated. Will it then be the new world that Eliot loves to contemplate, where a benevolent communism, throwing off the bloody gloves of Stalin, leads the whole world to peace and plenty?

And Elesina?

"No, my dear commissar," I hear her saying at dinner, "I never had any faith in the greedy structure of the old world. It is true that I fought for my husband's fortune. Why not? I sought to preserve this great collection for the people, and here it is today, in the Peoples Art Institute at Rye. What do you ask? The Steins today? Well, I understand that Lionel and Peter are *very* useful on a dairy farm. Yes, there was another son. David. Oh, he was much the best of the lot." Again the faraway look. "I think he would have been much heard from, had he survived the war. Oh, yes, I had a very special knowledge of him!"

I guess the present is good enough for me. I have few regrets. Mother will play one of her hymns if the worst happens. She will look very fine, very noble. The profile view will be the best.

PART THREE
ELESINA

GILES BENNETT began to live when he first came to New York in 1950. He used to tell people that it was as if he had died and gone to heaven. It was not, to be sure, that life was all hosannas and golden bells. Jobs were temporary and part-time: in his first year Giles worked as a waiter, a necktie salesman, a back elevator operator and a dog-walker. But he was young and high-spirited, and his looks were widely admired. Though small, he was neatly made. His reddish blond hair fell over his round pate in flat ringlets. His high, broad forehead and faintly olive complexion gave him the appearance of a bronze figurine of a boyish Roman emperor. But there was nothing imperious in his gentle hazel eyes, nor did his temper seem to correspond to the red tints of his hair. Giles was an affectionate creature who simply wanted to live and let live. He was always bewildered by the fuss that was made whenever he changed roommates.

He had grown up in Waverly Hills, a suburb of Pittsburgh, the son of a prosperous dentist, who was also a political rightist and active Legionnaire, and of a shy, self-effacing pretty little woman who drank. An older brother, with a great local reputation as an athlete, had disappointed the family by becoming a policeman. Giles, a dreamy and romantic boy, had never had the least congeniality with his noisy father or violent brother, and his mother's furtive sympathy had offered small support against their early campaign to keep him from being a "sissy." How had they known? As if he had divined their suspicion and taken it for a high truth, Giles turned at fourteen to the boys, and by junior year at the University of Pennsylvania he was a confirmed and contented homosexual. When his father learned of this, there was a frightful scene, and Giles was ordered to drop his friends and see a psychiatrist as the price of any further support. Giles, with a fire that surprised them all, refused out of hand and decamped for New York with his father's curse and his mother's nest egg. The latter, slipped to him surreptitiously, was barely enough to keep him a year.

But as it turned out, he was never uncomfortably hard up. The large male world in which he soon found himself was friendly and hospitable. He lived for three months in the apartment of a middle-aged decorator and for another six in that of two Chinese youths who ran a gift shop. He went to many parties and theaters, and had several romances, but nothing really serious occurred until his meeting with Eliot Clarkson at a cocktail party.

Giles was blithely ignorant of politics and current events, and he had had no idea who Eliot was. His host, the decorator with whom he had briefly lived, explained that the lean, angular, balding, disputatious-looking man who was talking so emphatically to an intently listening group by the window was a famous professor at Manhattan Law School, known for his brilliant and radical books.

"A communist?" Giles inquired. Communists bored him.

"Perhaps. The issue was certainly raised by the trustees at Manhattan. They only gave in when the students organized a mass protest." Giles's host had long forgiven Giles's desertion of him. He was a practical man, large, dark-complexioned, faintly piratical in appearance. "Come on over. He wants to meet you."

"Meet *me?* What on earth does he know about me?"

"What I've told him." The decorator laughed coarsely. "I wonder what that would be?"

"He's like us, then?"

"Of course, he's like us, stupid. Why the hell else would he be here? But he's the kind who's ashamed of it. Don't expect him to introduce you to his Knickerbocker folks."

"They don't know?"

"Oh, they must. Eliot would never conceal anything. He's

too proud. I only meant that he won't mix his worlds. And when I say he's ashamed of being like us, it's not for snobbish reasons. He's ashamed, deep down. Under all that atheism lurks a Calvinist heart. He thinks it's sin!"

Giles found this rather intriguing; he looked at the professor now with more interest. "But what will I talk to him about? I don't know anything about law or politics."

"Talk to him about his book."

"What book?"

"*The War Letters of David Stein.* It's having quite a vogue these days." He moved Giles toward the group.

"But I haven't read it!"

"What difference does that make, silly? Tell him you found it *divine*."

"Give me a clue then. What's it about?"

"The mysterious lady who betrayed David Stein."

"And who was David Stein?"

But already Giles was being introduced. Clarkson looked at him hard for a moment and then glanced down at his glass.

"I guess I need a refill. How about you, Bennett?" And placing a hand on Giles's shoulder he maneuvered him toward the bar. Giles was rather shocked by his abruptness.

"Oh, I mustn't take you away from your friends."

"I didn't come here to talk about why we dropped the A-bomb," Clarkson said impatiently. "I came here to relax. Phil tells me you're the only person he's ever known who's really learned the art of living from day to day."

"How else can one live?"

"As many other ways as there are people in this room!"

With refilled drinks they moved to a window seat that overlooked the garden at Turtle Bay. It was a warm, pleasant spring night. But Clarkson seemed moody. He stared out the window in silence. Giles decided that he had to say something.

"I hear you've written the most divine book. Everybody's reading it."

"I didn't write it. I edited it."

"Oh, you mean David Stein was a real person?"

"Why do you talk about books you haven't read? Does *The War Letters of David Stein* sound like the title of a novel?"

"Yes! But then I guess everything sounds to me like the title of a novel."

"I don't write novels. Or read them. There are too many grim facts in this world for me to bother with fantasies."

"Really? I'm just the opposite. I hate facts."

Clarkson at this seemed to relax. He almost smiled. "You and Justice Holmes."

"He hated them, too?"

"Brandeis used to give him statistical reports on labor to improve his mind in the summer recess. But Holmes would have none of it. He reached for his Plato instead. And he was right, too! But why do I tell you this? You probably never heard of Brandeis."

"I may not be one of your brilliant law students, Professor Clarkson, but I'm not a complete ignoramus. Brandeis is a college in Boston."

Clarkson laughed good-naturedly and took a gulp of his drink. "Tell me about yourself, young man. What do you do besides go to parties like this?"

"I go to the theater. And to art galleries. And I love ballet."

"But what do you *do?*"

"I guess I don't really do anything much."

Giles hated to talk about himself, and besides there was not much to tell. He liked to discover private things about the other person. He returned now to the subject of books, having heard that no author could resist this topic for long. Soon enough, indeed, Clarkson was talking about the little volume of war letters which had been so unexpected a best seller.

"Nobody was more surprised than myself," he confessed. "I thought people were sick of war books."

"And so they are. But yours isn't just a war book, is it? Wasn't your David Stein in love with a mysterious lady who treated him cruelly?"

"Mysterious only in the sense that the reader doesn't know who she is. Clarissa is an obvious alias."

"Has nobody guessed her identity?"

"Not so far as I've heard."

"But you know?"

"Of course, I know, dummy." But there was a note of friendliness in the gruff voice. "How could I not know? The letters were written to me."

"And she's still alive, this Clarissa?"

"You may assume so. It was only a dozen or thirteen years ago. *She* wasn't at Dunkirk." Clarkson smiled a bit grimly. "No, you can be sure she wasn't anywhere that bombs were flying."

"Ah, that gives me a hint."

Clarkson looked surprised. "As to who she is?'

"No. As to *what* she is. I'll bet you one thing. Her name's not Clarissa."

"But I told you it wasn't!"

"I mean it's not even a woman's name. What is the male for Clarissa? How about Clarry?"

For a moment Clarkson looked actually shocked. Then he shook his head emphatically. "No, no. David wasn't that way at all. Even if he was a friend of mine."

"But you spoke of Clarissa avoiding bombs. Why should that be reprehensible in a woman? I assumed this was a man who had not only treated David badly, but who had shirked the draft."

Clarkson considered this for a moment. "That, I admit, is

reasonably deduced. But it's still wrong. I meant that Elesina — Clarissa, I should say — was the kind of person who is
always at the head table, or on the grandstand, or wherever
the prizes are being given out. She is immune to the ugliness
of life."

"Elesina. What a curious name. It shouldn't take me long
to run her down."

Clarkson smiled ruefully, recognizing his slip. "Would a
dinner at Twenty-One buy your silence?"

"No. My respect for you will do that. But I should love to
dine with you just the same. At Twenty-One or at some
place less expensive. *I* should be honored if you would tell me
the story of David Stein."

Clarkson's friendly expression dissolved again to a mask,
but his voice almost shook. "I think I shall like to do that,
Giles. I shall like it very much."

Thus it began. In two weeks' time Giles had moved into
Eliot's apartment in the Village. In three, he was working for
Sam Gorman on *Tone* magazine. The job was arranged by
Eliot, an old friend of Sam's. It struck Giles as rather odd
that a man as austere as Eliot should be on such intimate terms
with a merry, gossip-loving old queen like Sam, but he found
that the relationship went back to the David Stein days, and
everything that originated *there* was sacred.

It was never a happy affair. When Giles's initial pride at
occupying so much of the attention and affection of this
strange, interesting man began to subside, he was surprised to
discover that he was actually bored. Eliot's friends, teachers,
law students, radical writers, finding Giles ignorant in all
subjects which interested them, ignored him. He was made to
feel like a pretty creature to be winked at or chucked under
the chin and then forgotten. If Eliot's friends had no disapproval of his relations with Eliot, they also had little interest
in them. On the other hand, Eliot's old world, his school and
college mates and the great host of his relations, was firmly
closed to Giles. If Eliot did not conceal his sexual tastes,

neither did he flaunt them. For nothing on earth would he have taken Giles to dine with his old mother, or with his aunts or cousins. There were certain things, he would say, that didn't mix. And he would make matters worse, when he was going out to such haunts, by leaving lists of suggested evening reading. He never quite abandoned the idea that Giles could be educated.

In the meanwhile, however, Giles was obtaining success at *Tone*. He had an eye for knickknacks, for tricky gadgets, for catchy designs, for all kinds of new household ideas; he was the perfect assistant to Sam. He went to fashion shows, to department store openings, to commercial previews, and he wrote up his discoveries and recommendations in a spicy style that soon made his column popular. Sam took a great fancy to him and asked him to all his parties. This was the cause of the first major falling-out with Eliot.

"I've gotten rather fond of Sam through the years," Eliot told Giles, "but I cannot abide his chattering parties of society hags and fashionable faggots. Spare me!"

"I mean to spare you, Eliot. There's no reason you should go. But the people at Sam's parties are just the ones I want to meet. They're my kind of people. You've got your brain trusts. You must let me have my feather trusts, as I suppose you call them."

Well, of course, there was nothing Eliot could say to this. It was too manifestly reasonable. And they both knew that what was really behind Eliot's reluctance to let Giles go to Sam's was his fear that he would be seduced. And, of course, Giles did find lovers there. He tried to keep this concealed, but the gossip in his world was fierce. There were scenes, terrible scenes, followed by days of moody silence on Eliot's part. Silence would at last give way to lectures.

"What you can't see, Giles, is that your whole life on *Tone*, that whole world, in fact, is going to limit you hopelessly. I know I was responsible for getting you into it, but I thought it was just a temporary job. People like Sam and Ivy

Trask only play at life. They decorate it, pulling up a corner here and pushing one down there, patting things. I want to send you back to school. I want you to start thinking."

"Look, Eliot. You've got to accept me for what I am. Because I'm going to continue that way. I want to enjoy my life!"

"But you're too young to know what you are! You're too young even to be sure that you're homosexual. You may be off on the wrong track altogether. Nature may have intended you for an intellectual, a lawyer . . ."

"And a wife and three darling children in a white cottage with a green lawn in Plandome. No, Eliot, I know what I am."

Giles spoke with greater assurance now that he knew about Eliot's own past. He had learned all about his passionate friendship for David Stein and his absurd marriage to an alcoholic. He saw in the seventeen years that separated their birthdays the division between the old-fashioned and the modern homosexual. Eliot was ridden with guilt and doubt. There was always a part of him that agreed with the con-temners of pederasty. He saw his life as an obscene tragedy and himself as a kind of Hamlet in drag. Giles was very clear that he wanted no part of such dramatics in his own life. He was perfectly willing to take advice in many things, but not in the question of sex. That had been answered once and for all in Pennsylvania.

Most of the young men he knew would have abandoned Eliot without a qualm, but Giles had a kinder heart. He had no wish to drive his friend to desperation. It was Sam who intervened at last.

"I've got an apartment for you, Giles. It's on top of a brownstone, a sort of studio. You can move in right away, and I suggest you do. Don't worry about Eliot. I'll take it on myself to break the news. He will be upset, but he will get over it. It's not the first time it's happened. I appreciate your wanting to let him down easily, but there's no easy way of doing these things."

Giles moved out, and everything occurred as Sam had predicted. Eliot wrote Giles a long, bitter letter and then accepted the situation. What else could he do? He was not a man to commit murder. Giles, who immediately before the separation had thought that he would have everything that his heart could desire if he could simply be free of Eliot with a good conscience, now discovered how quickly one could adapt oneself to good fortune. It even seemed a bit flat to be having no further arguments with the sardonic professor.

Sam, however, had another "patron" in mind. Giles met Julius Schell at one of the "respectable" Gorman parties. Schell was a rich, elegant bachelor of fifty, the grandson and namesake of a famous but unscrupulous manipulator of railroad securities. Everything, according to Sam, that Schell undertook he did well. He was an astute manager of family investments, a conscientious fiduciary of charitable and cultural institutions, an excellent bridge player and equestrian, and he had recently completed a successful term in the Assembly in Albany. His diminutive figure, plump but muscular, was always enveloped in the finest tweeds. His face was round, his skin smooth, his thick curly hair a rich chestnut. His lips were thin, his eyes bland, searching, suspicious, reproachful.

In the following month Schell came to two other gatherings at Sam's at which he talked only to Giles.

"Julius obviously likes you," Sam told Giles. "If he takes a real fancy to you, there's nothing he won't do. But remember: be careful. Julius is a public figure. He's planning to run for Congress. There can never be a whiff of scandal to his name."

"And why should I cause scandal?"

"I wonder. But the question shouldn't come up. You won't have to *do* anything with Julius. And just so long as you keep anything you do with anyone else concealed, all will be well and good. Julius may ask for little else, but he does ask for total devotion. Or the appearance of it."

"But what, my dear Sam, is there in it for *me?*"

"Don't be naive, darling. Julius is a very important man. He knows all the great people. And like his wealth, his ambition has no limit. His 'secretary,' shall we put it, might be a young man to be reckoned with."

"Would I have to leave *Tone* to become his secretary?"

"I like to think that nobody ever leaves *Tone*. Our alumni move onward and upward, but they always remember us. Look at Ivy Trask."

Giles laughed. "So we rule the world?"

"We set the tone, anyway. It may be the same thing."

Julius Schell, indeed, seemed to require very little in return for the handsome gifts which he now lavished on Giles. There was a gratifying succession of jeweled cuff links, old master drawings, tricky gold gadgets and the finest ties and shirts. When Giles dined at Julius' handsome Georgian town house on East 8oth Street, the chauffeur called for him and took him home, as was also the case when he went for the weekend at the Gothic castle in Rye which Julius inhabited with a widowed sister. All that Julius required was a first re- fusal on Giles's evenings. If he wished to take Giles to the opera or to the theater or to dinner with friends, he expected Giles to be free. If Giles were not, there would be no re- proach, only the slightest arch of those silky eyebrows.

For Julius never showed temper. He was always cool, always dapper, always seemingly on top of things. His voice was a mild monotone of mild sarcasm. He played the role of the kindly martinet, the down-to-earth aesthete, the poet who yet knew how to live in a world of prose. He never humili- ated Giles by a public correction, but he sometimes lectured him when they were alone.

"I was concerned, dear boy, when you told that dirty story to Babs Reardon. Not that Babs, of course, is unaccustomed to such revelations. And not that I object on grounds of morality. To me it is a question of aesthetics, pure and simple. It so happens that your looks are angelic. That story did not go with them. Angelic looks create an air of innocence which is quite charming and which is a distinct social asset. Let me reassure you at once that people will not take them as any indication of your true character. The very fact that they know you not to be angelic only intrigues them the more. But you must never, in social circles, do or say anything too obviously inconsistent with your principal aspect. It is like wearing a discordant tie and shirt."

Giles understood this lecture in a double sense. Not only was talk about sex to be disguised, action was, also. If Giles had affairs, they were to be kept not only from Julius' sight, but from the sight of Julius' world. Julius might have had the wisdom, for social and political reasons, not to appear homosexual, but he had also the vanity to wish not to appear betrayed. It was one of his solutions to the problem of his personality to pose before his audience as a continual enigma, a kind of Elizabeth Tudor, a creature not quite human, a superior sexless being, an awesome mixture of mortal power and divine clemency. Giles suspected, for all his friend's harsh comments on the financial antics of his grandfather and namesake, that Julius deeply revered his memory, that he yearned in his own way to be a tycoon.

"It's hard to know, isn't it?" Giles responded with a sigh. "Sometimes New York seems like Liberty Hall. And at others it's as rigid as the Spanish court."

"Heed my words, dear boy, and you will get by. The most difficult eras to live in are those of supposed tolerance and informality. Ours is a real bitch."

∾§ 2 §∾

Giles's apartment consisted of a single room at the top of an East Side brownstone, but it was a spacious, airy room, the former studio of an affluent amateur painter, and it was vividly decorated in the high fashion of what Sam Gorman, who had supplied many of the objects, called the "febrile fifties." There was a big black and white canvas, school of Franz Kline, an L-shaped sofa in beige that ran across two of the walls, a Calder mobile, two ebony-carved African figures flanking the marble Victorian mantel and a smell of incense. But the particular glory of the chamber was the chinchilla cover to the bed, a gift from Julius Schell. Giles had always wanted a chinchilla bedcover and had never dreamed (or had always dreamed) that he would have one.

On the night of Mrs. Mortimer Blake's party he had two hours to dress. Julius had told him to be there at ten. By that time dinner would be over and the late guests would be arriving for the music. Julius, of course, was dining there, but Giles did not expect that kind of invitation yet. A scant two years before who would have dreamed that a college dropout from Waverly Hills would be an assistant feature editor of *Tone* magazine, an intimate friend of Julius Schell's and an about-to-be guest at the triplex apartment of Mrs. Mortimer Blake, the best-dressed woman in the world? Giles smiled at his image in the eagle-topped mirror as he answered aloud what Sam Gorman's response would have been: "Any smart observer!"

The lavender telephone purred.

"I call to remind you that ten o'clock means ten o'clock and not ten-thirty or even a quarter to eleven."

Giles made a little pout into the mirror. "Of course, Julius. I'll be on the dot."

"And be sure you don't have too much to drink. A glass of white wine while you're dressing. Maybe a second if you're having anything to eat. That should be ample. Bear in mind that you will be making your debut in the highest society. Intemperance is never tolerated in newcomers. After you've made the grade, *je ne dis pas*." The sarcastic voice was kind. Julius was always kind. "Are you there?"

"I'm here, Julius. I shall do just as you say. Two glasses, no more."

"Good boy. Till ten, then."

Giles could not suppress a sigh as he hung up. Now that Julius was actively seeking the Republican nomination for Congress, he was more than ever the martinet. If only people did not have to be quite such big brothers! Julius was a big brother; Sam Gorman was a big brother, or big sister; Eliot — poor Eliot — had been the worst of all. They were nice big brothers, it was true, unlike Giles's own, real-life big brother who had beaten him up when he had caught him rouging his lips in the bathroom, but Giles was beginning to wonder if the time were not coming when he would be able to do without such condescension. After all, he might want to be a big brother himself.

He searched regretfully through his wardrobe. Julius had said that "black tie" at Mrs. Blake's meant just that, even for the younger guests — black tie, white stiff shirt, dinner jacket. No blue velvet jacket, no ruffled shirt, no red pants, no . . . The telephone rang again.

"I hear my little protégé is stepping into society," came Sam Gorman's grating voice. "Who would have thought, when you were walking dogs for Park Avenue matrons, that one day you would enter their sanctuary? You've gone from little bitches to big ones, my dear."

"It's natural for you to be dazzled, Sam. Where you come from, they don't even wear shoes."

"You told me that when you walked barefoot into *Tone*. But ta-ta, lovey. I just wanted you to know that if you're late tomorrow, old Sammy won't mind. Live it up!"

Giles decided to pour himself a glass of wine. He got the bottle from the icebox. Peering into the yellow depths of the tall thin glass, he considered Sam's reminder of how far he had climbed. But *had* he climbed? Had he not simply been yanked up? At the end of a leash? He had hated the dogs, big ones, little ones, snarlers, snappers, barkers, biters, sometimes as many as a dozen at one time, enmeshing him like a maypole in their leashes, defecating and pissing on every last patch of green left in the beleaguered city. But even that had been better than Waverly Hills. Let Sam jeer. All he had done was accept life.

Mrs. Blake's great, high-ceilinged chambers were filled with tapestries, consoles and people. Giles knew nobody, but he was happy to walk about and stare. Suddenly he had to pause to avoid colliding with a small woman hurrying across the room in an aggressive stride, her shoulders jerking, her shiny gold hair bobbing.

"Miss Trask!"

She paused to squint at Giles. Then she grunted. "Hello, baby. How did you struggle to this exalted rung? Oh, Julius, I suppose."

Ivy Trask appeared infrequently at *Tone*, but all the staff knew and revered her.

"You promised once to introduce me to the great Mrs. Stein. Is she here?"

"She is." Ivy looked at him as if his request had reminded her of something. "Follow me."

They found Mrs. Stein in the next room. By what was surely a rare piece of luck she was alone and walking toward them. She was in black, tall, regal, moving to rustling skirts. When she paused to clutch an earring, perhaps loose, she seemed to smile, though it might have been an involuntary twist of the lips as she bent her head. Her skin was white, very clear, the skin of a much younger woman. Her eyes were amused, friendly, as if she were thinking of something that pleased her. She saw Ivy and handed her both earrings.

"I told you they were loose."

Ivy put them in her evening bag. "This is the young man I spoke to you about. Does he remind you of someone?"

Mrs. Stein regarded Giles for a moment. "Not really. But I see what you mean."

"Talk to him. I'll get you some champagne."

Mrs. Stein struck Giles immediately as the type of woman that he would like to have been, had he been born one. For wasn't she a chameleon, all feminine one minute, all despot the next? As he followed her across the room to an empty sofa he pictured her as a czarina who at a snap of the fingers could summon her guard. Except that she was not going to summon her guard. She was going to be nice. With a certain air of greatness she seated herself on the sofa and patted the cushion beside her to bid him do likewise. When she turned her large dark eyes upon him, he seemed at once the only other person in the room. They might have been strangers on a park bench. The rest of the party were so many pigeons and sparrows.

"Would it be untactful of me to ask whom I remind Ivy of?" he asked.

"Not in the least. There's something about your eyes that recalls a young man who died in the war. His name was David Stein. You needn't worry. He was very handsome."

"You mean the David Stein of Eliot Clarkson's book?"

"Oh, you've read it?"

"But he was a hero!"

"Not really. Just another brave young man who happened to get himself killed. There were far too many of them."

"Was he related to you?"

"He was my husband's son."

This seemed, somehow, to conclude the discussion. Yet Mrs. Stein continued to look at him silently, with her curious half smile.

"Ivy tells me you're a friend of Julius'," she said at last.

"Yes! Are you?"

"Well, if I was, I wonder if I will be. I'm thinking of opposing him for the Republican nomination for Congress in Westchester."

"We heard that. Will you really? Poor Julius. He won't have a chance."

"I wouldn't say that."

"Anyway, why should it matter? Can't you run against people in politics and still be friends? I thought all that name calling was only play-acting to fool the peasants."

"Some of it. Not all of it."

"But you like Julius?"

"Why on earth do you assume that?"

He was pleased by her candor. "I thought everyone did. What have you against him?"

"He's a fraud. He uses charities the way his wicked old grandfather used railroads: to serve his ambition. But the grandfather at least wasn't a hypocrite. He made no pretense of philanthropy. I like my robber barons to be robbers."

"Aren't you afraid I'll repeat this to him?"

"Why should I be? I'll probably say it in public."

"That should be fun! Anyway, I shouldn't dream of telling him. I take no sides in politics."

"You mean you won't be helping Julius in his campaign?"

"Me? What on earth could he use me for?"

"You seem very perceptive to me. And Ivy tells me you're doing well on *Tone*."

"Oh, that." Giles made a little face, as if to indicate how far from Mrs. Stein's great world they had now strayed. "I guess I've done all right. But it all depends on what Sam Gorman's had for breakfast."

"On the contrary, it depends on what *I've* had for breakfast." Seeing him stare, she explained. "I bought *Tone* some years back. During the war, when people had stopped reading it. Ivy persuaded me, and it turned out to be a very good thing."

"You bought it!" He clapped his hands. "Just like that?"

"Just like that."

He marveled at her power and at the ease with which she seemed to wield it. "Maybe I should work on *your* campaign."

"You'd be quite welcome. But Julius would think me a seducing witch."

"Oh, Julius!" Somewhat to his surprise Giles found himself shrugging at the picture of Julius' interfering. "Julius could never afford to let anyone think he took me that seriously."

"Why not?"

He glanced at her shyly. "Don't you know?"

"Perhaps."

"He's terrified of whispering campaigns. Because of his not being married and my being so much younger."

"Not so much younger, I suppose, as to be quite without a past?"

He looked at her more seriously now, but she was still smiling. "No, not so young as that."

"Well, you can assure Julius that he has no reason to fear any such whispering in *my* campaign."

"Really? You'd never use anything like that?"

"Never."

"Even if it were . . ."

"True?" she answered for him. "Certainly not. I think sex has no place in politics."

"I think that's admirable. But then you're obviously an admirable woman."

"No. But it's not impossible that I may become one. Or something not too unlike it." She seemed amused by her own candor and conceit. "I believe that people can change. Don't you?"

"No. But, anyway, you don't need to."

This seemed to please Mrs. Stein, but she did not have a chance to answer. Ivy Trask returned in her usual flurry.

"Elesina! The mayor's come in. He's asking for you."

Mrs. Stein's glance at Giles seemed to include him in the privileged circle of those who found mayors faintly comic. "Would you like to meet the mayor, Giles? Come with me."

Giles reflected that it was almost too easy a way to make him her slave for life. Then he excused himself and went back to join Julius. The latter, for once, was very dry of tone.

"I saw you charming my opponent. I trust you did not forget your old loyalties."

"Oh, Julius, you must admit she's wonderful!"

"Elesina? Must I?"

The name brought its reaction at last. "Elesina! Then she's Clarissa! Of course!"

"Clarissa? Who's Clarissa?"

"The woman in Eliot Clarkson's book. The woman David Stein was in love with. Oh, my God, she was his stepmother!"

Julius' brown eyes seemed for a moment to glimmer. "Perhaps I had better read that book. Clarkson? Wasn't he a communist?"

"But you wouldn't use it in the campaign!"

"That she had a thing with her stepson? No, I think not. Sex is a notorious boomerang. But I think I'm still going to read Clarkson's book. Yes, my dear Giles, I think that you may have given me an excellent idea."

"But what, Julius? I wouldn't want to hurt Mrs. Stein."

"Never mind, dear boy. It will not be you who does it. It will not even be your responsibility. But I think, if things work out, it may net you a small gift. What would you say to a set of moonstone evening studs?"

Giles reflected that Julius must never have heard about him and Eliot Clarkson. He decided that the less said about it the better.

❧ 3 ❧

Ivy Trask loved offices, and now she had them to her heart's content. She had an office at Broadlawns, just off the library, hung in black and gold Chinese lacquer panels, from which she ran the house and gardens; she had another in Rye, at Elesina's campaign headquarters, hung in banners and posters, and she had a third in New York, at *Tone*, a small yellow box of a room with green curtains and yellow walls from which, as the owner's vicereine, she supervised the operations of the magazine.

Some weeks after the evening at Mrs. Blake's, when the fight for the Republican nomination was in full fray, Ivy came in to the city to spend a quiet day at *Tone*. She needed to get away from the racket of the Rye telephone and the intrusion of political callers to the unrelated and relatively restful world of fashion. Nothing stimulated her mind like contrast. After twenty minutes of solitude, during which she perused the mockup for the forthcoming issue, she sent for the assistant feature editor.

"I like your piece on greenhouses," she told Giles Bennett, pointing to it, when he hurried in. "Anyone might think you could build this one for twenty G's, but you and I know it would cost forty. A luxury economy must be based on the stimulation of envy and discontent."

"Do you tell that to your voters, Miss Trask?"

Ivy looked up in surprise. "Perhaps I'd better watch my tongue before a friend of Julius Schell's!"

"Oh, I don't get into that. And even if I did, how could I not be for the divine Elesina?"

"Is that what you call Mrs. Stein?"

"Well, not to her face, of course. But how can anyone so beautiful interest herself in grimy politics?"

"They're not so much grimier than fashions. And don't forget Elesina was an actress. She's seen her share of sordid things."

"But there was always the goal above the grime! She could be Hedda Gabler. Or Juliet! How can she descend after all that to such dingy things as rent control and sales taxes?"

"Precisely because she's an actress. Elesina never forgets that she's still in the entertainment business. And she entertains! That's her secret."

Ivy did not go on to say how instrumental she had been in

persuading Elesina to this approach. But she paused to look back now with wry amusement on the day when she had found Elesina in the library in tears over the complexities of the federal pension law and had taken the heavy statute book to fling it in the scrap basket. "What's your money for, angel? Get researchers. And good ones!" Oh, yes, it had worked well enough, then, and Elesina had been such a quick and willing student. But how rapidly she had mastered the art! And now, already, she had less need of Ivy. Worse, far worse, she was beginning to be bored with Ivy.

"Miss Trask! You look as if you were in pain. Can I help you?"

"Call me Ivy. Everyone at *Tone* does."

"Ivy. I like that! Are you all right, Ivy?"

"Oh, I'm all right. It's old age, that's all. I never thought I'd have to worry about old age because I was born old. But that's nonsense. Everyone has to worry about old age. And my temper gets worse. I tell myself, Ivy Trask, you're going to have to watch that temper of yours . . ." She broke off. "Why should I tell you this?"

"Because I care!"

Ivy stared at him in astonishment. "You're really a nice child. And you like Elesina, too?"

"I'm in love with Elesina!"

Ivy grunted. "Everyone is. Even the boys. Oh, sweetie, I didn't mean to be nasty. But life can be hard. I see myself getting quarrelsome and vindictive, and I tell myself: 'Now, Ivy, you must be lovely to Elesina, because Elesina wants people to be lovely to her, and she doesn't have to put up with people who aren't, not for a single, solitary second, why should she?' And yet, oh, Giles, the temptation to be nasty, to remind people of their obligations, the urge to take them down a peg, becomes a kind of compulsion, not to be resisted. Why are we all driven to suicide? Or why am I? What would I be without Elesina? A nothing! A gnarled old hag, a witch. And yet, I simply cannot do the things I ought to do. There's the yearning, the deep yearning, to spit in the face of all I love and care about. Do you know, Giles, there are moments when Elesina seems to be my old aunt whom I resented so in Washington?"

"Who was your aunt, Ivy?"

The question helped Ivy to pull herself together. She stared coldly at him.

"What business is that of yours, I'd like to know? I must see Sam Gorman."

She brushed past the young man, who appeared to take her abrupt change of mood as an entirely natural phenomenon, and made her way down the narrow corridor to Sam's office. He was dictating, but he dismissed his secretary at once and rose to close the door behind Elesina's friend and counselor.

"I am honored, distinguished Ivy! Will you sit?"

"No, I like to wander." Ivy paused at the window, her back to Sam. "Little Giles seems to be doing very well. You must be proud of him. And I gather the great Julius has lost his heart. If he has one."

"Surely you don't begrudge him Giles. What could you or I or Elesina do with Giles? Besides, the boys never vote."

"You think that's all we care about now? Votes?"

"Until you've got them. Then you'll care about something else."

Ivy prowled around the office, which looked more like a decorator's shop than an editorial center. She squinted at the signed photographs of persons famous in cosmetics. But she knew everything in the room, and Sam knew she knew it. He watched her suspiciously.

"If you had to bet between Elesina and Julius, Sam, how would you bet?"

"On Julius."

"Because he has more money?"

"No. Elesina has quite enough, and enough is as good as a

feast. That is not where Julius' edge lies. He has a male asset."

Ivy sniffed. "Not so you'd notice it."

"Not so *you'd* notice it, but enough to make the difference. You see, as women, he and Elesina are evenly matched: same realism, same ruthlessness, same bitchiness."

"Sam! I won't take that!"

"Oh, calm down, Ivy. Who introduced you to Elesina, after all? I know her, and you know I know her. What she lacks is Julius' sense of the forest. A woman's danger is looking too closely at trees."

"She may find something under them," Ivy retorted grimly. "Particularly after Julius, speaking of bitchiness, has lifted his dainty leg. But why does Julius have to be bitchy? Didn't God endow him with enough?"

"Do you remember the Shakespeare evenings in the old days at Broadlawns? And how Pemberton used to hold forth on Richard the Third? Because he had a hunchback, he had to seize the crown."

"But Julius has no hunchback. His appearance, if anything, is moderately pleasing."

"True. His hump is within. He cannot love women, and he dares not love men. So he must have the world. Even if he has to take it away from Elesina."

Ivy came abruptly back to Sam's desk at this and sat down, ready for business. "They tell me he's going to use the Red smear. But how can he? How can he use that against Elesina?"

Sam's eyes showed his amusement. "Guess."

"Because the Steins are Jewish? International conspiracy?"

"Do you think he's out of his mind? Do you think he wants to commit political hara-kari?"

"Well, it might do for a whispering campaign in anti-Semitic circles."

"He's got those on his side, anyway. No, Ivy, he has more direct ammunition. But I learned it in confidence."

"You mean you won't tell me? Your oldest friend?"

"See if you can guess. Then I won't be betraying a confidence."

Ivy reflected. "It has something to do with Giles Bennett."

"Warm. Very warm."

"But where do I go from there? What connection is there between Elesina and Giles?"

"Think, Ivy." After a pause, he offered her a hint. "Who introduced Giles to *Tone?*"

"Oh. Eliot Clarkson. And Eliot's a communist. Or *was* a communist. I see. And Eliot wrote a book about David Stein. But it still seems remote from Elesina."

"Oh, Ivy."

"What?"

"You can't bluff me. I know. I didn't know till Giles told me, though I'd always suspected it. Clarissa is Elesina."

Ivy jumped up, as if in response to the eruption of her wrath. "The filthy swine! He plans to use that? Well, I shall open a campaign against him, whispering or shouting, that will blow him right out of the polls!"

"You'd better watch your step, Ivy. There are laws of libel. Julius has batteries of expensive counsel. And you can't prove a thing. What is there to prove?"

"That's just what you're going to tell me, Sam Gorman, before I leave this room! I want to know just what Julius *has* done and who can prove it. You know, because you know everything."

As Sam took in her meaning and her seriousness, he became suddenly grave. "You can't ask me to betray friends, Ivy."

"Why not? Who's betraying mine? Your friends won't have anything to worry about. All I need is a few names to keep Julius from suing."

"I can't!" There was a note of shrill distress in his voice as he began to take in the full measure of her determination and advantage.

"You know who owns *Tone.* You won't have a job tomorrow morning if you don't give me what I need! Just reflect how easy it will be to get another job at your age. Think of it, old man! And don't kid yourself we can't replace you. We've got Giles!"

"Ivy, you're a fiend!"

"Never mind my fiendishness. Are you ready for questions?"

"How do you know I won't make up the answers?"

"Because you won't dare, Sam Gorman. I have your career in my hands, and I'll break you in two if you betray me. I repeat: are you ready?"

Sam turned sullenly away from her, facing the wall. "Go ahead, then. But I warn you: I'll never forget this."

"I don't mean you to! Now to begin with, is there any chance of running down proof of an affair between Julius and another man?"

"Very little."

"Any?"

"I don't know. I can't help you there."

"Does he go to brothels to get whipped or to peek at others?"

"Possibly. I don't know."

"What *do* you know?"

"You ask the questions, Ivy. I'll try to answer."

"Very well. Have you ever known him to expose himself in public?"

"What do you mean by public?"

"In front of other people."

"Well, there was an art class where he once posed as a model."

Ivy's eyes fairly glittered. "In the nude?"

"Of course, in the nude."

"What sort of a class was it? Mixed? Boys and girls?"

"Actually, it was an all-male class. But that may have been a coincidence."

"Did he do this frequently?"

"I should say a dozen times. At least in the winter when I attended the class."

"But why would they want Julius for a model? He can't have been all that pretty."

"It was a life class. They wanted a middle-aged male."

"I don't believe it! They always want young models."

"Not always, Ivy."

"And why would he be a model, anyway? Not, God knows, for the money. Oh, that gives it to me! I've got it!" Ivy sprang to her feet. "He *paid* to be the model. He paid for the privilege of all those men seeing him. That's his thrill and joy!"

"Ivy, you really *are* a fiend."

"So I've got it! Good. And now you may write down for me the name of the art class and its director and when this all happened."

As Sam reluctantly proceeded to write down the information, Ivy once again paced his office, talking triumphantly to herself as she did so:

"Well, it's not much, but I guess I can make do with it. Posing in the nude to art students! Yes, it's something. And I'm sure I can find one little whipping incident. One usually can in these cases. Of course, we haven't got him in an act of pederasty, but this ought to do. Oh, yes, it ought to do. But what a strange man to want people to sketch his bare ass!"

"Everybody's strange," Sam retorted bitterly as he watched her pounce on the paper he had written. "Even, methinks, Ivy Trask. Who knows what fantasies move *you*? It seems to me an unworthy thing to go about collecting the oddities of others."

"Only when they attack Elesina! Julius could show his ass to the President and Congress assembled for all I care, but when he calls Elesina a communist, I'll have his heart. I will, Sam! You can warn him if you like!"

"Warn him? And tell him what I've told you? He'd have *my* heart."

"That's your lookout," said Ivy with a sniff, as she left his office. She was ready to go back to Rye, but a sudden recollection directed her steps to Giles's office.

"What is it, Ivy? You look like a figure of doom!"

"Well, if I am, it's to offer you a refuge. Remember, my friend, you'll always be welcome at Broadlawns."

"Am I to be sacked at *Tone?*"

"Oh, no. But I'm doing things today which may have repercussions. Remember that I like you. And that Elesina likes you."

"Ivy, you darling!" He rose and went to the doorway to kiss her.

"How's my old cheek? The girls in stenographic say I insist on a private john because I have to shave. They think I don't hear them, but I do."

"You listen to those bitches?"

"Oh, I listen to everyone!"

"Well, listen to me. I adore you. Even if I know you only want to add me as another piece of tinsel to Elesina's Christmas tree!"

"Does Sam say that?"

"Indeed he does."

"He's wrong. I want you on mine!" And Ivy gave him a swat on the seat as she turned to hurry off.

◄§ 4 §►

Elesina had discovered in politics her ultimate role. She suffered no longer from her old hankering for the stage. She had discovered the joy of being applauded by an audience which had not paid her to perform, by people who had no reason to clap except for their hope that the speaker might be able to effect an improvement in their lives. How shallow by contrast seemed the small, strutting role of the actress, uttering made-up lines about made-up people, catering to dreams and fantasies, hypnotizing the pit to believe for an hour that the great dull world outside did not exist! Watching herself on television she learned how to correct each note, each gesture, each dress. She saw that she was best in black, with a hat that was no more than a beret to dramatize her tallness, her pallor, her eloquence. She would rehearse sudden changes of mood, shifting from the nobly sublime to the familiarly ridiculous, joining her listeners in their hesitant but soon uncontrollable laughter at a bit of daring wit with a fine, infectious low chuckle. She could soar, but she must not forget how to stoop, to perch, even on occasion, all smiling and happy, to waddle.

Ivy taught her to emulate Franklin Roosevelt in never condescending to her electors, never allowing the least note of folksiness to mar her speech. She had to be always what they knew she was, the great lady of Broadlawns who had transformed a vast estate into a museum and park for the people and who now felt that her duty obliged her to offer herself as well to the service of her district. But if she would never insult her hearers by pretending to be other than she was, she had still to remember that in a democracy class lines must always be made to seem easily crossable, and she would illustrate her own knowledge of poverty and despair by a reference to the Depression years when she had spent dull days waiting for bit parts. She would even imply, with a slight shrug, a half smile and a brief sideways glance, that as a single woman she had had to master every aspect of the art of surviving in a city of sin.

If Elesina, the actress, had learned not to play the proletarian, she had learned also not to play the man. She relied boldly on her beauty and her femininity, and never allowed her speeches to be dull. Her aides learned how to make tangled topics clear. Elesina would demand a single page on each issue, stating the principal arguments pro and con. She never allowed her attention to be squandered on details. She made a merit of superficiality by giving the impression of always going straight to the main point. It was frequently the only one she knew.

Because of her looks, her social position and her speaking ability, she had achieved a public recognition far above what any ordinary state assemblyman could have expected. Her picture was carried in *Time*, in *Life*, in *Newsweek*, and she faced her first congressional primary as a cosmopolitan figure, whereas Julius Schell, the favorite of the ultraconservatives, was hardly known outside Westchester County. But Elesina had disadvantages, too. She was a woman, she had been twice divorced; she had been on the stage. Ivy proposed to make up for these liabilities with a whispering campaign to spread three responses: that Julius Schell was not really a man; that if he had never been divorced it was only because he had never been married; and that he, too, was known for his enthusiasm for the stage, and in particular for handsome, young actors.

"I want a clean campaign, Ivy," Elesina warned her sternly when she heard these suggestions.

Ivy abruptly changed the subject. It was always difficult to tie Ivy down. Elesina suspected that she rigidly separated the morality of the candidate from that of the campaign manager. It was all very well for the former to proclaim a belief in ideals; it was even acceptable that this belief should be sincere — so long as the manager had a free hand in the sewers. Elesina was determined, however, to bring matters to a showdown. She was perfectly aware of all that she owed her friend, but she knew, too, that gratitude was the cause of half the sinning in public life.

Was she a hypocrite? She put the question to herself occasionally. Where had her new sense of virtue come from? Was it not possible that it had come from her own admiration of her own portrait: that of the noble matron on the podium, the tall lady in black with one arm raised to assert her faith in the better life? Well, what of it?

Certainly her daughter considered her a hypocrite. Ruth

had passed from Mummie-worship to Mummie-envy. In reaction to the splendors of Broadlawns she had married a
tedious, radical journalist, and, unhappy with him, seemed to
live to find fault with her increasingly successful mother.
Elesina's only cruelty was to be sweet to her. Poor Ruth,
who had not lost her childhood weight or looks, was not
worth a quarrel. If Elesina read the resentment of a whole
world in her daughter's eyes, she knew that it was only one
world in many. But it was unfortunately the world that
contained the two persons closest to her.

That Ivy, for all her refusal to discuss the issue between
them, was well aware of it, became evident on the morning
when she entered the library in Broadlawns to deposit a typescript triumphantly on Elesina's desk. Before she stamped out
of the room, she grunted:

"Read Julius' speech to the Rotary and then tell me that old
Ivy is unscrupulous!"

Alone, Elesina read the following:

"Some of my listeners tonight may have heard of a touch-
ing little volume entitled *The War Letters of David Stein*.
The letter writer was a young resident of this very electoral
district who enlisted in the British army in nineteen thirty-
nine and, unhappily, was killed in the Allied evacuation of
Dunkirk. His letters have been edited by his good friend and
cousin, Eliot Clarkson. In them the reader will find many
references to a certain married lady with whom David Stein
was romantically involved. This married lady is given the
alias: Clarissa.

"Now why am I telling you this tonight? Is it because I am
in a position to prove that the mysterious Clarissa is none
other than my worthy opponent? And stepmother of the late
David Stein? No. I have no wish to pry into family scandals
or long-past romances. I have no wish to have others pry into
mine! In revealing this fact, then, do I not seem a hypocrite?
Perhaps so. But, racking my brain, I have not been able to
think of any other way to bring before you certain other

facts which are of vital importance to every voter in this district. To do this I am duty bound to unveil Clarissa.

"My other facts are these. David Stein could not await his own country's decision to go to war. He was the kind of impetuous young man who lets his enthusiasm outrun his discretion. Idealistic and confused, he dreamed fuzzily of a better world for all. In his hurry to achieve it, he was inclined to disdain the means. Young men of hot blood and careless thinking have always been an easy prey for their radical friends, and David found his carnivore in a seemingly quiet and scholarly cousin, Eliot Clarkson. But this same Clarkson, my friends, was a card-carrying member of the Communist Party! Read these letters if you can bear it! Read David's juvenile onslaughts on our American free-enterprise system! And remember when you do so that the third musketeer of this tight little trio was the lady now seeking the Republican nomination for Congress, Elesina Stein!"

Elesina sat in silent contemplation of the typescript for several minutes. Then her telephone buzzed.

"You'll never believe who's here, Mrs. Stein!" the cheerful volunteer operator's voice communicated. "It's your honorable opponent himself!"

"He has his nerve. What does he want?"

"To speak with you on a matter of the greatest urgency, he says."

"Send him in."

Julius Schell, standing in the doorway of the great library, glanced at the high shelves of the Stein collection with his usual contained smile. It was the smile of the extreme Tory. It seemed to profess that the wearer, who had seen all, knew all, was now beyond passion, beyond anger, almost beyond disgust. It purported to accept at last the sorry fact that men were blind beasts and seemed to say: "Well, let us not tear our hair about it, let us see what little can be done."

"Good morning, Julius. I am surprised that you expose yourself to this communist den."

"I am impregnably armored in my virtue," Julius replied in his mocking tone. "I take it that my remarks at the Rotary Club have not altogether escaped your notice?"

"Have you come to gloat?"

"No. I have come because I believe, despite what my campaign managers assert to the contrary, that you are a person who fundamentally believes in telling the truth."

Elesina stared at the strange, soft, fanatical brown eyes of her opponent. "And *I'm* the one who hasn't been telling it?"

"Perhaps it has not been altogether your fault. Perhaps advantage has been taken of your confidence. It happens in politics. But are you aware of the filthy slander the woman Trask is spreading about me?"

"What slander?"

"She is saying that Giles Bennett and I are lovers."

Again Elesina stared with astonishment into those glinting eyes. "And that's a lie? You needn't get so excited, Julius. In the theater we used to take those things very lightly."

"Damn the theater! I've never touched Giles. I've never touched any man that way!"

"Or boy?"

"Or boy!"

"Well, Julius, suppose I believe you? What earthly difference is there between Ivy calling you a homosexual and you calling me a communist?"

"I didn't call you a communist! I said you had a communist association. And you had! Can you deny it?"

"Certainly I deny it."

"Do you deny that you were a lover of David Stein's, whose best friend is — or at least was — a communist?"

Elesina's indignation began to subside a bit before her now awakened interest in his evident sincerity. "I think I begin to see your point. It doesn't matter that I wasn't a communist. It only matters that I had a communist association, is that it? Like a game of hearts? So many points off if I hold the

Queen of Spades? No matter how hard I've tried to get rid of her?"

"The point is that in such dangerous times the voters must be told of *all* affiliations with Moscow. They can then judge which are innocent and which are guilty."

"Well, then, isn't it *my* duty to bring before those same voters your association with Giles Bennett?"

"Because of his reputation for inversion?"

"No! Because of his affiliation with Eliot Clarkson."

"What are you talking about?"

"It was considerably more intimate than any that existed between Eliot and poor David."

Julius' air of utter amazement could hardly have been faked. "You mean . . . ?"

"Simply that Giles was kept by Eliot for a year."

"It's not true!"

"I suggest you ask him. He can hardly deny it."

"Ask him? I'll never see him again!"

"But the communist association has already been established. According to you, isn't that enough? Aren't you as contaminated as I? Isn't it my duty to illuminate the electorate?"

"There is the difference, of course, that I never knew of the connection with Clarkson."

"Shouldn't you have known? Shouldn't you have inquired? Isn't that the duty of every aspirant for public office in these troubled days?"

"I admit my negligence." Julius seemed at last to be genuinely humbled. "I shall even admit it publicly." As the idea became clearer to him, he raised his head with renewed assurance. "I shall repudiate Giles!"

"Another person to fling in the fire. What a pity you weren't born in Toledo in the reign of Philip the Second. How you'd have loved it!"

"But you, Elesina. What will you do about Ivy Trask? Will you muzzle her?"

"Oh, Julius, get out. You bore me. You bore me inexpressibly."

"You will continue, then, I gather, your sewer campaign?"

"What I shall do or not do you will learn from my actions. Just remember that Pandoras shouldn't go around opening boxes."

But as soon as the door was closed behind him, she rang for Ivy. When the latter appeared she cried out angrily:

"What have you been saying about Julius and Giles?"

"Don't ask about things you're not supposed to know."

"I think, if you don't mind, Ivy, I'd like to know everything about my own campaign." Elesina paused to let the authority in her tone have its effect. Ivy, approaching the desk, began nervously to play with a paperweight. "Is it true that you've been spreading the word that they're lovers?"

Ivy sniffed. "Some news!"

"Have you?"

"Little-known facts about well-known people!" Here Ivy gave vent to one of her jeering laughs.

"Do you believe that a candidate's sexual taste is relevant to his qualification? I had thought you more tolerant."

Ivy shrugged. "I suppose there's always the danger of blackmail."

"If Julius' homosexuality is as well known as you imply, where is the danger of blackmail?"

"If it's that well known, where is the harm in saying it?"

"Because I suggest it's not true!"

"Not true? That Julius has hot pants for little boys? Be your age, Elesina!"

"I intend to be. And I still have reason to believe that Julius is a virgin. With both sexes."

"The more fool he! Am I to blame for his inhibitions? I know what I'm doing. Trust old Ivy. If Julius wants to sue me, I can prove enough about his posing for art classes to convince any jury in the land he's a bugger!"

"Posing for art classes?"

Ivy explained.

"But that doesn't prove anything," Elesina retorted. "A man can do those things without being a practicing homosexual. Indeed, the mere fact that he does them suggests to me that he isn't."

"Well, what does it matter?" Ivy exploded. "If he *did* do anything, you know what it would be. He wants to prove you a Red by association. Well, I'm proving him a faggot the same way!"

"I've noticed, Ivy, that when you like a homosexual, he's a free soul. When you don't, he's a faggot."

"What's wrong with that? If I don't like him, you can be sure he's a son of a bitch. So anything goes."

"Not with me. And certainly not in my campaign. I am going to answer with the truth. I shall tell the story of me and David."

Ivy looked aghast. "Elesina! There's not only Eliot Clarkson and all those radical letters. My God, there's incest! Have you never heard of a senator called Joseph McCarthy?"

"I wonder if people aren't getting a little tired of McCarthy. Can he last forever?"

"No. He's a loudmouth, a lush and a faggot, too. And when he slips, it'll be just as dangerous to be for him as it is now to be against him. But the first ones to resist a demagogue always get clobbered. Wait for the second wave. The timing in these things is everything."

"Ivy, do you believe in nothing?"

"I believe in you, baby. My faith there never wavers. I'll bring you through, never fear. Sometimes I think I have a kind of second sight where you're concerned."

Elesina shook her head firmly. "It's not enough, my friend. It won't do. I must run my own campaign my own way. Let me therefore give you an explicit order. There is to be no further use of sex smears. Shouted or whispered. Is that entirely clear?"

Ivy leaned over the desk and began now to rummage desperately with paper clips, with pencils, with anything. "I
hear you," she said hoarsely.

But Elesina was inexorable. "Is it entirely clear?"

"Haven't you made it so?"

"Very well. And I warn you, Ivy, if you fail me, I shall
replace you in the campaign."

"Elesina!"

"I mean it. I am determined to do things my own way.
The fact that in the past I have used methods that I now
dislike does not mean I must always do so."

"Oh, darling, don't turn Christer on me."

"One can change, Ivy, without being a Christer. And now,
if you will forgive me, I want to write my speech for the
Veterans on Saturday night."

"I've already written it!"

"Save it for the League of Women Voters. I am going to
write this one myself."

"May I see it before you deliver it?"

"No, Ivy, you may not."

In the town hall of Chester, four days later, Elesina rose to
address an audience of five hundred veterans and their wives.
Never had she more looked forward to a speech. But as she
had listened to the colonel who was introducing her, she had
had a shock. "Why do you think you're enjoying yourself?"
an inner voice, like Ivy's, had sneered. "Do you imagine you
are brave? Do you have the effrontery to surmise that you
have more guts than all the poor slandered fools who tremble
before Joe McCarthy and his ilk? Don't you know it's just
because you have nothing to lose, nothing, that is, that you
really care about? Can McCarthy touch your money? Hell,
no! So go ahead, be Hedda Gabler, be Portia! Have the time
of your life, kid!"

Elesina found that she was shaking her head angrily.
Quickly she stopped and rose to bow to the applause. She

looked out over the upturned faces and smiled as radiantly as she knew how.

"My opponent has thrown the name of David Stein into the campaign. I am not sorry that he has done so, because it gives me the chance to talk about David, and that is something I am always eager to do.

"David, I am afraid, was a hero. But he was the kind of hero you would all have liked. He was a friendly, modest, companionable hero. He was a hero for weekdays — not just for Sunday wear. David was a young man who had everything to live for. He had a charming personality, a first-class mind, exuberant health, good looks, lots of friends, a loving family and — wealth! What more could a young man ask on this beleaguered planet? He was indeed among the blessed.

"But a wicked fairy godmother had tossed a rather horrid little bundle on the glittering pile of his christening gifts. She gave David a conscience. Oh, yes, my friends, David Stein never faced the world with the freedom of Julius Schell! David cared about the poor. He cared about the sick. He cared about the oppressed. And more than anything else he cared about the victims of the Nazi terror.

"You all remember how many there were in our community back in nineteen thirty-eight and nineteen thirty-nine who cried out shrilly that Germany was not our problem, that we had no duty but to ourselves. David did not seek to answer them. He did not raise his voice. He did not criticize others for turning their backs on the problem any more than he praised himself for facing it. He believed that each man must make up his own mind for himself and act accordingly. One day those who loved him, of whom I was one, found that he had quietly departed. He knew what he had to do, and he did it. He reached for his gun and was gone. A year later he was dead.

"Eliot Clarkson, his dearest friend and cousin, went with him. Eliot Clarkson survived. My opponent says that Eliot Clarkson was a communist. I know nothing about that. I do not even know Eliot Clarkson, despite what Mr. Schell alleges. But what I do know is this. When it comes to presumptions, mine are for the brave men who crossed the sea to fight the bloody tyrant and against the spoiled darlings like Julius Schell, who stayed at home to wave the Stars and Stripes.

"But let me state the case even more broadly. I think the time has come in the history of our great nation when we should cease to tremble before every communist bogy. We have now reached the sorry point where the greatest of our national names, that of General George Marshall himself, can be dragged in the mire by any Tom, Dick or Harry who has the impudence to allege a Red affiliation. Why do we put up with it? My friends, we are still free! We *can* choose our associates. And I choose to be associated with a hero like David Stein who gave all that he had gladly for a great cause rather than with Julius Schell, the unctuous squid who hides behind his own black cloud of venom and falsehood!"

She could proceed no further, for the hall was filled with uproar. Some people were standing to applaud and cheer; others were booing and shouting imprecations. The room had begun to seethe with Elesina's mention of General Marshall, and the tumult exploded altogether with that of Julius Schell. Elesina remained standing, with a half smile, occasionally waving her arms for silence. When she saw that it was no use she turned to the orchestra and signaled for them to play. They struck up "God Bless America," and half the audience joined in singing while the others continued to shout and gesticulate. At the end of the stanza Elesina bowed deeply to the assembly and strode from the podium.

In the limousine going home her assistant silently handed her a cartoon depicting Julius Schell and a young man, hand in hand, walking down toward a landscape where the dome of the Capitol appeared. Elesina, overwrought, burst into tears.

At Broadlawns she went straight to Ivy's office. "They telephoned me about the commotion!" Ivy cried, jumping up in alarm as she took in the grim expression on her friend's face. "Are you all right, dear?"

"Half that commotion was applause," Elesina retorted. "But never mind that." She flung the cartoon down on Ivy's desk. "Shirley Lester said you gave her five hundred of these this afternoon."

Ivy stared glumly at the cartoon. "Somebody's got to save your bacon. You seem determined to throw away the nomination. It's not fair to the people who've worked for you, Elesina."

"I'll be the judge of that!"

"Very well, we'll do it your way." Something in Elesina's tone had cowed Ivy. "I promise, dear. In the future I'll be good."

"I'm afraid it's too late for that, Ivy. As of now you are relieved of all further duties in my campaign. You will continue, of course, as manager of Broadlawns."

Ivy said nothing. She seemed to huddle, to shrink into something even smaller than she was. There was a dull, sullen, brutish pain in her green eyes.

"I'm sorry, Ivy. I warned you!"

But Ivy remained silent, and Elesina, unable to bear the sight of her discomfort, hurried from the room. Why should Ivy always put her in the wrong? She was like a death's-head. In the library Elesina pressed her back against the door which she had slammed as if to keep her friend out. Why, if she had a vision of a new Elesina, an Elesina who had at last found the right role, the right costume and cue, should she not adapt her soul to the part? A conscience to go with a hat? Well, why *not?*

◅§ 5 §►

The first thing that Elesina did when she arrived in her office on the morning after her speech to the Legion was telephone

Sam Gorman at *Tone* and instruct him to send Giles Bennett out to Broadlawns for the rest of her campaign.

"We've cost him the favor of the great Julius," she explained, "and I want the poor boy to know that he won't be the loser."

"But he doesn't know anything about politics!"

"He can learn. Besides, that's not what I really need him for. I want a buffer between me and Ivy. I've taken her off the campaign, and things are going to be rough for a while."

"You've *what?* Oh, my God, Elesina! If Ivy gets the idea that Giles is going to replace her, she'll murder the child. She will!"

"I can take care of that."

"Remember! Ivy can be a fiend."

"Oh, shut up, Sam. You're just peeved because you know you'll have to write Giles's column. Now do as I say."

"Working for women, what a life!"

Giles, seemingly unsurprised by his promotion, came out to Rye that very afternoon and fitted himself almost at once into the Broadlawns family. In a couple of days he was on first names with everybody. Elesina, in turning the estate into an arts center, of which she was president, had retained title to the mansion in which she lived and kept her offices. The big rooms on the main floor were opened on certain days to the public, but the second story, where Elesina and Ivy had separate apartments, was always private. Ivy managed the staff and grounds; Elesina directed the artistic events. Giles established himself as the friend of both.

"Poor Ivy is absolutely shattered over the Julius episode," he told Elesina. "Can't you give her a second chance?"

"Is she using you as her advocate now?"

"Well, why not? You mustn't be hard, Elesina. Great politicians should have great hearts."

"Great politicians must also know when they're badly served. Keep out of it, Giles."

She was sure that Julius would know that Giles was at Broadlawns, and it amused her to imagine the intensity of his discomfort. It would never occur to Julius that she did not intend to make nefarious use of his relationship with a young man, now in her camp, of easily impugnable morals, and she was perfectly content to let him suppose so. After all, he deserved it. But what pleased her most about the presence of Giles at Broadlawns, even more than its effect on Julius, was the way that he filled the hole which her breach with Ivy had made. Giles was the perfect assistant, at least in her lighter tasks. He seemed to have no moods; he was always cheerful. If he knew little about politics, he knew everything about how to project her. Soon she was reciting her speeches to him in the library.

"Look, dear," he would coach her, with the intimacy of a stage director, "you must never show your audience that you expect applause or laughter. Keep on going, and then, when it comes, look up with that little-girly expression of surprise that you do so well."

The fact that Giles had little or no feelings about the McCarthy issue was a balancing factor in the hectic days that followed. Letters poured into Broadlawns, abrasive, critical, threatening, praising, ecstatic, and the telephone rang without cease. Elesina varied between moods of exhilaration and moods when she felt frightened. It was a relief to let Giles read the mail and hear his little squeals of laughter at the most violent diatribes. To him it was box office, pure and simple, and Elesina was putting on a terrific show.

"Listen to this," he would exclaim. "Here's a man who thinks Broadlawns is a center for Russian propaganda. He lists five pieces by Russian composers played last summer!"

When she thought she was a heroine, Giles was there to remind her that it was all a play; when she thought she was in danger from the apes who wrote the letters, Giles was there to turn it all into a joke. And he was willing to lend a hand in anything, high or low, from writing a speech to filling in as a guide on days when the mansion was open to the public. He had his meals with Elesina in the big dining room, and sometimes, late at night, she would sit up with him alone in the library. She told him almost the whole story of her life. He told her nothing of his, but he was too young, presumably, to have much to tell.

"Don't bother about my past, Elesina," he told her. "Let's say that my life began the day I came to Broadlawns."

"Why on earth do you like it so?"

"Because it isn't real! All these flowers and statues and paintings, all this beauty and luxury. And presided over by a fairy queen! I don't want to go back to *Tone* now. I want to stay here forever and ever."

"Well, you're certainly welcome, dear boy. You've made a place for yourself here already. I begin to wonder how we ever got on without you."

Giles was thoroughly discreet about his sex life, if indeed he had any. So far as Elesina could make out, nothing untoward occurred on the premises; presumably he took care of such matters on his weekly visits to the city. She liked the fact that he never mentioned the subject because it allowed her to fantasize that his demonstrative affection for herself was total, like a faithful dog's. Indeed, in lonely moments she caught herself treating him as a pet, chucking him under the chin and rumpling his hair.

One day, when she did this in the presence of her mother, Linda sharply reproved her.

"He's not a lap dog, Elesina!"

Elesina flushed and moved away from the unembarrassed Giles. But when she had recovered from the slight shock, she took a high tone. "Indeed he's not," she retorted coolly. "But he's the dearest of dear friends. Aren't you, Giles?"

"Yours in the ranks of death!"

Was it true? Was *this* the friend she had always wanted? But was that any stranger than finding herself on the threshold of Congress? When had her life been logical?

One morning, when she was working alone in the library, the receptionist telephoned to say that a Professor Eliot Clarkson wished to see her. A moment later he walked in, very tense, and ignored her friendly greeting. "I've been abroad," he explained abruptly. "Which is why I've only just heard about your speech to the veterans. I came right out here. Would you like a public statement that this is the first time we've met?"

"Sit down, Mr. Clarkson. I'm so happy you're here. Let's make a public statement that *at last* we've met!"

Eliot seemed taken aback. "You're very kind."

"Kind? But you were David's friend! Did you think I would deny you?"

He rubbed his temples anxiously now with the fingers of both hands. Then he sat down. "I thought you might have taken exception to my book."

"Why? It was David who said the harsh things. He had great fun imagining how I would behave if the Nazis won. Perhaps he was right. Perhaps I would have been that way."

Eliot shook his head emphatically. "No, you've proved your guts. David would have been proud of you if he'd heard that speech."

"He'd have found something else to object to soon enough. I could never have been the woman David imagined I was. He was too much of an idealist. He was always looking for beautiful damsels to rescue from dragons. He never found the damsel, but he did find the dragon. Perhaps in the long run that was just as good."

"I'm beginning to wonder if he didn't find the damsel as well."

"That's very charming of you, Mr. Clarkson. But if he did, he never knew it. He was bitter to the end."

"Yes, but he didn't see you as I do. Now."

"*Do* you see me? We've only just met. I'm the kind of person who continually looks as if she were going to be somebody's damsel. People are always putting their faith in me. And being disappointed."

"Not your constituents, I'm sure."

"Well, maybe not them. Maybe that's just the point. That I can fool *them!*" Elesina suddenly laughed. "By being what they expect! Anyway, I can try. For I have a bit of David's idealism in me, too. Just a bit, mind you. There are times when I, too, want a dragon. A small one anyway."

"Like Julius Schell?"

"Oh, he'll do. For those of us who weren't lucky enough to find a Hitler!"

"You'll gobble Schell up!"

But Eliot's expression changed now as his eyes took in something behind her. When he smiled, it was not an agreeable smile.

"Hello, Giles. Are you in politics now?"

Giles had appeared from the librarian's office with a handful of papers. As always, he seemed perfectly unsurprised.

"Hello, Eliot. You're looking very well. No, I'm not really in politics. I just help Elesina in any way I can. I guess that's what we all end up doing, isn't it?"

"Not I, thank you."

Here it was again, Elesina reflected with dry amusement. Clarkson had not been in the room two minutes, and he was repudiating her already! She smiled with deliberate artificiality.

"Why, Professor Clarkson, how ungallant of you! Now that you've been thrown into the issue, why not join me?"

"Because, my dear Mrs. Stein, if I have moved somewhat to the right of my former position, I am still many light-years away from even a liberal Republican. But in the McCarthy matter I will help you any way I can. The best way, no doubt, is for me to remove myself entirely." He turned now to go. "Giles will know where to reach me if there is anything I can sign."

"But surely we can meet sometime?"

"Oh, Eliot, say yes! You'll adore Elesina."

Eliot glanced coolly from Elesina to his former friend. "I assume you knew of my relationship with Giles?"

Elesina nodded, still smiling. "Ivy Trask took care of that. What does it matter?"

"It doesn't, of course," Eliot shrugged. "But let me depart on a Shakespearean note. The Steins always went out on that. We're in *Twelfth Night*. Only Olivia prevails over the Duke!"

Giles turned a bland countenance to Elesina. "Isn't he horrid?" he asked calmly. When he turned back, Eliot was gone.

❧ 6 ☙

Elesina won the nomination by a very small margin and the election by a larger one. The district was prevailingly Republican, and the Democratic candidate a political hack drafted to fight a losing battle that no abler party leader cared to take on. The only real issue had been that raised by Julius Schell about Elesina's supposed communist connections. What had brought her to national attention was not the accusation of this, which was easily rebutted, but her refusal to limit her denial to the simple fact that she had not known Eliot Clarkson. Instead, she had chosen to attack the whole McCarthy technique of character assassination. Her beauty and eloquence had created a sensation wherever she had spoken. People hissed and people applauded, but it did not make much difference which. They listened, that was the point; she was always stage center. She was at last a star. The tall dark-haired lady with the challenging eyes and the uplifted arm made the cover of *Life*.

The week after the election, when Elesina had gone with her mother for a few days' needed vacation to Hobe Sound, Ivy received a visit from Ruth at Broadlawns. Elesina's daughter, now Mrs. Robert Pix, was like a piece of expensive pink stationery on which an obscene note had been written; those round fat cheeks and pale blue eyes had been made for cheer and not complaint. Her business with Ivy, as always, was financial. Elesina was perfectly willing to help her daughter whenever necessary, but not to listen to her lamentations. Ivy had brought Ruth quickly to the point with a promise of needed assistance, and now they had a moment to chat.

"What do you think of your mother's success?"

"What can I think? Triumph after triumph! She's way beyond us now." Ruth gave a little wave of her hand to indicate the sweep of Elesina's arc and at the same time slightly to denigrate it.

"And the victory is not just here below. I seem to hear the chorus of the angels on high in solemn '*Te Deum.*'"

Ruth smiled sourly. "You're always so sarcastic, Ivy. Do you admire nothing?"

"I echo your thoughts, honey. But, seriously, there's no stopping your mother now. Her timing is perfect. Politics is like surf bathing. You have only to watch the breakers. I had an uncle who used to tell me a warning story. He said that in the eighteen nineties every observing man could see that the future belonged to the automobile. So he bought shares in all the companies that were making them — there were seventeen, I believe. And do you know what? He lost his shirt! Because the big boys rode in on the second wave and knocked out the beginners."

"I take it you believe that we're in the second wave of anti-McCarthyism."

"Elesina has just proved it! Oh, it will take a while yet, but the signs are sure. People are getting tired of being ranted at. Your mother knows just how to hop about in that turbulent water, waving her lovely arms and giving an occasional shriek and knowing all the while she's as safe as a rubber ball."

Ruth's steady gaze intimated that even she did not want to

annihilate the maternal image. "Are you saying that nobody's been really hurt by McCarthy?"

"No, dear, of course not. All those poor actors and radio people who had no savings and got blacklisted — they were ruined, I know. But people like Elesina have nothing to lose. The only trick is to get your licks in before the world knows it's a paper dragon. And, oh, the bliss of it, Ruth!" Ivy jumped to her feet and raised an arm in a brutal parody of Elesina's dramatic gesture. "Think of it! To stand before the howling crowd, a beautiful martyr, and receive only a little spray of slander on the cheek! And to know that that spray will soon turn to incense! Oh, if Joe McCarthy had never lived . . ."

"Mummie would have invented him, I suppose," Ruth finished for her dryly. "I think you go too far, Ivy. Do you have to hate being good to be good?"

Ivy looked at her bitterly. "She'll bring *you* over to her side easily enough. If she ever has five minutes to spare for it."

"Mummie's side? What makes you think I'm not on Mummie's side? Just because I criticize her . . ."

"Oh, skip it, skip it."

"Ivy, you're in such a funny mood! This ought to be your finest hour. Why should you be so jaundiced?"

"Because it's not my finest hour, even though it should be. I missed the boat, Ruth. I didn't think the time had come to attack McCarthy."

"What does that matter? So long as Mummie did?"

"Because she did it against my advice!" Ivy exclaimed fiercely. "She proved me wrong. Worse than that, she proved me useless!"

"Anyone can make a mistake."

"Not me. And it's more than that. Your mother has outgrown me. She doesn't want me around — to remind her."

"You don't mean she's dropping you?"

"I mean I'm not going to Washington." Ivy gave a little groan as the full effect of her own words struck her. She buried her face suddenly in her hands. "I'm to stay here and manage Broadlawns."

Even Ruth was capable, for once, of taking in a sorrow that was not her own. "Oh, Ivy," she murmured. "That *is* bitchy."

"No, no, Elesina is right. Elesina is my pupil, my star. I wouldn't want her to behave any differently. She's outgrown me, and she knows it. And *I* know it! She wouldn't be my pupil if she didn't keep growing. So let her keep on." Ivy slumped back in her chair. "Besides, she has Giles."

"Giles?"

"Giles Bennett. She's using him more and more. On her campaign, at Broadlawns. She's taken him off *Tone* altogether. He's perfect for her."

"But, Ivy, isn't he just a silly little pansy?"

"He's not a bit silly. And he learns fast. He's what your mother's always wanted."

"You mean as an assistant?"

"I mean as a lover!" Ivy cried brutally. "Oh, Ruth, you're such an ass. I'm sorry to say it, but you are. You put people in drawers. Young men like Giles are perfectly capable of making love to older women. He sees Elesina as the mother he's always wanted, and she pets him like a kitten, and they get cozier and cozier, and the first thing you know they're in the sack together, having really quite a lovely time!"

"Ivy!" Ruth's eyes shivered with disgust. "How can you? Mummie must be thirty years older than Giles!"

"Oh, go home, Ruth. You've never understood your mother. I tell you, she doesn't want a man. She wants a poodle! And she's got one. They're perfect for each other!"

"I think I *will* go home. And I assure you, I don't believe a word you've said!"

When Ruth had gone, Ivy sat for a long time without moving. She thought of the old family place in Auburn and of all the uncles and aunts. She thought of Washington and of Edouardo. She thought of the years with *Tone*. One had to judge life by the hand one was dealt; hers had had no quick tricks. What she had done she had done with nerve and grit, with spit and sealing wax. If in the end there was nobody to applaud but Ivy Trask, who else could there have been?

Nothing had to be put in order, for everything was in order. The photographs of her parents, looking absurdly young, she took from the desk and placed in a drawer. Then she straightened the objects on her blotter, placing the paper cutter which she had never used exactly parallel to the scissors which she had never used.

"Tell Alfred to be ready to take me to the station," she telephoned her secretary. "I'm going into New York."

"Can't he drive you in, Miss Trask?"

Ivy paused. Ordinarily she did not take the Broadlawns cars so far from their base. "Well, why not?"

Passing into the patio she paused to watch the visitors coming in and out of the rooms opened to the public. She noticed, standing before the marble bust of David Stein, an elderly woman of ample frame, evidently in the deepest meditation. The stillness of her erect, darkly garbed figure isolated her from the nervous females who poked about the patio making estimates of the costs of things. It was Clara Stein. Ivy went up to her. Clara's features had lost none of their high serenity.

"Are we still enemies, Clara?"

"I was hoping not to see you. But of course I knew I might. And I knew if I did, you'd ask me that. So I have my answer ready. Somebody asked Talleyrand the same question about himself and Lafayette. 'After seventy there are no enemies,' he replied, 'only survivors.'"

"Yes, we've survived a lot," Ivy said grimly.

"I came to see the bust of David."

"Do you like it?"

"Very much."

"I don't. It isn't David to me." Ivy shrugged as she saw the look of proprietary surprise in the eyes of the subject's mother. "I know. You think you own him. But nobody owns the dead. The sculptor who did it never saw him, you know. He worked from photographs. But what he did was the bust of a hero. He saw, quite correctly, that that was what Elesina wanted."

"But David *was* a hero!"

"Heroes are banal. To me, anyway. That was what you all wanted out of poor David, a blond, blue-eyed hero to convince you there was something in life worth living for besides your tawdry selves. Take Irving. David was going to justify his mishmash of compromises. And yourself. David was going to prove that your marriage had not been entirely futile. And for Elesina — he was the love she could never feel. And for Eliot — he was a man. There it is, all in that pretty bust, the young Apollo, ready to fly into the wild blue yonder!"

"You're very articulate."

"I've lived with that piece of statuary for five years now."

"And what was my son to *you*, Ivy Trask?"

"Oh, to me he was a cute little Jewish boy with an infectious laugh. But at least for me he lived, the poor darling. For the rest of you he just died."

Clara surveyed Ivy now with something like curiosity mingled with her disdain. "You take a very high tone to someone whose life you ruined."

"I didn't ruin your life, Clara. You were half dead, and I awakened you. You could still have lived. There was time."

"Lived? Like you, I suppose."

"No, not like me. I've failed."

"How have you failed? Aren't you mistress here, where I was? Haven't you got precisely what you were willing to rob and murder for?"

"Those are strong terms."

"I don't think so." There was a faint tremor in Clara's serenity now. "You've been very frank with me. I should be the same with you. If you had never come to Broadlawns

neither Irving nor David would have died when they did. I
repeat: how have you failed?"

"I've lost Elesina."

"Perhaps there is a God, then, after all."

Ivy threw back her head and cackled. "Oh, Clara, you can
believe it! Your God is going to have some very good news
for you!"

Ivy left her abruptly now and strode to the front hall.
Alfred was already there. Instead of sitting in front with him
and picking up useful bits of gossip about the help, as she
usually did when traveling alone, she sat in the back of the
limousine and closed the glass partition. Alfred made no comment about this, for nobody in Broadlawns ever questioned
the actions of Ivy Trask. All the way to New York she
looked out the window and wondered at the vividness of the
landscape. She might have been seeing it for the first time.

At the Althorpe she told Alfred to return to Broadlawns.

"And, Alfred . . ."

"Yes, Madam?"

"Goodbye. I shan't be coming back."

She turned away from his astonished face and entered the
building. The old elevator seemed slower than usual. In her
apartment, which was hot and musty, she went to the big
window and threw it open. Immediately the room was filled
with a cold wind. Ivy felt her heart beating very fast, and she
stood motionless until it had calmed down. Then she began
to talk aloud to herself:

"There is nothing to be excited about. You've always
promised yourself you wouldn't live to be a useless old
woman. Well, now you won't! You're being logical, sensible, realistic, just as you've always been. Ever since that
terrible day in Florence when Edouardo's sister told you to
go away. Yes, you've been fine ever since, almost without a
deviation. So don't let yourself down now. A little brandy
may help."

She went to her liquor closet and drank quick gulps from a

bottle of brandy until she felt her flesh hot and tingling. Then, with a sudden dullness of heart and mind she climbed onto the window seat and sat on the edge of the open windowsill, facing into the room, her legs on the cushion. She sat there for a minute and then, with a sudden cry, kicked up her heels and fell backward.

⋖§ 7 §⋗

Ivy was buried at Broadlawns in the rose garden beside Irving Stein. Elesina felt that their common interest in the place nullified any lack of sympathy that might have existed between them at death. Linda Dart was not sure that she agreed with her daughter's reasoning, but it was not her business, and she said nothing. Besides, she was too much concerned with the effect of Ivy's suicide on Elesina's already overcharged nerves. After the interment they walked together on the lawn and in the gardens. Elesina from time to time shook her shoulders as if she were trying to rid herself of a troublesome insect.

"If she'd only given me a chance, of course, I'd have done something," she moaned, speaking more to herself than to Linda. "Why should she think me such a fiend? I could have found her a place in Washington."

"Darling, you can't be sure that was why she did it."

"Oh, it was the Washington job, Mother. I know it was!"

"Well, if it was that, do you think that just finding her a place would have been enough? Didn't she have to be your right hand?"

"Well, that she couldn't be!" Elesina exclaimed, almost in anger. "That was impossible!"

"Exactly. And she wouldn't play second fiddle. So she had to die. That's the way she was."

"You think I *should* have given her the first place!"

"My dear, I'm not blaming you."

"Oh, Mother, you're always blaming me!"

"No, Elesina, that's not fair. I do not think you were responsible for Ivy's death. Ivy was. She knew exactly what conditions had to obtain to make life worthwhile. When these conditions ceased to obtain, she chose not to go on. She did not fuss or recriminate. She simply ceased to exist. There's a certain style to it, you must admit." Linda paused because she saw that Elesina was now sobbing. "My poor child, it's very hard. Believe me, you did nothing wrong. And, anyway, you gave Ivy all the joy she had in her life."

"Why do people want to own me?" Elesina wailed in anguish. "I never asked them to. Irving did, and so did David. And Ivy most of all! It wasn't right to expect all they expected of me. And I told them so! I was always frank. I told Irving about David . . ."

"You did!"

"And I told David that I wouldn't give up my inheritance. And I warned Ivy that she'd have to give up her dirty tricks. I was always willing to risk the truth!"

"I know that."

"And now she does this to me! She turns my victory to ashes. She knew it was the one way to destroy any satisfaction that I might feel at what I've accomplished." Elesina stopped walking and turned to her mother, her eyes glittering. "Well, she won't succeed. I shall continue to enjoy my life. In spite of Ivy!"

"I am sure that is what she wanted, my dear."

Elesina stamped her foot. "Oh, damn Ivy! She always has to have the last word. Anyway, I'm glad I'm a public figure. I'm glad that I've ceased to belong to greedy individuals! You watch me, Mother. I'll be great!"

Linda stared at her remarkable daughter. Elesina for the moment anyway seemed to have transcended the ordinary limitations of fatuity or complacency. Had she escaped herself? It would be interesting to see — a good enough occupation for an old woman. Linda wondered if she might not herself move to Washington.

"I had such confidence in Ivy's judgment," Linda said, "that I cannot really question her acts, even her final one. It sounds brutal to say it, but at my age one can afford to be brutal. What Ivy did was probably for the best."

Meals are a great help when there is grief in the house, and Linda was relieved when lunch was announced. Giles Bennett joined them and provided a welcome distraction. Linda supposed that Elesina would appoint him Ivy's successor at Broadlawns. Certainly she seemed very fond of him. Linda even wondered at times if it were something more than fondness.

"Do you know what poor old Ivy's last project was?" Giles asked them at table. "She wanted someone to write a history of Broadlawns — how Judge Stein put together his collection and how the place was converted to what it is now. She even thought I might write it."

"Well, why not?" Linda asked politely.

"Do you really think I could?" Giles seemed elated even by perfunctory approval. "What about you, Elesina darling? Do you think someone like me, without any real background in art or literature, could do the job?"

"Yes, because it's essentially the story of a man with a dream, rather than a piece of art history," Elesina replied. "You might be just the person to do it, if you can write the way you talk. Would you really like to try?"

"I've been reading some of the files Ivy gave me. Judge Stein might have had something of the same sort in mind, for he left notes. Then there are all the thank-you letters of the famous people who stayed here, with references to the discussions they had. It must have been a fascinating time. And I found a guest book, full of poems and drawings and funny stories."

"Was it really such a salon?" Linda inquired of Elesina. "I thought you and Ivy used to rather laugh at Irving's little gatherings."

"Laugh?" Giles protested. "What was there to laugh at?

Imagine having been present when Frederic Pemberton delivered his theory of the ghost in *Hamlet*. Or when Erna
Cranberry read aloud from *Paradise to Come!*"

Elesina smiled. Linda thought her smile proud, proprietary, almost maternal. "You certainly have been doing your
homework, dear boy," Elesina said.

"Would you help me with it, darling? Would you tell me
about those weekends? Oh, we might do a wonderful book
together! And you know you really ought to. It's terrible
for all those things to be forgotten. Or do you believe, as
some people do, that no sounds are ever lost, that all our
words are somehow preserved in the air around us? Think
what this room must have heard!"

Giles glanced up at the arched roof of the big dining room
as if to imagine the golden discussions accumulated under its
vault. Linda smiled at his naiveté, but she noted that her
daughter's expression was penetrated with an air of great
interest. Elesina, following Giles's gaze, seemed to be recognizing the discovery of a treasure long lost.

"I suppose you may be right, Giles," she said. "There *were*
extraordinary conversations in this room. It is always true, I
imagine, that most of those who are present when great men
talk are more conscious of their personal idiosyncrasies than
of their ideas. Think of all those eighteenth-century aristocrats who sneered at Dr. Johnson for his bad table manners!
Yet Boswell, writing everything down, made it immortal.
Maybe you and I can do something like that on a small scale.
I recall, for example, that the first time I dined in this room,
there was a discussion of Shakespeare's sonnets . . ."

Linda listened in astonishment as her daughter proceeded to
take over the past. Of course, it was all that was left to her.
She had already taken over the present.